ELEVATOR *Ride*

A ROMANTIC COMEDY MYSTERY

BY

BETHANY MAINES

Blue Zephyr Press
2661 N. Pearl, #360
Tacoma WA 98407

Cover art by **LILT**.

ISBN-13: 979-8-9867745-6-5

CONTENTS

BETHANY MAINES

ELEVATOR
Ride

1

Rowan

THE ELEVATOR

Rowan Valkyrie adjusted the gun on his hip, flapped his suit jacket over it, and then walked straight through the lobby of the Hoskins Building. Ignoring the glares from the variety of suits, ties, and dresses that made up the assorted business persons who occupied the majority of the building, Rowan led his team toward the elevators. Valkyrie Security, the premier security firm on the West Coast, rented one floor and a large chunk of the parking garage and basement, but the rest of the tenants were an elite roster of Seattle's high-end lawyers, accountants, and financial planners. Rowan had hoped that their shared clientele list might make them better neighbors, but after six months, it was clear that most of the Hoskins Building hated him and his team.

Rowan had to admit that he hadn't exactly fostered a neighborly vibe. But he put most of their dislike down to the fact that while neat and tidy professionals liked feeling secure, they didn't want to be reminded that security frequently came with guns. There had already been a slew of angry emails when they'd first moved in about letting his *stormtroopers* traipse across the lobby with their weapons out. The guns hadn't been out. They just hadn't been concealed. Moving in all their equipment without flashing something around wasn't easy. Ultimately, Rowan had gone back and rented the basement so they could load in and out from the parking garage. That seemed to tamp things down for a bit. There had been more emails recently, but he had ignored them. He didn't have time for whatever bullshit complaints the business casual set had come up with.

Meanwhile, the renovation on the warehouse complex he'd purchased had run into one snag after another. What had promised to be a short six-month stay in the Hoskins Building now seemed like it would be a year.

Rowan headed for elevator three, followed by his second-in-command, Mark Goldman, as well as Teddy and José, but car three was crowded with giggling, over-caffeinated baby executives. So he switched to car one. He never took the same elevator from day to day. If he asked his clients to be careful, he should do the same. A woman was in the back corner of one, but she didn't look up as they entered.

Curvy, late twenties, reddish-tinted brunette—too young for him, but that didn't stop him from admiring her like the damn work of art she was. Oversized glasses and a messy bun combined to give her a sexy nerd look. She carried a folder, and, like everyone under thirty-five, had her eyes fixed on her phone. Rowan gave her plenty of space and made the other three crowd into the opposite side of the car as he tapped the button for twenty-six. She had already pushed twenty-three. That was the law firm Hoskins, Branch, and Kato. One of the partners, Howard Hoskins, owned the building but found renting out the top floor more profitable. Rowan appreciated the practicality of that, and he also liked the tactical advantage of being at the top.

Another suit approached the elevator, took a look inside, and then backed away. Rowan glanced back at his team. They all wore well-tailored black suits, but to his eye, only Teddy had any weaponry showing. The idiot had attempted to tote the Mossberg in from the car by discreetly covering the shotgun with his overcoat. Teddy aside, Rowan didn't think they looked scary. Teddy shrugged apologetically, and Rowan shrugged back as the doors slid closed. Some people were just chicken shit.

The doors shut, and the elevator lurched into motion.

"Mr. Valkyrie," said the girl, her voice smooth and pleasant. It was a tone that set off alarm bells for him. "Good morning."

Rowan turned to look at her more fully as she straightened up and slipped her phone into the pocket of her dress.

"Good morning," he said cautiously. The girl looked up at him, considering him very coolly, while he lost himself in her storm-gray eyes.

"This would seem like an excellent opportunity to discuss building protocol," she said.

Building protocol had been the subject line on the most recent email.

"I'm busy," he said automatically. It was usually true.

"We have exactly one hundred and nine seconds until we reach my floor. But don't worry, it will only take sixty."

"Were you waiting for me?" he demanded.

"Considering that you've been avoiding all attempts from my firm to talk to you otherwise, it seemed like a good idea."

"How did you know which elevator I would take?"

"It's Tuesday," she said as if that explained everything. "You tend to take one or three on Tuesdays, and I stacked car three with interns."

Rowan wasn't sure whether to be impressed or furious that he'd just been ambushed by a lawyer. He was both, he decided. Furious with himself and impressed by her. He checked his watch.

"You promised it would only take a minute. You've used thirty seconds."

She opened her folder, withdrew a piece of paper with a crisp snap and held it out to him. Rowan refused to take it, and she shoved it at him again with an angry glare. He mutely shook his head, reveling in her fury. Her eyes narrowed and she ruthlessly folded the paper in half. He leaned in, silently daring her to make a move. Grabbing him by the lapel, she tucked the sheet aggressively into the front of his suit jacket and he stared down at her in disbelief, shocked by her audacity.

"You will cease-and-desist with open carry in the lobby and all public spaces. You are a tenant, and you will follow the tenant code of conduct."

"Are the sheeple scared?" he asked sarcastically, confident that there hadn't been any open carry recently.

Her eyes flared with anger. "You do not own this building. It is the Hoskins Building, and it is my firm's job to ensure all tenants feel comfortable and safe within their workplace."

"So the flock sent you, by yourself, to talk to four armed men in an elevator? If you're not worried about our guns, then why would they be?"

"As a woman, every time I enter an elevator alone with men, I am at risk. The fact that you have guns only brings the risk factor up a tiny notch."

Rowan felt Teddy shift uncomfortably and move further away from the girl. Teddy was young enough that it probably had never occurred to him that virtually all women thought he could be a threat. Having it pointed out probably made him feel like a bad person and his discomfort came out in his body language.

"But let's get a few things straight," the girl continued. "My flock, as you describe them, are not scared of the substitute dicks your pack of assholes insist on flashing around."

"Really? That doesn't have them quaking in their loafers?"

"You want to know what keeps us up at night? What everyone around here prays for?"

She advanced an extra step, and Rowan leaned in, refusing to give ground. She smelled like something sweet. A fruit he couldn't quite name.

"It is our very fervent hope that you pay your junior twat monkeys enough to afford that escort on Saturday night because the last thing we need is for one of your inbred incels to start shooting up the place due to a misplaced sense of entitlement, access to weapons, and the fact that Becky in accounting turned him down. You don't get to mock people for feeling threatened when you know damn well you're a threat. Now stop treating the lobby and plaza like you own them because you don't."

The elevator dinged as it arrived at floor twenty-three.

"Thank you for your time, Mr. Valkyrie. Have a nice day."

She turned on her heel and exited the elevator with a determined stride.

Rowan waited until the doors closed again. He took the paper out of his jacket and opened it. The letter demanded—in flagrant lawyer-ese—that they cease-and-desist using the front entrance when armed.

"I thought we gave everyone strict instructions to use the basement entrance. Where the hell is she getting this shit about treating the lobby like we own it?"

Teddy cleared his throat, and Rowan raised an eyebrow at him.

"Actually, I've been meaning to bring it up. With the road construction on Fifth and all the one-way streets… everyone has to do the detour to get to the garage entrance. That's four extra blocks, and at peak traffic times, that can add like fifteen extra minutes. So I think some of the guys have been pulling onto the plaza to unload and then sending the car around."

"What do you mean *onto* the plaza?" demanded Rowan icily. It could not mean what he thought it meant. "You mean the loading zone."

"No," said Teddy. "They use the emergency services access ramp and pull up to the front door."

"Onto the plaza, with all the pedestrians, during peak times, when literally everyone can see them," clarified Rowan.

"Yeah," muttered Teddy.

"Oh, for fuck's sake," said Mark, taking off his glasses and pinching the bridge of his nose.

Rowan looked in disbelief at his team. "Gentleman, do you know what is worse than being called an asshole *and* a dick by a beautiful woman?" They all shook their heads. "It's when she's right."

2

Vivian

THE OFFICE

Vivian Kaye collected her tea from the breakroom and checked the hall before stepping out. As yet, no one had said anything about her encounter with Rowan Valkyrie, but she didn't think that silence would last.

She had gone into that elevator so incredibly full of confidence. Howard Hoskins had given the problem of Valkyrie Security to Belinda Erikson—the Harvard Law Bitch who thought delivering a cease-and-desist letter was beneath her—but Belinda hadn't been able to figure out how to do it. The Valkyrie website had only a generic *info at* email address. Phone calls were trapped in the morass of automation and well-trained front desk staff. Visits to the office were met with polite refusals of access. Registered mail would have gotten the job done, but Howard wanted to know that Rowan Valkyrie himself had received it, and he wanted it delivered by the end of the week.

So Belinda, with a smile, had dropped the problem on Vivian. Belinda hated that the top partner treated a lowly paralegal like Vivian with such respect. Vivian knew that Belinda was absolutely gleeful at the prospect of Vivian disappointing Howard.

What Belinda didn't understand—what none of the privileged lawyers who walked the halls of Hoskins, Branch, and Kato understood—was that Vivian did *not* fail. If her father had left her nothing else, it was the Marine Corps motto: Improvise, Adapt, and

Overcome. Her father, a decorated Marine Corps veteran, had died from cancer due to chemical exposure in Afghanistan when Vivian had been eighteen. It had slowed her college career and left her adrift in grief, but she had done what she knew would make her father proud—she had survived and excelled. And never, not for one second, was someone like Belinda going to take her down.

Vivian had taken on the mission to find Rowan Valkyrie and deliver the letter personally. The number of locations he was exposed to interaction were limited, so she'd had to discover his patterns. A few hours of watching the security recordings had given her Valkyrie's habits. The security guards disliked the Valkyrie crew and were happy to oblige. The interns had loved riding the elevator for a paid half hour and free coffee. All Vivian had to do was hand him the cease-and-desist letter, and it would have been mission accomplished.

Vivian heard the drawling, confident voice of Belinda from up the hall and took a quick left, hurrying into the secretarial cubicle nest. Belinda made secretaries come to her, so it was a safe place to hide.

Vivian hadn't failed in her mission—she *had* delivered the letter after all. But it was only a matter of time before Rowan Valkyrie placed a phone call and demanded an explanation as to why Vivian had unloaded an insult and profanity-laced tirade on him as well as the letter.

The worst part was that Vivian couldn't even explain herself. She'd looked all the way up into his hazel eyes with their green flecks and smug expression and realized that Rowan Valkyrie was someone who had gotten double helpings of handsome and powerful. Then she'd realized that she was leaning in.

She was not supposed to be affected by his charm. She liked sensible, practical guys! Not whatever the hell Rowan Valkyrie was.

Gorgeous and charismatic.

No. He was a jerk.

A challenge.

He'd been sarcastic and rude. And that was why Vivian had unloaded everything she thought no one would ever dare tell him.

Not because she wanted to prove that he didn't get to win at every aspect of life just by looking like that. Definitely not that.

"Hey, Viv," said Courtney, looking up from her desk. Vivian grimaced, and the younger girl looked startled. "Did you need something? I was going to email you about the research you asked me to pull."

"Oh, yeah, don't sweat that," whispered Vivian. "I'm good until tomorrow. I'm just hiding."

"Hiding?" she whispered, and Vivian nodded. "Belinda?" Courtney guessed, her expression souring. Vivian knew the administrative assistants took twice the flak from Belinda that Vivian did, and she tried to buffer them, but there was only so much she could do. The secretaries still appreciated it, but that only pissed Belinda off because Vivian was better-liked as a result.

Courtney stood up and checked a mirror that hung behind her monitor.

"Front hallway is clear," she said giving her blonde hair a little pat.

Vivian realized, in admiration, that Courtney could see the reflection from the windows in the hall from her carefully angled mirror. Courtney could easily spot visitors from either direction. The willowy assistant had ambush-proofed her desk.

"Thanks," Vivian whispered, hurrying out to the corridor.

Outside the window, the Seattle waterfront skyline made for gloomy viewing. The weather had broken with sunny September tradition and rain smacked the windows in a passive-aggressive drizzle that no one was prepared for. Through the rain drops she could see the Ferris wheel on the waterfront illuminated in Seahawks blue and green for the upcoming game.

The hall route led through the front lobby and was the long way around to get to her cubicle in front of Mr. Hoskins' office, but it was better than a short walk and a long talk with Belinda. Hoskins, Branch, and Kato was the city's premier law firm, and Vivian was lucky to work there, but she had worked her ass off to get the job and was good at what she did. Belinda, however, always managed to make Vivian's community college and state school education sound like a black mark on the company's reputation.

All but certain she'd escaped for at least the rest of the day, Vivian rounded the corner—the safety of her desk mere steps away—and stopped in horror.

Howard stood in the doorway of his office, chatting with none other than Rowan Valkyrie. Having stalked him in the course of her mission, Vivian knew that the handsome forty-two-year-old with just a sprinkling of gray in his near-black hair was retired Marine Force Recon. She knew he had multiple medals. She knew he had government security clearance and had worked for billionaires, ambassadors, foreign dignitaries, and rock stars. From shoving her letter into his jacket, she also knew he had a rock-solid chest. And from being in the very close proximity of an elevator for one hundred and nine seconds, she knew that he smelled like pine trees, had a scar on the back of his left hand, and practically vibrated with an intense energy that probably had women falling at his feet. What Vivian didn't know was why the hell he was here.

Howard was in the middle of a sentence. Considering that he'd been a lawyer for thirty years, that sentence could go on for a while. Rowan checked his watch.

"Howard," he said, holding up his hand in a stop signal. Mr. Hoskins stopped talking from sheer surprise. She doubted that anyone had interrupted him in years. "I appreciate your time and your thoughts. However, as I mentioned, I have exactly five minutes, and we're at four ten and counting."

"Ah," said Howard.

"I don't want to impose a time limit on you, but my

recommendation is that you use Vivian to communicate with us. She appears to be able to be succinct."

He knew her name? She hadn't told him her name. Fuck.

"She does have a talent for brevity," agreed Howard, nodding thoughtfully and not looking the least put-out.

"Great," said Rowan, nodding. "I'm glad we could carve out this time." He wheeled around and looked her up and down. "Vivian, you're with me."

More fuck.

"Uh," said Vivian, looking toward Howard, but he had gone back into his office.

"You're walking me to the elevator."

Fuckity fuck fuck fuck.

"OK," said Vivian, trotting a little to keep up with his long strides. Only when they were well past her desk and into the foyer did she realize she still had her tea mug in one hand.

"This is my card." His hand snapped out, producing a white card like a magic trick. Vivian took it from him because she didn't know what else to do. "I have spoken to my employees. However, if there are any further complaints, you will call me. If I have concerns regarding building protocol, I will call you."

They stopped in front of the elevator bank, and he jabbed the button.

"Do you have any questions?" he said, finally turning to face her.

She shouldn't. Rowan was a CEO, older and rich enough to buy everything she owned about twelve times over. He was in charge—he practically radiated in-chargeness. Actually, what he radiated was big daddy energy of the kind that made her want to bend over and say she'd been naughty. That kind of person, even when they asked for questions, didn't get asked questions.

"Why did they do it in the first place?"

It was possible that she had a tiny authority problem. Maybe Rowan could discipline her for it?

Damn it. What was wrong with her?

"They didn't want to take the construction detour, and they are used to getting away with things. I'm sure you understand."

"Me? Why?" Vivian was offended at the idea that she shared any affinity with his hooligans.

"You seem to have figured out that being brave enough to do something usually gets you what you want."

Vivian wanted to make a retort but couldn't think of a single thing to say. Even worse, he looked like he knew it.

"Right," Rowan said with a cocky smirk, his hazel eyes sparkling maliciously.

As if on cue, the elevator door opened, and he got in.

"Have a nice day, Miss Kaye."

3

Rowan

HOME & FAMILY

Vivian Kaye. Twenty-six. Paralegal with an associate's degree from a community college and a B.A. from a state college. Her background check came back with no criminal record and some college debt. In short, she was a poor kid who had managed to get a job at a top law firm where the head partner described her as *rather brilliant.*

Rowan clicked off the Hoskins, Branch, and Kato website. Vivian's picture was two-scrolls down on the "Our Team" page, and he'd already looked at it too many times. Instead, he opened the latest emails from his contractor about the warehouse renovation.

There had been progress on the west wing but a fresh delay while they investigated whether or not there was a buried propane tank that hadn't been marked. In a location that had been part of Seattle's industrial complex for over a century, that was entirely plausible. If he had learned anything about construction in this process, it was that humans in the 1950s gave zero fucks about the environment and just assumed that burying something would take care of whatever problems existed. So much for the good old days.

His contractor wanted permission to spend more money to do an exploratory dig. Yes, because he had money leaking out of his pockets. Valkyrie Security charged top rates, but he also put out a lot of cash to attract the best talent and use high-grade equipment. As a Marine, he understood the pressure of having lives depend on him, and he'd foolishly thought that starting his own business would be less pressure. But he hadn't understood the pressure of having paychecks on the line. It wasn't life or death—it was dreams, goals, and Mark and his wife feeling confident enough to start a family. It wasn't lives; it was only everything that made life worth living.

Rowan ran a hand through his hair. He wondered when it would be his turn to start living.

His thoughts turned back to Vivian. None of the facts he'd found about her online encompassed the way her storm-cloud eyes snapped when she was mad. The way she smelled like apricots. Or the slight bounce of her goddamn luxurious set of tits as she walked. Not to mention her slender waist and distractingly curvaceous ass. She was a fucking wet dream in a little black dress and sensible flats.

Rowan stretched his neck. He'd gone down to the law firm intent on making Vivian pay. Not a lot. Just a little. He thought an apology would have been appropriate. He was pissed that a paralegal, who apparently rated barely above a secretary, had managed to predict his movements. Worse, he still didn't know how she'd done it. And he'd wanted a little payback. Only somehow…

Howard's face had lit up at the mention of Vivian. Vivian was tough and resilient. And always taking care of her co-workers! Howard had been so happy to have someone else recognize Vivian for her talents.

It was the care-taking that had clicked for Rowan. Vivian had been genuinely angry. And she'd been angry because she thought Rowan was not taking proper care of *her* people. Rowan wanted payback because his pride was hurt, and she wanted to protect people. Which one of them was the security professional again?

So Rowan had adjusted the plan and devised a new form of payback.

He relished having one-upped her. Leaving her speechless at the elevator gave him a warm glow. The problem was that a second encounter had only confirmed his first opinion—Vivian Kaye was gorgeous but far too young for him. And then there was the fact that she seemed to hate his guts.

His phone pinged, and he saw a message from his closest brother, Forest. Forest had entered fatherhood in bewilderment three years ago, but now he could barely talk without saying something about little Oliver. Not that Rowan minded that every day came with at least one fresh photo of Oliver in the family text thread.

Rowan opened the message, saw Oliver's beaming spaghetti-covered face, and grinned. When he saw Oliver's face, he never regretted the sacrifices he'd made to make sure his brothers got a decent start to their careers. Seeing their lives unfold was everything.

"That is the *my nephew is cute* face," said Mark coming into Rowan's office. "What's the little guy up to today?"

Mark had taken the plunge to retire from the military instead of re-enlisting and had come to work as Rowan's Vice-President. Rowan felt lucky to have convinced him to jump ship, but knew the selling point had been that Mark and Jenny could settle down and start a family.

"Spaghetti," said Rowan, holding out the phone.

"Aw!" Mark made pinchy fingers at Oliver's cheeks. "You know," said Mark, looking up at Rowan, "you could get yourself one of these. Oliver might want a cousin."

"Uh-huh," said Rowan. "I feel like you and Jenny just want me to spawn so you're not the only ones in the company with kids."

"I mean..." said Mark and then grinned.

"I will do a lot of things for this company," said Rowan, "but reproducing isn't one of them. Besides, I'd have to have a partner for that."

"Well, it wouldn't hurt you to find one of those either," said Mark, looking at him over the top of his glasses. Since leaving the military, Mark had invested in multiple pairs of glasses. Rowan had suggested getting eye surgery, but Mark chose to spend money on more fashionable eyewear than the Marines had allowed.

"And where am I supposed to find the time to date?" asked

Rowan.

"Mmmm... You could ease back," said Mark. "Our crew is pretty solid. Our client roster is on track. You could take a tiny more time to yourself." Rowan gave him a look. "Anyway," Mark dropped his stack of papers on Rowan's desk, "I'm out for the day. You are going home eventually, right?"

"I'm going home now," said Rowan, making the decision. "I'll walk down with you. See? This is me taking time."

"Uh-huh. Let me grab my jacket."

Rowan opened the wardrobe he'd had installed to pull out his overcoat. He didn't understand why offices didn't get built with closets anymore. Did no one hang up their jackets? What about rain gear? Spare shoulder holsters? They all had to go somewhere. It looked unprofessional to have them hanging out for everyone to see.

He walked out to the hall and realized that he and Mark were the only ones still there. Everyone else had quit at a reasonable hour and gone off to their lives. Which is what he wanted them to do. The point of starting his own firm was to get all the fun of the military with a better work-life balance and a much better fucking paycheck. Except getting the company off the ground had been an all-in proposition and for the last four years, it had been his entire life. This year was the first extended period that he'd felt good about easing back even a fraction. Which was also why Mark and Jenny had chosen to have kids now. The dream was becoming reality. Rowan had no fucking clue what to do with that, and he was more than a little petrified that he would screw it up.

They rode down in the elevator, and Mark showed him the latest baby ultrasounds. Rowan looked forward to having Mark's kids running around the place and made a mental note to start baby prep and gun lock-down now.

"And then, apparently," said Mark, as they stepped out of the elevator, "there are some people that eat the placenta. I mean, what the fuck kind of cannibalism shit-show are we running here?"

"It's all-natural?" Rowan offered because he had nothing else. Then he frowned. Ahead of them, Vivian was being dogged by some asshat in a white linen suit. Every few steps, the man would dodge in front of her, and she would go determinedly around.

"Uh, who is the asshole threatening the lawyer girl?" asked Mark.

"We don't know that he's threatening Vivian," said Rowan.

"She does not like him," said Mark, scrutinizing the set of Vivian's shoulders.

"And if he touches her, I will pound his face into the pavement," said Rowan, surprised to realize how much he meant the sentiment. "But I don't think we can preemptively stuff him into the garbage chute if she doesn't ask for help."

"No," snapped Vivian, finally turning to face her follower, which allowed them to hear what she was saying. "No, Mr. Tate. I cannot discuss client conversations with you."

"You're not a lawyer. That doesn't apply to you," said Mr. Tate, reaching out to touch Vivian's arm. She side-stepped the outstretched hand, but Rowan felt a growl of anger in his chest.

"As a third party agent, privilege does apply to me. Privilege belongs to the client and only the client can wave it. So if I want to keep my job, we will not be talking about it. Goodnight, Mr. Tate."

A security golf cart trundled into view, an overweight security guard behind the wheel.

"Evening, Vivian," said the security guard, eyeing the man in the suit and letting the golf cart idle in place.

"Hey, Bill," said Vivian, turning to him with a smile. Mr. Tate stormed back toward Mark and Rowan.

"Stupid bitch," Mr. Tate muttered as he passed them and got into a Porsche parked in a handicapped stall. If Rowan had been ambivalent about Mr. Tate before, the comment and his sallow, dissatisfied face was enough to put him on Rowan's shit-list. If he saw that jackass again, Rowan would be making a more direct intervention.

The security guard and Vivian nodded to each other and

continued in their separate directions as the Porsche raced out of the garage. Vivian had made it safely to her own car so Mark and Rowan continued into the parking garage.

"Oh, my God, I love her car," said Mark, laughing as Vivian drove past them in a mint green Mini-Cooper.

"Too bad she doesn't love us," said Rowan.

"I don't know," said Mark. "We may have made a bad first impression, but I bet you could bring her around."

Rowan gave him strong side-eye.

"What? Based on her car alone, she is clearly more our kind of people than theirs." He gestured to the tidal wave of cars where Rowan's blue Ferrari and Mark's red Tesla stood out among the sea of black and charcoal German automobiles. "She swears like a sailor. She knows how to strategize and plan an ambush. She's not scared of… apparently anything. And she had a POW-MIA sticker on her back window. Honestly, since you brought it up, if you're looking for a potential partner, I'd start with her."

"I did not bring it up. You brought it up," said Rowan. "And I'm going home now before you come up with some sort of bizarre rom-com plot for us to fall in love and have eight babies."

"Eight does seem like a lot," said Mark with a grin. "See you tomorrow."

Rowan grabbed some take-out on his way home and brought it into his condo. The building was on the south side of Lake Union and had a great view, but was a run-down eighties monstrosity that had once been three condos. The building had cost him a million and a half but he had the luxury of being able to renovate everything to his liking and security tastes. Compared to the million-dollar two-bedroom apartments next to the Space Needle, it was a steal. It was also still under construction and costing him an arm and a leg. Like the rest of his life.

His phone rang as he separated his chopsticks.

"Hey, Forest," he said, putting the call on speaker. "What's up?"

"Hey! Two things." His brother had taken to itemizing his conversations, probably because Oliver had condensed his time and attention span. "Can you babysit next Tuesday afternoon for a couple of hours?"

"Yes, if you don't mind him being in the office."

"As long as no guns are lying around, then sure. I need Olly out from underfoot while I interview nannies."

"Don't you want him there for nannies?" asked Rowan, confused. "And what happened to Mrs. Brown?"

"Mrs. Brown is moving back to Colorado to take care of her own grandbabies. I offered her triple the salary, and she said *that's sweet* and patted me on the head, but the answer was still no. And these are the first round of interviews where I get rid of the gum chewers and college kids. Once I've got a couple I like, I'll introduce them to Olly."

"Got it," said Rowan. "Yeah, bring him by. The guys all love him. We will feed him sugar and let him play with whatever Doc's invented this week."

"OK, do we need to have another talk about child safety?" demanded Forest.

"Hey, I basically raised the two of you, and you both still have all your fingers."

"Considering some of the shit we got up to, I don't know how you managed that. But if we could have slightly higher standards for Olly, that would be great."

Rowan chuckled. "Well, you're home every night and feeding him some amount of spaghetti, judging from the pictures, so you're already doing better than our parents."

"Yeah, our parents aren't exactly a high bar to clear," said Forest sourly. Their father's disappearing act when Rowan was eleven had actually been an uptick in the quality of their lives because although it had taken income out of the house, at least he wasn't there to hit them anymore. "But that does bring me to item two. Have you heard from Ash lately?"

Their younger brother Asher was some sort of tech investment whiz, and Rowan readily admitted that he didn't understand half of what Ash did. What he could tell was that sometimes Ash's schedule ran heavy and then opened up for a lot of free time, which meant it was sometimes hard to connect if their schedules didn't run hot and cold at the same time. The family text thread had been helpful for that.

Rowan flipped open his messages and skimmed through.

"No, I haven't heard from him, and he hasn't done more than thumbs-up pictures of Olly all week."

"Yeah, I tried to call him yesterday, and it went… badly?"

"What kind of badly?" asked Rowan.

"Like, I think he was at work and wasn't willing to say anything but yes or no to anything I asked."

"Do we think someone is holding him hostage?" asked Rowan with a laugh.

"No," said Forest hesitantly, "but I asked about Emma, and I got ultra frosty Ash telling me that Emma would not be attending anything for the foreseeable future and that he would appreciate it if I didn't discuss her with anyone."

Rowan let out a low whistle. Ash had been dating Emma Van Lanken for two years, and Rowan had assumed they were stable. Rowan hadn't liked Emma—he thought the heiress was cold, snobby, and selfish—but all indications had pointed toward a solid relationship.

"Maybe I'll hit him up and see if he wants to get dinner on the weekend. We'll get more out of him in person."

"Good idea," said Forest, sounding relieved. "What night, though? Because my babysitting options are limited."

"We'll do Saturday night, and I will find you a babysitter," promised Rowan, thinking he could make Mark and Jenny practice their parenting skills on Olly.

Forest sighed, sounding tired. "Thanks, Rowan. I know this probably sounds dumb, but sometimes arranging Olly's schedule is one more thing, and I can't handle it."

"You're making it," said Rowan encouragingly, thinking that Forest could outsource more.

"Yeah, I'm making it," said Forest. "But that's all I'm doing. Most nights, I just pass out on the couch."

"You could call in for reinforcements more often," said Rowan. "I don't mind helping out."

"I know, but you're busy."

Rowan made a note to start dropping in on Forest more often. Uncle Rowan could definitely be taking Olly off for a few adventures. Forest needed some downtime.

"Well, clear your Saturday evening," said Rowan. "I'll pin down Ash, and then we'll figure out what's going on, and you can spend time with an adult for once."

"You mean Ash, right?"

"Ha. Ha."

Forest chuckled. "No, we all know you're the adult. You've always been our grown-up."

"Maybe that's why I feel ancient," said Rowan.

"Well, let's go out and get drunk, then," said Forest. "That's sure to make us feel better."

Rowan laughed. "Not so sure about that, but we can try."

4
Vivian

THE PARKING GARAGE

Vivian picked up her tea mug and took a sip, only to discover it was cold. She also wasn't entirely sure it was today's cup. She checked her email and saw with relief that there was nothing new in the inbox. That meant the Victory Mission Gala was under control, and all of the work fires had yet to explode for the week. She had a meeting with the Tates and Howard at two-fifteen, and while she was prepped on the paperwork, she probably ought to run a brush through her hair and check that she didn't have anything in her teeth. Not that it would matter. Charles Tate Junior was a sleazebag. She could have an entire salad hanging out of her mouth, and he'd still say something inappropriate. He was a puffy-faced smarmy jackass who made Vivian feel dirty with his lingering glances, and she couldn't believe he'd shown up in the parking garage to try and weasel information out of her.

She checked her email again. Still nothing. Not one peep from Valkyrie security since the previous week. Which was disappointing.

No, it was great.

Rowan Valkyrie was a big, grumpy jerk. She didn't want to see him again.

Her cellphone rang, and she saw with horror that the caller ID read ROWAN VALKYRIE. It was as if she had Beetlejuiced him into existence.

"Hello?" asked Vivian cautiously.

"Vivian."

Vivian shivered at the sound of Rowan's voice on the other end of the call. How he managed to make her name sound like a promise or possibly a threat, she didn't understand.

"Would you care to explain what is going on in the parking garage?"

"Um... People are parking their cars?"

The silence on the line said that her answer was incorrect.

"Mm-hm. Vivian." Once again, the sound of her name in his pissed-off growl sent a little shiver down her spine. It was probably supposed to scare her, but it wasn't fear that was fluttering her stomach. "Perhaps you could join me on parking level one near the elevators." It should have been a question, but there was no question mark on his command.

"Well, I have a meeting shortly," she began, although she was already standing up.

"Now, Vivian!" he snapped.

"You are not my boss!" she barked back, but the line was dead. He'd already hung up on her.

Vivian marched out to the elevators and angrily punched the button for the parking level. Who did he think he was? Just because he was a wealthy, handsome CEO, who could probably kill people with his pinkies or something did not mean he got to order her around.

She arrived at the parking level and found him waiting directly outside the doors with his arms folded across his chest.

"I'm your liaison, not your personal parking service," she snapped.

"I have no problem parking. I'm having trouble leaving." He paused slightly and frowned. "You have pencils in your hair."

Thrown off, Vivian tentatively put her hands up to her bun.

"Multiple pencils," he said, plucking one out and handing it to her.

"That is for..." A lock of hair unrolled and fell against her face. "Structural integrity," she said, sweeping the hair behind her ear and shoving the pencil into her pocket. One of his eyebrows went up like he couldn't believe she'd just said that.

"Noted. Now, can we discuss my car?"

"You brought me down here to show me your car?" she demanded. What kind of rich guy weirdness was this?

He stepped aside and swept an arm behind her, pushing her gently forward with a soft hand on the small of her back.

"Well, technically, I brought you down here to show you my wheels."

His car was a Ferrari. Sleek and a gorgeous custom blue, it looked fast standing still. Which was an illusion since it had a bright yellow parking boot clamped around the front driver's side wheel. It was also parked in a loading zone.

"Ah." Well, at least now she understood his problem.

"Would you care to explain why I have been booted?"

"Unpaid parking tickets?" she offered, taking out her phone and dialing Barb, who was head of building security.

"I don't have any parking tickets," he said through clenched teeth. "What I do have is one hour for lunch, and this is making food difficult to achieve."

It was nearly two, and she knew he arrived between seven and eight. How had nobody fed the poor man already? No wonder he was grumpy.

"Hey, Viv," said Barb, picking up. "I've got you on the security feed. I see Mr. Hot Shit finally realized his fucktard mobile is on lockdown."

"Yes," said Viv.

"Well, maybe he should stop acting like he owns the fucking place. We got eighteen complaints about his squad this month, and he's been avoiding all attempts to communicate, so now playtime is over. We've been letting him park in the loading zone for long enough. This is his warning shot."

"Yes, actually, I believe I had a breakthrough on that front last week. Have there been any new complaints since then?"

"No, nothing new, now that you mention it. Hoskins put you in charge?" asked Barb drily.

"Yes. I'm the new Valkyrie Security liaison, so you should let me know about all issues."

"Sucks to be you," said Barb. "You want me to unboot him?"

Vivian glanced at Rowan. His scorching glare and folded arms were probably supposed to communicate the heat of his anger, but all Vivian got was hot.

"Um... yeah. I think we could do that."

"OK, your call. But I fucking want his ass on notice."

"I will express that."

"Uh-huh. Zots will be down in a minute."

"Thanks!"

"This is for you, not for him. He's a shit stain," said Barb and hung up.

"Ah, Naval communication," said Vivian. "Such an art form."

"What?" he asked, frowning.

"That was Barb. She's in charge of Security and is also a retired Chief Petty Officer."

Rowan put a hand up and itched his eyebrow, which was a blatant tell that he knew he was in deep shit.

"Which you would know if you had bothered to talk to her when you moved in. In fact, her crew could have been buffering you against the other tenants, but... you would rather act like they're E1 and you're Recon."

"I *am* Recon," he growled furiously, and Vivian nearly laughed. Sometimes pissing off Marines was too easy.

"Well, right now, the Chief Petty Officer says you're a shit stain and has your car in her pocket, and you've used up all the leniency they were giving you."

"They were giving me leniency?"

"That *is* a loading zone," Vivian said. "They probably assumed you could read the sign *and* between the lines."

If looks could have killed, she would have been toe-up on the pavement.

"We were only supposed to be here for six months! We were supposed to be a blip on everyone's radar. There wasn't supposed to be a need for leniency, buffering, or... anything!" He waved his arms in frustration. Mr. Bigshot CEO was having a minor meltdown. He definitely needed a snack.

"But now you're here for longer, so maybe you should try acting like you're part of our community," said Vivian, fishing in her sweater pocket.

Rowan opened his mouth, but he was cut off by a smooth voice from behind her, and Vivian's spine instinctually stiffened in dislike.

"Ah, Vivian."

"Mr. Tate," she said, pivoting and giving Charles Tate Junior a wintery smile. Privately, she called him Chucky, but she tried not to be anything less than professional to his face.

"You're not going to be late for our meeting, are you? I'd hate to tell Howard where I found you." His look said he had every intention of doing just that and would probably also imply that she was down here selling herself to the nearest stranger.

"Actually," snapped Rowan, stepping forward to stand next to her, "regardless of the location, this is a tenant meeting that you are interrupting. Ms. Kaye will be available when we are done and not before. Feel free to tell Howard whatever you like. Don't let us keep you."

Vivian relished Rowan's clear dismissal and sharp use of *Ms. Kaye*. Chucky gave Rowan a surly glance that lingered on Rowan's watch and correctly assessed that Rowan was a match for him financially.

Vivian wanted to stick out her tongue at him. Rowan might be a grump, but he wasn't an icky little turd. Tate's eyes returned to Vivian, and she felt Rowan shift his weight, moving closer to her. She didn't feel in need of protection, and she didn't really think Chucky was a threat—at least not one she couldn't handle—but she liked feeling Rowan next to her. And she liked that he wasn't posturing or making grandiose threats. He was just making himself very, very present.

"Building business," said Vivian, with another plastic smile. "I'm sure I'll be up shortly for the meeting with you and your father."

"Of course," said Chucky and stalked off toward the elevators, but he ruined his grand exit by awkwardly glancing over his shoulders at them as if uncomfortable at being watched.

"He exists in the universe, but I'm a shit stain?" asked Rowan when the elevator doors had closed.

Vivian couldn't help the snort of laughter that escaped her.

"I wouldn't be concerned. I believe that Chucky could only aspire to achieve the rank of shit stain."

"Chucky?" he repeated, his eyes twinkling as a lazy grin spread across his face.

"Mr. Tate," Vivian corrected guiltily.

"Mm-hmm. Sure."

"Zots will be down to unlock your car momentarily," said Vivian, trying to get back on track.

"Great. Thank you."

"Well, you should probably also thank Barb."

"I will do that. Thank you for your advice," Rowan said, and Vivian blinked. "I appreciate the operational insight."

Vivian found herself with nothing to say. CEOs didn't take advice. She could barely get lawyers who liked her to listen when she spoke. His eyes twinkled again. His smug expression said he knew damn well he'd thrown her and clearly enjoyed rendering her speechless.

"Well. Then." In the pocket of her cardigan, her fingers locked around the granola bar she'd stashed there as emergency rations. "You may have a squirrel snack." She held out the bar, and he looked like he could not believe what he was seeing.

"Squirrel snack?"

"It's mostly made of nuts and chocolate," she said, already wishing she could take it back. "Your lunch is very late." Why was she such a dork?

He took the bar out of her hand. "Squirrel snacks. Got it."

"OK," said Vivian, backing up. "I'm leaving. Try not to be an asshole to anyone while I'm not around."

"Being an asshole is my specialty," he said, tearing open the wrapper. "And I stick to my strengths."

Vivian rolled her eyes. Men. Well, this man, anyway. God, why did he have to be so annoying and good-looking at the same time? It was unfair. Vivian marched back to the elevator and *almost* managed to not look back before she got in. But she wasn't as strong as she would like to be. Her last glimpse of Rowan was of him leaning against his car, enjoying his granola bar, as he watched her leave.

5

Vivian

OFFICE MANAGEMENT

Vivian shook her head and returned upstairs, trying not to feel like she'd just left the best part of her day. Courtney rushed by as Vivian exited the elevator, then pulled up and reversed course.

"Ack! You're here. Thank God! Howard sent me to find you, and I heard Chucky Tate say you were in the parking garage flirting with some guy." Courtney looked horrified.

"I was talking to Rowan Valkyrie about a parking issue," said Vivian.

"Oh. How'd that go?" Courtney's expression said that she would rather eat slugs than have that conversation.

"I... Fed him a squirrel snack out of my pocket and told him to stop being an asshole."

Courtney let out a sharp giggle of hysterical laughter.

"No, seriously."

"No, seriously," said Vivian. "I think I have something wrong with me."

"It's probably called having a spine and no filter," said Courtney. "Meanwhile, you're late for the Tate meeting, and Chucky is being a douchehole."

"Yeah, Rowan told him to get lost, and I think Chucky was pissed about it. I'll get in there."

"OK, but um... Maybe..." Courtney gestured to Vivian's hair.

"Right," said Vivian, remembering the pencil situation.

Once in the bathroom, she saw it was even worse than she'd feared. Her charmingly messy bun had somehow transformed into something that looked like it had been styled by a tornado. And she had talked to Rowan that way the entire time. No wonder he'd looked at her like she was insane. Vivian pulled out the second pencil, managed to sleek it into something less disastrous, then grabbed the Tate file off her desk and headed into Howard's office.

"Sorry, I'm late," she said, smiling at the group. "Mr. Valkyrie had an issue with building security."

"Ah," said Howard, nodding. "That makes sense. I hope you were able to resolve matters."

"Yes, I may have to do a formal introduction between him and Barb later, but I think we're resolved for now."

Howard nodded again. "Good. Thank you for taking care of that. Meanwhile, Charles and I have just been discussing his will and trusts. Did you pull the paperwork?"

"I did," said Vivian, coming forward and placing the file on his desk. She had already told Howard about Chucky's after-hours visit in the parking garage to finagle information out of her, but apparently, they weren't mentioning that. Mr. Tate Sr. had three trusts and a will. Depending on any recent tax law developments, he liked to periodically restructure them, but any movement in his father's accounts made Junior nervous. "The 1997 trust could be decanted, and the will was last updated in 2013."

"I want to update the will," said Charles Sr., taking a piece of paper from his jacket pocket and handing it to Vivian. "And I want to restructure the trusts."

"I don't think we need to restructure all of them," said Chucky, his tone colored by annoyance.

"Well, I'm getting up there," said Charles. "And while it's all well and good to name you as a trustee and executive while I'm fiddling around, I don't want to die and leave matters like that."

"What do you mean?" demanded Chucky.

"Oh, come on," said Charles, patting his son's shoulder. "You go through money like water. I want to ensure there's something left in the estate for your sister and mother."

"Stepmother and half-sister," snapped Chucky. Charles Sr. visibly rolled his eyes.

"Anyway, I've put my wishes down there, and I don't know quite how to adjust the trusts, but I thought we could at least amend the will today."

Vivian handed the paper to Howard. Having recently reviewed Mr. Tate's will, she could see that the changes would mean Chucky's portion had dropped to well below half the estate.

Howard took the paper and looked over it. She and Howard had played a lot of poker over the last three years of her employment, and she recognized his game face as he read over the document.

"Not a problem," said Howard. "We'll draw up the paperwork and have it ready to be signed and notarized next week. And in the meantime, we'll talk to some of the tax guys on staff about recommendations for the trusts."

"Great," said Charles, beaming.

"However, why don't you do me a favor." Howard picked up a pen and slid it and the letter across the desk. "Why don't you just sign and date that for me so we have it on record for our files."

"Of course," said Mr. Tate, picking up the pen and signing with a flourish. Chucky craned his neck, reading over his father's shoulder.

Charles signed the letter and then stood and handed it back to Howard. Behind him, Chucky turned a violent shade of furious red.

"I'll have one of the girls call your assistant and set up an appointment for next week," said Howard, standing to shake Mr. Tate's hand.

"Perfect," said Charles. "It's so nice to be able to count on friends like you."

The pair left the office, but Vivian heard shouting from Chucky by the time they reached the elevator.

"Should I call security?" asked Vivian, looking after them.

"No, but you should scan this letter and put the original in the vault, not the file cabinet. If Chucky isn't back up here by tomorrow trying to get it back from us, I will eat my hat."

"You're not supposed to know I call him Chucky," said Vivian.

"But it's so very right," he said with a grin that sent the wrinkles around his eyes into a crinkly cheerful squint. "How are things with Rowan? Did the parking thing really get smoothed over? I know Barb can be a bit of a stickler when she gets P.O.'d."

"Oh. Hm." Barb had never been a problem for Vivian. She wondered if other people had a different experience. "I think it did. He seemed fine when I left anyway."

Howard scrutinized her for a moment. Awkward silences were one of his top lawyer skills. Vivian made a conscious choice to not blurt out the part about squirrel snacks or pencils in her hair.

"Great," he said at last, smiling. "If this goes well, I'd like to channel you into more building relations duties."

"Oh," said Vivian. She wasn't sure what she thought about that. She *did* feel stagnated at paralegal. She didn't have much further to advance unless she wanted to go to law school. She kind of did, but the price tag scared her, and she wasn't sure if she loved law or if she just didn't like being bossed around by lawyers. She could also stay where she was until Howard retired, but she wasn't sure it would be fulfilling.

Who was she kidding?

It would not be. Vivian already knew that. She'd just been pretending it would be OK because she adored Howard.

"We'll talk about it more later," said Howard. "It's just that with your legal background and people skills, real estate management might be a good fit. You're too smart to stay a paralegal forever. Not that I mind because you make my life easy, but still... I've got to find some way to keep you from jumping ship!"

"I'm not going to do that," said Vivian, laughing.

"Darn tooting, you're not," he agreed, with a fierce expression that made Vivian laugh again.

Vivian returned to her desk, but the smile dropped off her face as she slid back into her desk. Her inbox had magically filled itself while she was gone. Most of it was busy work she could do with her eyes closed. There was a fat stack of emails about the gala, and the email thread about her birthday on Saturday had resurfaced. It seemed basic, but she had decided to make it a Triple D night—dinner, drinks, dancing. It had been too long since she'd been out with the girls, and she wanted some actual, non-technology-assisted face time.

With a sigh, she opened the top email on the gala. Her father's dying request had been that she keep volunteering with the Victory Mission, the charity he'd helped found. She didn't mind. She believed in the mission, and as it had grown, she'd tried not to interfere with the operational stuff. It wasn't fair to staff to pop in and tell them, *well, actually...* when they were older and had a degree in fundraising. She just had a lifetime of reading all the research that had gone into making the organization and still got Christmas cards from most of the past board members. But no one needed to be second-guessed, so she'd tried to keep her head on the volunteer segment. Assisting with the annual fundraising gala had been a great place for her. She'd pushed and shoved and used all of Howard's connections to make the gala one of the top fundraising events in the city. It was now big enough that they'd had to bring on event planners for the third year in a row. That was how she'd met Ashley, who was now a firm part of her girl squad.

The gala email was someone who couldn't remember where they'd stashed the centerpieces they'd bought on sale months earlier. Vivian dashed off a reminder that they were in the storage unit. The following two emails were similar in nature—asking her was easier than figuring it out for themselves. Vivian knew she had unintentionally become their walking continuity of operations database.

Theoretically, if she were an employee, she would train others to be auxiliary databases. But she wasn't, so she sucked it up and she considered it part of her volunteerism.

But it also meant that the gala didn't *really* need her. Howard needed her, but she spent most of her time supervising two junior paralegals and writing first drafts of his briefs. These days, every time she turned around, it felt like she'd outgrown her job.

She was supposed to have been *something* by now. Instead, she was a legally savvy, non-profit volunteer who knew a lot about the military without having any service experience and was good at managing people. She was a jack-of-all-trades, trained for nothing in particular.

Vivian stared angrily at her email as a wave of anger hit. If her father had lived, she would have gone to a four-year university and found a career instead of a job. But here she was, facing twenty-seven and not one step closer to being anything other than a glorified secretary. She was stuck with the fact that her job was unfulfilling because she couldn't afford the time or money it would take to discover her perfect place. So she kept busy helping everyone else, but far too often, she felt terribly alone.

Vivian sighed and tried to let the rage go. One of the more surprising aspects of grief was how often she got angry—something that did her no good. She wished she had someone to talk to about it, but most of her friends wouldn't understand, and a therapist was too expensive. The nagging thought that a boyfriend would be nice showed up in her head like a pop-up on a website. Of course, the pop-up was accompanied by Rowan Valkyrie's face. With a sigh, she hit the X to close that thought out.

6

Rowan

THE BOYS CLUB

Rowan rode past the law firm's floor on the elevator and thought about pushing their button, but the only thing he had to tell Vivian was that she had been right—he should have talked to Barb before even moving into the building. The sixty-something Naval retiree was his kind of people, and she knew all the ways to keep him and the other building tenants apart.

He could have gone in to tell Howard that *he* was right—Vivian was brilliant—but Rowan didn't have a reason to do that either. She was an adorably disastrous little genius, with pencils in her hair, food in her pockets, and the rest made up of sass and brains, but telling someone that would only let everyone know about his massive crush.

"Building relations seem to be going better," said Mark, also eyeing the twenty-third floor. "The meeting with the Security Chief went OK?"

"Yeah," agreed Rowan. "I brought bourbon. She cursed me out, then called me *son* and told me to get my head out of my ass. I said *yes, ma'am,* and now we're friends."

"Aw, the Navy," said Mark fondly.

"The gift baskets went out?" asked Rowan.

"Arrived yesterday," said Teddy, rubbing his hand over his recently buzzed hair. His scalp looked pale. Teddy didn't usually maintain his hair at military standards and always said he was growing it out. But after it reached about three inches long, Teddy would freak out and shave it all down. Rowan had been expecting a freshly shaved head for the last few weeks. Having PTSD from military service wasn't entirely unexpected, but no one ever mentioned it would be from the barbers.

"We got a round of thank you emails," continued Teddy. "Estate planners and associated industries seem very formal. They all said, *Dear Mr. Valkyrie.*"

Rowan shrugged. He couldn't explain why Estate Planners always had to have everything be so *appropriate*, but he suspected that they handed out the sticks for everyone's asses on the first day of employment. Vivian being the exception. He thought her hair alone kept her from being allowed in the Estate Planning club, not to mention her swearing abilities. Being called an asshole by Vivian had pretty much been the highlight of his week.

He needed to stop. Stop thinking about Vivian. Stop fantasizing. Just stop. It wasn't going to happen. Vivian didn't like him. Well, maybe she liked him a little. She *had* fed him squirrel snacks. But Rowan was fifteen years older than she was. The idea was ridiculous.

He focused back in on what Mark was saying. More about the upcoming workload. Rowan's brain wanted to go back to Vivian and the things she could do with that pretty, filthy mouth. Instead, he refocused and tried not to glare at Mark for talking about a computer upgrade. He managed to make it through most of the morning without thinking about her again—primarily by keeping busy—so he was surprised when his phone popped up with Vivian's number. He was even more surprised to hear himself say he would come down to talk. Apparently, his dick thought another encounter might further help flesh out his fantasies. It probably would, but it wasn't going to do his crush any good.

Vivian's hair had been forced into tameness, and she had accessorized with high-heels today and her usual mug of tea, although the glasses had been left somewhere. But there was another oversized cardigan to compensate for the lack of proper nerd wear and sleek hair. He liked the heels, which had little ankle straps, like naughty Mary Janes, but he suspected they only meant she had a meeting later. He missed the tousled hair, though. Polite buns were no fun.

"You didn't have to come down," she said. Rowan couldn't tell if she was flustered or annoyed.

"I prefer to keep my communications in-person, if possible," he said. Which was mostly true. "And I was on my way down anyway." Also, mostly true. He could have left any time in the next half hour.

"It's really not..." She was getting a little pink, which was fucking adorable.

"Why am I here, Vivian?" he asked suspiciously.

"It's your own fault," she said, getting even pinker. "You made me the company liaison, and now I'm obligated to tell you things even when..."

"Even when what?"

He liked pink and uncomfortable Vivian. He wanted to run his tongue down her neck and see if he could get the same result. As if she'd heard his thought, she put her hand up to her neck. She had long, graceful fingers. He wanted to see them wrapped around his cock. He tried to focus on what she was saying, but that just brought his attention to her mouth. That he also wanted wrapped... damn it.

"Well, obviously, what you do with this information is up to you. You could choose to act, make a response, or... ignore it."

The look on her face said that, personally, she would ignore it.

"Thank you for clarifying my options. Tell me what it is," Rowan said, attempting to sound detached and professional.

"When you rented basement space, you were allocated parking spots that historically have been used as... incentives. And now that you've extended your contract beyond six months, *some* people think you should relinquish those spots since Mr. Hoskins refuses to co-opt more of the employee or public parking."

"So *some* people think I should give up the spots that I negoti-ated and paid for and am currently using because they would like a reserved spot with their name on it?"

Rowan wanted to laugh. Vivian was practically biting her tongue trying to keep her mouth shut. She knew it was ridiculous and hated that she had been forced to mention this to him.

"And they think I would do this because they are under the impression that I'm a nice person?" He didn't see how that was possible.

"You did send those nice apology gift baskets to the businesses." She didn't look like she was taking her own argument seriously.

"Those were bribes."

She nodded understandingly. "Food and alcohol do go a long way."

Rowan had never felt more frustrated in his life. He had managed to get her to stop fighting and agree with him... about the fact that he was not a nice person. This was not winning.

"I think that, in this case, I will take your suggestion and go with option three. I'm ignoring this."

Vivian's eyes went wide in alarm. "I did not suggest that!"

"Your face did. I believe your face."

She almost laughed. It was right there, and with a heroic effort, she swallowed it back down.

"No proof. You can't subpoena my face," Vivian said.

"And now you know why I like to communicate in person."

He needed to get out of this conversation before he said something else ridiculous. He pushed the elevator button and turned back to give a polite goodbye as the doors trundled open.

"There she is!" trilled a patently fake cheerful voice.

"Oh, shit balls!" gasped Vivian, and dove into the elevator.

He stepped in after her and pushed the door closed button as a woman carrying a cake rounded the corner. Vivian slammed the L button in a panic, the tea in her mug sloshing dangerously.

"Vivian, is it possible that we are fleeing your own birthday party?"

"That's not a birthday party. That's a passive-aggressive excuse for Susan to make me eat shit cake while she continues her rampage against anyone under forty. I thought I managed to avoid this! My birthday isn't until Saturday! How did she even find out? I have told *no one*. It was that bitch Stephen in HR. I bet they looked at my file." Her eyes narrowed in a way that promised retribution.

"Forced celebration is against the Geneva Convention. You should file a complaint."

"You're making that up."

"Yes. Well, no. Committing outrages upon personal dignity, in particular, humiliating or degrading treatment, is a war crime, but you're just at work, so it probably doesn't count."

"Funny, but some days, it feels like war."

"I know what you mean."

"It's all very well for you," she snapped. "You probably get Scotch and cigars on your birthday."

He did, actually.

"Do you know what I get? I get shit cake and those disgusting chocolates with the alcohol in them."

"Those are neither alcohol nor chocolate."

Her tea nearly decorated the wall as she flailed her arms in rage.

"Exactly my point! And that is worse than getting nothing because now I have the chore of disposing of them along with the cruelty of knowing that if I put those in my mouth, I will only be disappointed, yet having them right there mocking me."

They stared at each other while he tried very hard not to laugh.

"And now you are laughing at me."

"Quietly. On the inside."

She wilted—just sagged in defeat—and he wanted to hug her so much he took a half-step forward. Shitty birthdays were the worst. With a visible effort, she straightened up and lifted her head.

"Well, it's nearly the lunch hour. I will go for a walk and get lunch somewhere."

"It's raining, and you don't have a purse."

She looked down at her cute shoes.

"I will... sit in the lobby. I have tea." She put her chin up as if daring him to argue the value of tea. "I'm not going back until they've forgotten about me and eaten the cake themselves."

She was being so brave, and it was the saddest thing he'd ever seen.

"I know where there is chocolate," he said. He knew it was a bad idea even as the words came out of his mouth. He also realized he would be doing it anyway. He wanted Vivian to like him.

She looked at him suspiciously. "Where?"

With a sigh, he pulled out his badge, swiped it under the security sensor, and pushed the button for basement level two. She watched him with an expression that looked torn between curiosity and confusion.

The problem with owning a private security company was that, at some point, he'd had to admit that he had his own tiny army. But that meant he had to perform all the duties of the logistics branch of the military. And *that* meant that somewhere on his property, there had to be what amounted to a clubhouse for boys to do boy things. He held his breath as he entered with Vivian.

Teddy and three others were in the midst of gun disassembly and cleaning, and a poker game was in full swing because... of course it was. He was pleased to see that no one was day-drinking. He'd put his foot down on that, but as had recently been demonstrated by their trips across the plaza, sometimes behavior codes needed to be monitored. Everyone looked up and froze as he walked in.

The other thing about being in command of his own private military was that they expected him to tell them what to do, and they didn't generally require much explanation.

"This is Vivian. She will be here for an hour. You will feed her chocolate. You will not embarrass yourselves or me."

There was a general chorus of *yes, sirs*. He looked down at Vivian to see how she was taking being placed in the care of the inbred incels.

She was beaming at him. A genuine smile. For him.

"Thanks," she said.

"I suggest you vet the chocolate before saying thanks," he said drily.

"As long as there's no singing, we're fine," said Vivian.

"I believe I can guarantee that."

Rowan made eye contact with Teddy, who nodded his understanding. Vivian would be politely taken care of, or it would be Teddy's head on the chopping block.

"Have fun," he said, turning to go. Maybe she'd wish he'd stayed. Who was he kidding? She'd probably be happier with a group more her age, anyway. God, when had he gotten so old?

"So," he heard Vivian say as he left, "poker? That sounds fun."

He almost turned around and went back in but made himself keep walking. Vivian was a big girl and could handle herself against those sharks.

Probably.

7
Vivian

THE NIGHT CLUB

The boy in front of her turned to high-five his bros, and Vivian hurriedly slipped away, heading back toward her table.

"He was cute!" beamed Christine, giving a little shimmy that made her gold dress sparkle.

"Yeah, real cute giant twenty-five-year-old man-baby," said Vivian, sliding into the booth beside Ashley, who chuckled. Her birthday outing had turned out to be a great girl's night, but so far it hadn't included any decent dating prospects.

"You don't know that," protested Christine. "You spent five minutes talking to him. You complain about all the hot guys. I swear it's like you don't actually want to meet anyone."

Vivian sighed. Over the last few months, Christine had become increasingly disapproving of Vivian's negative attitude toward dating. Christine was the youngest of their friend group, and although Vivian was only two years older than Christine, she frequently felt as if they were a solid decade apart. She felt closer to Ashley, who was thirty-two. Loretta and Rachel were still on the dance floor, and Vivian did a head check on them. They looked like they were having a blast.

"I do want to meet someone," said Vivian. "But of those five minutes, he spent at least two responding to texts on his phone, talking to his boys, and last, but definitely not least, he called me bro."

Christine paused, her nose wrinkling. "OK, well, being bro'd is not ideal," she admitted. "But what's wrong with being twenty-five and having friends?"

"Oh, my God," said a man with a beer in one hand and too much chest hair peeking out of his unbuttoned shirt. "Is this a meeting of the U.N.?"

"What?" Vivian stared at him, completely puzzled by his out of the blue question, but Christine made a growl of anger.

"Well, like, you're white, and they're..." He petered out as he realized that pointing out that Ashley was Black and Christine was Korean might not go well.

"Oh, I'm sorry," said Ashley. "This a gathering of W.A.A.A., the Women Against Assholes Association. And we only let the assholes speak once a month."

"What?" he asked, looking confused.

"Tonight is not your night," translated Vivian. "Keep walking."

Christine laughed into her wine as the asshole slunk away.

"That douchebag threw me off. I forgot what we were talking about." Vivian hadn't forgotten. She was just hoping to change the subject.

"What's wrong with a boy having friends?" Christine had no intention of letting it go.

"Nothing," said Vivian, with a sigh. "And if all I was looking for was a hook-up, then maybe... sure. Well, OK, probably not. I'm not going home with someone who tried to high-five me. But someone like him would be fine. It's just that... I would like to have someone with more..."

"More what?" demanded Christine, as if she had caught Vivian out. Vivian paused, trying to wrap words around what she wanted to express. "See? You don't even know. Any of the guys you shoot down could be good boyfriends."

"I'm not looking for a boyfriend," said Vivian. "I'm looking for a partner. I want someone who has his head on straight and knows what he's doing with his life. I want excitingly stable."

"Excitingly stable?" asked Ashley, laughing, while eyeing a sexy hunk of man candy at another table.

"Passionate about his life, but reliable," explained Vivian.

Like Rowan Valkyrie. No, not like him. What was she thinking? Well, she was probably thinking about his rock-hard chest, hazel eyes, and sharp jawline. But that was just physical stuff because she was hetero and not blind.

Another girl walked up to the guy Ashley had her eye on. They were clearly a couple, and Ashley let out an annoyed breath that ruffled her natural curls.

"What guy in his twenties is going to be Mr. Career and make six figures?" said Christine. "You've got to adjust your expectations."

"It's not the money!" protested Vivian. "It's more like I want..."

"You want someone who meets you where you're at," said Ashley.

"Yeah," agreed Vivian.

Christine raised an eyebrow. "What does that even mean?"

Ashley sighed. "Look, the way I figure it, life is a train track, and we're all little trains zipping along it. And all the trains have to pull in at every station. Childhood, puberty, living on your own. Life is full of all these big and little stops, and we have to go to all of them. The problem is that we're not all moving at the same speed. Due to her life being the way it is, Vivian had to stop at some of the stations very quickly. She had to figure out life insurance, death benefits, funerals, career, bills, school, and everything you don't even know exists yet because you're still on your parent's health insurance and have three roommates."

Christine glanced guiltily at Vivian.

"And there isn't anything wrong with that," said Vivian, in Christine's defense. "I wish I hadn't had to think about those things either!"

The death of Vivian's father didn't come up a lot, but when

it did, Christine always looked awkward. Christine meant well, but Vivian thought the topic caused her to panic.

"No, there isn't anything wrong with it," said Ashley, making a placating motion with her hands. "There isn't anything wrong with either life. It's literally just life. But it does mean that Vivian has arrived at some of the stations earlier than other people her age. And what she wants is a train that's going her same speed. Which will be hard to find in a twenty-five-year-old who still calls everyone bro."

"Oh," said Christine, seeming to chew on that. "That does kind of make sense."

Vivian wanted to add that it wasn't really the paperwork that made her different from people in her age group. It was the grief. Knowing what it meant to lose someone was a gulf that was hard to cross. Christine was sunshine cheerful in a way that Vivian remembered but couldn't ever go back to. It wasn't that she was always sad or couldn't be happy, but she couldn't remember how to live like death didn't exist. Vivian glanced at Ashley, who smiled at her. Ashley had lost her mom the previous year in an unexpected heart attack. Vivian gave half a shrug back, knowing that Ashley understood but didn't want to try to explain that part to Christine either.

"OK, so..." Christine's brown eyes narrowed, and she began to wind one long black lock of hair around her finger.

"Recalculating," murmured Ashley, and Vivian laughed. Christine worked in data processing, and the group joke was that she operated on Javascript and Java.

"What you need is a train that has been to all the same stops as you."

"Not all of them," said Ashley. "Just enough to know what she's talking about."

"And you need someone who is heading for the next stop at a similar speed. Next stops being partnership, monogamous or otherwise." She added that part for Ashley since she was currently exploring polyamory. "Followed by kids, yes?"

"I mean... ideally. I'm not in the kid zone right now, but yeah, I think that's one of my upcoming train stations," said Vivian.

"How do you feel about other people's kids?"

"I like them for other people?"

"But you don't want to be a stepmom?"

"Uh... No, thanks. That looks like something I don't have the energy or skills for."

"So, you need an older guy with no kids who is invested in his career but is also looking for someone."

Vivian's thoughts went to Rowan Valkyrie again, and she forcefully pulled them back to Christine's serious expression.

"Yes?" agreed Vivian, tentatively.

"You're twenty-seven, so we'll put a cap at forty-seven and the bottom at thirty-two."

"What?" asked Vivian.

"To re-do your dating profiles. We'll need to adjust your parameters, and then you should swipe right on some older guys to re-jigger their algorithms."

"I don't know..." said Ashley. "This is sounding like you're going to get creepy old dudes with dad-bod."

"Thirty-two isn't old," said Christine.

"Thanks," said Ashley drily.

"And we can lower the top-end if you want and then add a physical fitness preference. I'm going to run some keywords and see what would be good to include."

"You can't scam the dating site algorithms," protested Ashley.

"Sure I can! I do it all the time. You figure out what keywords the algorithm is hitting, and then you put those in your profile, and it matches you with people you're into."

"Then why are you still single?" asked Vivian.

"Because I'm bi and I'm having a hard time finding one person that ticks all my boxes right now."

"Or you could find two people who check both your boxes,"

suggested Ashley.

"Except philosophically, I'm a monogamist," said Christine and Ashley rolled her eyes. "And besides, right now, a relationship sounds like a lot of work."

"Then why are you pushing me into it?" demanded Vivian, outraged.

"Well, you keep saying you want to meet someone, but all I see you do is rejecting people. But now I see that your parameters are set wrong!"

"Oh, it's your parameters," said Ashley with a wink at Vivian.

"But it is! If she isn't targeting the right user pool, she won't get the desired results."

"I may be drunk," said Vivian, "but that actually sounded like it made sense."

"It did to me, too," said Ashley, "and that scares me. I may need to stop drinking."

"I was thinking I needed to order another round," said Vivian.

"Mmm," said Christine, raising her glass of white wine. "Sorry, this is the max of my budget. I'm sipping slowly."

"On me," said Vivian.

"It's your birthday!" protested Christine.

"Yes, but I... got a bonus today, so drinks are on me." Vivian fudged the poker game since her friends disapproved when she suckered her coworkers. It wasn't her fault that most people saw her boobs and assumed she couldn't play poker. But the girls said it led to bad vibes at work, and she had to stick to strictly legit poker games. They were probably right, but it wasn't as much fun. "Also, a gorgeous new lingerie set that arrives tomorrow," she added to distract from her hesitation around her lie.

"You and your lingerie," said Ashley, shaking her head.

"Expensive lingerie is my secret armor against the drudgery of the world," said Vivian.

"I love your boobs," said Christine with a sigh.

"I'm not bi, but I also love your boobs," said Ashley.

Vivian laughed and looked down her own shirt. "Yeah, the girls aren't bad, and they look so good in lace. Too bad I don't have anyone to show them to currently."

"It's like I don't even exist," said Christine sadly.

"I'll show you my boobs anytime, and you know it," said Vivian, rolling her eyes.

"Not in a fun way," said Christine.

Vivian took a quick glance around. No one was looking. She lifted her shirt and flashed Christine, who went wide-eyed and choked on her wine. Ashley laughed so hard that she slipped off her chair and nearly onto the floor but managed to hang onto the table.

"I may need a cigarette and a donut," said Christine when she could breathe.

"Just the donut for me," said Ashley.

Vivian laughed. Thanks to her friends and Rowan's clubhouse poker game, this was turning out to be the best birthday she'd had in a long time.

8
Rowan

THE DONUT SHOP

Rowan looked at his drunk younger brothers in the rearview mirror. He'd never seen Asher quite so on his ass before. The kid was absolutely nearing the puking stage. Not that Ash was much of a kid these days. But this breakup seemed to be hitting him hard. It was good riddance as far as Rowan was concerned, but it still surprised him.

"Donuts!" yelled Ash and kicked the back of the seat, managing to sound exactly like he had when he was four.

"I would also like to have the fat-fried breads," said Forest. Forest had reached the pompous stage of drunk.

"I will get you donuts," said Rowan, "but you will stay here, and you will not—I repeat, *not*—puke in my car."

"I promise nothing," said Forest.

"Promish," said Ash, nodding as though his skull was loose, his sandy blonde hair flopping into his face.

Sometimes, Rowan wondered if he'd excelled in the military because he already had a decade of experience managing his brothers by the time he enlisted. He also sometimes wondered if he'd always been gun-shy about marriage and kids because he didn't want to raise another set of hellions like Forest and Asher. Although, lately, with the arrival of Oliver, Rowan had started to think maybe having kids while he wasn't a kid himself might be OK. Not that he was likely to get a shot at kids at his age. Perhaps he should have given in when Melissa had demanded he pony up on the marriage and children front. Being tied to Melissa for all time probably would have been a nightmare, but he couldn't help wishing that things had turned out differently.

With a sigh, Rowan got out and crossed the street to the only open donut shop that had popped up on his Google search. A group of women were ahead of him—heading for the donut shop too. They looked like they'd been clubbing. The heels were high and the hemlines were short. He focused on the leader whose ass was a curvy dream in a green skirt. Her long, auburn hair, the same color as Vivian's, swayed in counterpoint to her walk, and he couldn't help shaking his head at himself. His various run-ins with Vivian had left his libido in overdrive.

He stretched his legs and entered right behind them. They had barely crossed the threshold when the group fractured, two women heading for the restroom and another two answering phone calls, leaving the woman in the green dress alone to stand in line behind two guys who looked and smelled incredibly high.

"Just order us whatever you're getting," chirped one of the girls heading for the restroom.

"But I didn't even want donuts," the girl in the green skirt replied, sounding bewildered, and Rowan found his pulse rate jumping by about ten points.

"Post-club birthday donut binge?" he asked, and Vivian squeaked in surprise and spun around to face him. He grabbed her arms as she teetered in her heels. He got her stabilized and tried to pretend that he hadn't pulled her closer to him.

"Rowan! I mean… Mr.—"

"Rowan's fine," he said before she called him Mr. Valkyrie and made him feel like a dinosaur.

"What are you doing here?" she asked, shoving her hair behind her ear. There were no nerd accessories tonight. She looked gorgeous.

"My youngest brother is in the middle of a break-up."

"Ah," she said, nodding sagely. "And he's drunk off his ass and demanding donuts?"

"Yes," he said. "And my middle brother is just drunk. I made them stay in the car, but I'm not sure it was the right tactical decision."

"Always a crapshoot. They could puke, but if you let them out of the car, then you've lost containment. Who knows where they'll go from there?"

"Next thing you know, someone is assaulting a police horse."

"That is a felony," she said severely.

"I'm aware of that *now*. Although, in his defense, it was a very rude horse."

She laughed, a delightful burbling chuckle. "I try to limit my squad to public indecency and property damage. I can't afford the bail on felonies."

"Oh, I don't bail them out," said Rowan. "At least not for a solid twenty-four hours."

"Ooh. Tough love."

"Self-preservation. I'll have to deal with their hangover if I get them out before then. I take it this is the real birthday party?"

"Yes," she said, standing up straighter, which coincidentally shoved her breasts out at him. He kept his eyes firmly on her face, but it was a struggle. Her top was a slinky thing, and he wanted to pull it off her shoulders.

"And did they feed you proper chocolate and alcohol?"

She opened her purse and revealed a stack of Theo chocolate bars in varying flavors.

"They gave me the entire product line," said Vivian, beaming proudly. Whatever else she had been about to say was curtailed by the presence of one of her friends—a pretty Asian girl in a gold metallic dress—who, despite being on the phone, had come close enough for drill sergeant worthy inspection.

"One second," the girl said and took the phone away from

her ear to look him up and down. "His tailoring says gainfully employed." She squinted up at him as if assessing. "But is he passionate about his career?"

"Christine!" hissed Vivian angrily.

"I am, actually," he replied, confused by both her question and academic tone.

"Excellent. And you're thirty-eight-ish?"

"Forty-two."

"Perfect. Now, do you—"

"Oh my God, Christine, if you don't walk away right now, I will never show you my boobs again."

Christine vacillated and then stomped her foot. "Fine!" she said in response to Vivian's angry glare. "But I'm just saying!" And then she waved at Rowan as if he was evidence in her argument before putting the phone back to her ear and going outside.

Meanwhile, Rowan discovered that the mere thought of Vivian's naked breasts snatched all the air from his lungs.

"I'm sorry," said Vivian in what he thought of as her professional voice. "That related to a previous conversation. Please disregard anything that she says."

"I'm not sure I can," said Rowan with more honesty than he'd meant to express. "I'm also having difficulty figuring out what the conversation could have been."

"That is... umm... there were things." Vivian's face was a picture. She clearly hadn't been prepared for the question. She was going all pink.

"Oh, I want to subpoena that face," said Rowan, grinning, and Vivian laughed. Her head ducked down, and she shuffled her feet. Maybe it was his imagination, but he thought she shuffled a few inches closer to him.

He opened his mouth to say something—although he had no idea what—and then the two customers in front of them got their orders and moved away from the counter.

"Hey, Vivian," said the young man behind the counter, smiling wide enough to annoy Rowan. Vivian jumped a little and turned around to face the clerk.

"Hey, Paolo! What are you doing on the night shift?"

Paolo was probably in his early twenties, with a mop of curly hair. Rowan didn't think Vivian would be interested in the boy, but he didn't particularly care for the way Paolo leaned toward Vivian's side of the counter.

"Picking up extra hours," Paolo said with a shrug.

"Your Dad giving you shit again?"

"Yeah," admitted Paolo sheepishly. "I think you were right. I need to save up and move out. I applied to that apprenticeship program you showed me."

"Good for you! That is a guaranteed union job when you get out. I think it's great."

Rowan couldn't help smiling. Howard had been right about Vivian's constant caretaking.

"Thanks," he said, looking embarrassed but genuinely grateful, and then he glanced at Rowan and flushed as he realized his crush was showing. Not that Rowan could blame him, considering that he and Paolo were in the same boat. "What kind of donuts did you want?"

"The girls and I better get a dozen. Half chocolate and half powdered sugar. And then I think Rowan will need the break-up special."

"You are *not* buying my brother's donuts," said Rowan firmly.

Vivian chuckled delightedly.

"It's the least I can do after all your hospitality and letting me play poker in your clubhouse."

Roman grimaced. He'd been feeling guilty about that. He hoped they hadn't taken too much of her money.

"I'm not sure hospitality is the right word for letting you play poker with—"

"Oh, God," exclaimed one of the girls as the duo returned from the bathroom. "You let her play poker? Vivian, is that why you've been buying us drinks all night?"

"You said it was a bonus," said the other.

"Well, sort of a bonus," protested Vivian, looking like she'd been caught with her hand in the cookie jar. "Rowan said I could." She looked up at him nervously. "You didn't say I couldn't win."

She could win with him any day of the fucking week.

"How much did you take them for?" he asked, pretending to be stern, although it was a stretch.

"Four hundred dollars," she mumbled. "And I already spent most of it." Her bottom lip puckered out. God, she was so sexy when she was being naughty. He could feel a stupid grin spreading across his face.

"Vivian!" exclaimed one of the girls. "We talked about this! You can't take money from those unsuspecting idiots who wander the halls of your building. They're too dumb and misogynistic for that. They get mad. It isn't good for your career!"

"It's fine," Rowan said, laughing at Vivian's pouty expression. "I'm pretty sure they had it coming."

Vivian's chin came up, and she gave him a smile that was worth a lot more than four hundred dollars.

"Break-up special," said Paolo, plunking down a massive box.

"Holy hell. How many donuts is that?" demanded Rowan in shock.

"Two dozen," said Vivian. "But if he's really broken-hearted, he will eat them all."

"No cap," said Paolo as if he were all too familiar with the facts of donuts and breakups.

"Donuts!" Asher's faint voice echoed through the front windows of the shop.

Christine opened the door and looked in.

"There's some yahoo wailing for donuts out a car window. Does he belong to someone?"

"Oh, God," said Rowan in exasperation. Vivian giggled and shoved the box into his arms.

"Good luck," she said, and he couldn't stop himself from smiling back, even as she pushed him toward the door. Maybe he just liked having her hands on him.

"Thanks. See you on Monday." He paused when he got to the door. "And happy birthday."

"Thanks!" she said, smiling at him. "See you Monday." The way she said it made it sound like a promise.

9
Vivian

MONDAY, MONDAY

"Hey Tyrique!" said Vivian, seeing the Valkyrie employee coming toward her as she entered the lobby. Tyrique was one of the younger members of the Valkyrie team and had sharp cornrows and a wide, friendly smile.

"Hey, Viv!"

Tyrique had lost a lot of money to her, so she thought he deserved extra niceness.

"How'd this weekend go?" he asked.

"Championship mode!" Which was the most hilarious phrase she'd picked up from hanging out with them.

"Up top!"

She held up her hand, and he high-fived as they passed each other.

"See ya!"

It was only after she'd high-fived that she realized that Rowan was with Teddy and Mark by the elevators. She couldn't tell what his expression meant.

"Hey, Viv," said Teddy.

"Hi, Teddy," she said, smiling.

"Championship mode?" repeated Rowan.

"The mode you enter when you have bested the weekend and are the top player," said Vivian. She didn't add that part of the afterglow of the weekend had been sending him off with donuts and the way he'd smiled at her when he'd said *Happy Birthday*. Ashley and Christine had instantly agreed that she needed to reset her parameters to Rowan Valkyrie, but Vivian had tried to wave them off. Rowan was out of her league. Which is also what she had also told herself when she'd put on her newest lingerie purchase in the morning, stared into the mirror, and wished she would be showing it to him later.

"Vivian is currently in championship mode," said Teddy. "She took all our money."

"I spent it on girls and alcohol," said Vivian. "It was great."

"Well, that's what they were going to do with it," said Rowan, laughing. "So at least it went to its intended purpose."

"Yeah, but I wanted to spend it on buying girls alcohol so that they would like *me*," protested Teddy, and Mark laughed.

Vivian sighed and shook her head. "Teddy, no. Never spend money to *make* someone like you. Only spend money on girls that *already* like you."

"Oof," said Mark. "I feel like my twenties just got bullseyed."

"Truth hurts," said Vivian. "Not to say that we all haven't fallen into that trap occasionally." Like when she had bought her work crush two dozen donuts.

"Please. Like you have ever needed to spend money to make someone like you," said Rowan skeptically.

"Believe it or not, I'm not everyone's cup of tea," said Vivian tartly.

"What? Not everyone enjoys being accosted by strange women in an elevator?"

"Are you saying you do?" she asked, feeling a slight flush on her cheeks. Why the hell did Teddy and Mark have to be there? There was a ding, and instead of replying, Rowan looked around at his elevator choices.

"Which elevator am I getting in?" he asked.

"What?"

"You seem to be an expert on my elevator habits. I thought I'd inquire."

"Well, it's Monday, so I'd put money on one or four," said Vivian primly.

"Three it is," Rowan said, heading that direction.

"You're going to throw my odds off," she said, trailing after him, unable to stop herself from checking out his ass.

"Good," he said forcefully.

"Is there a pool?" asked Mark. "How do I get in on the action?"

"You can't be in it," said Vivian. "You can influence the outcome."

"I'm starting to think you have a gambling problem," said Rowan.

"Not really," said Vivian, leaning forward to press her button. "I only put money on games I can win."

Rowan had already pushed her floor, and her hand bumped into his just as she caught his eye, and suddenly she was breathless.

"I didn't realize I counted as a game," he said. His pine-scented aftershave wafted the very short distance between them, and she had to physically repress the urge to stroke her fingers across his chin.

"Yes, but you're Russian Roulette, and no one wins that game, so refer to rule number one," she said, keeping her tone light. There was no way she could play with a guy like Rowan. He was an all-or-nothing proposition.

"Only bet on games you can win?" he asked, raising an eyebrow.

"I'm Candy Land," said Vivian. "So, it's OK to bet on me."

"Mmm. Sure you're not Crazy Eights?" The twinkle was back in his eye.

"Maybe Clue," mused Vivian, refusing to be baited.

"You are a mystery," he agreed, which might almost have been a compliment.

"Can I be Monopoly?" asked Mark, and Vivian laughed.

"Sure," said Vivian. "Do not pass go. Give me two hundred dollars."

"Pretty sure we already did," said Teddy, which made Rowan chuckle.

"You're welcome to try to win your money back," said Vivian. Teddy might have a shot at it. The cards had not been going his way, but he'd seemed like a decent player.

"No thanks," said Teddy with a grin. "I learned my lesson."

Vivian shrugged.

The door opened on her floor, and Vivian saw Belinda Erikson, looking gorgeous in a cream and black ensemble that screamed money and sophistication, talking to Howard. Vivian tried not to let the stratified class culture of her workplace bother her, but Belinda seemed to particularly delight in showing Vivian up. And Vivian couldn't quite give up comparing herself to the tall, slender lawyer. It was probably because Belinda had the hair Vivian had always wanted in high school.

"Well, why not just have Vivian do it," said Belinda, her voice sounding coolly amused.

"Vivian has enough on her plate. Ah! Rowan! Just who I wanted to see."

Vivian shuffled off the elevator, feeling under-dressed like she always did around Belinda. Vivian glanced regretfully down at her pale blue dress and flats. The A-line skirt and wide belt had seemed retro and fun in the mirror at home, but confronted with Belinda's streamlined style, it suddenly seemed childish. But she was also aware of the three very large men who were flanking her like reassuring sheepdogs.

"Hi, Howard," said Rowan, eyeing Belinda, who smiled at him. Vivian tried to unclench her jaw and not grind her teeth. It wasn't healthy. "Is there something I can help you with?"

"Want to spend money on a good cause?" Howard asked bluntly.

"Probably not," said Rowan, and instead of being offended, Howard's face crinkled into a smile.

"Of course you don't, but I'm going to talk you into it anyway.

I'm on the board of this non-profit that Vivian is involved in. It's a fantastic organization that raises money for veterans. They do a gala. That means it's my job to convince all my wealthy friends to buy seats."

Prior to having Howard minding the table captains, Vivian had watched the ticket sales nervously. But Howard usually had all the tables nailed down by the time early bird ticket sales ended.

"I'm supposed to have my tables sold by now," continued Howard, "but one of my table captains dropped the ball, and now we've got an entire empty table."

Vivian groaned, instantly knowing which person it had been. "George?"

"Yeah, completely spaced off," said Howard. "What do you think, Rowan? It's ten seats. Great dinner."

"Can I just give you money and not show up?"

"No! The whole point is to have butts in the seats, so we can ask for more money. I usually get a company table. It's a great opportunity for the younger kids to network and meet people in the community."

Rowan made a thoughtful noise like he thought that was actually persuasive.

"Viv," said Howard, turning to her. "How much did we raise for the Victory Mission last year at the gala?"

"Quarter million, I think?" She looked at Rowan and shrugged, feeling embarrassed. She hated asking veterans for donations unless they were in the Howard category. On the other hand, Rowan was rich, so maybe it would be OK. Truthfully, she'd been planning on hitting up most of his staff for volunteer time, not money.

"The Victory Mission works to prevent veteran suicide," she said. "Which sounds depressing, but the gala is a good time. We have food, dancing. The guys would have fun. It's usually a lot of military folks."

"That's the event you mentioned last week, right?" asked Teddy, and she smiled gratefully at him. "I'm down for a ticket."

"I don't like to push it on people," she said. "Especially vets, but..."

"Way to sell it, Vivian," said Belinda with a condescending laugh, and Vivian gritted her teeth again. Having Belinda tell her how to pitch the Victory Mission was beyond belief. "Vivian does a lot of work, but maybe she's a little better behind the scenes. Hi," she said, stepping forward with an outstretched hand, forcing Vivian to step aside. "I'm Belinda Erikson." As always, she said her name like the other person should recognize it.

"Nice to meet you," Rowan said with a chilly smile and a brief handshake. Belinda's head tilted like she was about to speak, but Rowan turned back to Howard. "Howard, you're right. It sounds like a good opportunity for team development. Have Vivian get me the information."

"Will do," said Howard, with a wave as the men got back on the elevator.

The elevator doors slid shut, and Howard clapped his hands together in a pleased fashion. "Whew! It's great to fill that space without too much trouble. Vivian, thank you for developing that relationship. Things have been going much more smoothly with them. Now," he checked his watch, "I think I've got the partner meeting next. Then, Viv, we're going over the Latimer file before lunch?"

Vivian nodded mutely. The Latimer file was already prepped and ready to go.

"Belinda, I'll see you at two to review the Fargo case?"

"Yes," said Belinda, with a tight smile.

Howard bustled away, looking happy with his schedule.

"Yes, thanks so much for developing that relationship," sneered Belinda. "He seems all warm and fuzzy now."

Belinda stalked off, and Vivian clamped her mouth shut on every angry retort that sprang to mind.

10

Rowan

LAND DRONE

"I don't think I like Belinda," said Mark when the doors closed. Rowan made a grunt of agreement. He hadn't liked her tone or how she'd pushed Vivian aside. But Rowan *had* appreciated Vivian's low key insistence on not pushing a Veteran's event on him. He sometimes felt they were on everyone's ask-list because of his service record. And how sweet was it that she volunteered for a military charity?

"She kind of had mega asshole vibes," agreed Teddy. "Not that I wouldn't bang her. But what was that crack at Vivian?"

"They seem like they have a lot of workplace drama up in there. Glad I just work with you bitches," said Mark.

"Well," said Teddy, "now that our cycles are synched up, it's a lot better."

Rowan snorted. "Idiots."

Rowan didn't want to admit it, but he also had trouble with how friendly Vivian had been to Tyrique and Teddy. High-fives, teasing— everything had been so sociable. She was the same age as they were. It made sense. But damn it, he was selfish enough to want her to himself.

With his current bank account, finding a girl to fuck was relatively easy. He had enough cash to get whatever size and shape he wanted. As long as what he wanted was to spend money on a girl who was only mildly interested in talking to him, then everything was fine. But what he wanted was a curvy, auburn-haired girl who cared enough to argue with him. One who wasn't afraid to call him on his bullshit. One that could conquer the poker table as long as you fed her enough chocolate. But those kinds of girls wanted someone who didn't need to have *championship mode* explained to them. Vivian was not going to be interested in him, and that was all there was to it.

His phone beeped, and Rowan checked it as he got off the floor. New prototype TODAY!

"I haven't been paying attention to Doc," said Rowan. "What is he excited about?"

Mark chuckled. "It's his new land drone for interior surveillance."

"Land drone..." Rowan tried to make that into something that made sense. "Isn't that just a remote-control car?"

"Yes, but it sounds like we play with toys if you put it like that," said Mark.

"We do play with toys. Expensive toys that do really cool shit. But, I mean, come on," said Rowan.

"I don't think our egos are prepared for that kind of honesty," said Mark.

"I know mine's not," agreed Teddy.

"OK, well, apparently, there's a new prototype of our land drone, which is good because I think we'll want it if we're vetting the Al Shamsi property."

"We do? I thought that was a sweet 'fly to the Caribbean to make sure the house was secure' gig?" asked Teddy.

"We cannot confirm that the house is secure without checking the utilities and crawl spaces for threats," said Rowan.

Teddy groaned.

"They have rats the size of your head down there," said Mark. "Have fun in the crawl space."

"Right. So where's my remote control car again?" demanded Teddy.

"Land drone," said Rowan and Mark simultaneously and then

they all laughed.

Rowan managed to work through most of the morning without thinking about Vivian. Most of his to-do list was paperwork and there weren't even any pending problems to worry him. It occurred to him that there hadn't been any work-related emergencies for over year—the company really was stable and that was a huge relief.

It was nearly lunch when Doc popped into his office.

"Is this a good time for the Land Drone prototype?" he asked. He was carrying a small vehicle under one arm.

"Yeah, Doc, come on in."

Goodwin Brown, AKA Doc, was a nerd. To be specific, he was Valkyrie Security's top nerd. He was their R&D department and Mr. Fix-It all rolled into one. Rowan had lured him away from MIT with a fat paycheck and the promise that they would let him shoot things occasionally. Two years in, Rowan thought Doc was even weirder than when he'd hired the kid, but also thought it was quite possibly one of the better business decisions he'd made. But then, Rowan believed that all of his success really boiled down to picking the right personnel. Without Mark, Teddy, and the rest, Valkyrie Security was just another mercenary group.

"OK," said Doc excitedly, setting the vehicle down and flipping switches on top of it. There was a whir as a tiny arm with a camera extended a few inches. "I widened the lens aperture, so it's got more visual range. I reinforced the housing so it's got greater resilience against impacts and built a wider base so it's harder to flip. And it uses Bluetooth, so you can connect it to a designated screen or phone."

"Sounds good," said Rowan. "Will it be ready by the end of the month?"

"Yeah, absolutely." He pulled up a screen on his tablet and handed it to Rowan. "OK, here you can see the resolution."

Doc flipped a switch on his remote control, and the knobby wheels slowly turned and then began to trundle across the carpet.

"See, you can turn the camera 360 degrees."

"Cool."

Doc pivoted the camera, and Rowan was amused to see his office from the floor. He and Doc looked like giants.

"And with this button…" Doc fiddled with the controls, and the tank drove about four feet and then stopped. Rowan saw that the light on the controller also died, but Doc fiddled with the disks frantically. "I don't understand."

"Probably needs new batteries in the remote," said Rowan.

Doc looked up and blushed. "I did play with it a lot yesterday."

"Just go grab batteries," said Rowan, trying not to laugh at Doc's embarrassment.

"Right. Be right back."

Doc zoomed out, and Rowan shook his head as he went to check his email. Doc could probably design a Mars rover if he put his mind to it, but couldn't remember to pack lunch. That was fine. Rowan had guys who could work the logistics of what to pack down to the smallest item. Doc would get lunch and batteries, and they got a tiny camera tank in return. It was a symbiotic relationship.

In the lobby, he heard the faint ding of the elevator and echo of voices through the thin partition wall to the foyer.

"Hey, Teddy! Can I see Rowan?"

"Sure, let me buzz you in."

"Vivian's here to see you, Sir," Teddy said over the intercom.

The sound of Vivian's voice in their lobby brought Rowan to his feet. He looked around and tried to figure out what he was supposed to be doing. Probably not standing at his desk like an idiot.

"Thanks," he said into the intercom. He heard the buzz of the door lock as Teddy unlocked the door to the private portion of the office and tried to decide if he should sit down again. That seemed like a big dick CEO move, and he felt more in control when he moved, so he went around the desk, preparing to meet her halfway.

"Hi." Vivian carried a handful of papers and sorted through

them as she walked. Now that her jacket was off, he could see that the fluttery blue skirt was attached to a figure-hugging top that was giving serious retro Marilyn Monroe vibes. "I have info on the gala. Do you have a minute?"

"Yeah," he said, adding a smile, but she was already looking at her papers.

"OK, I can help with registration if you get stuck. Howard and I usually badger everyone and their brother this time of year, so I've practically got the form memorized. He was in the Army, so we're the charity he actually cares about."

"I didn't know that," said Rowan, feeling surprised. He'd liked Howard. Although he would have liked him more if he could finish a sentence in under a minute. But he respected Howard for still finding a way to serve the veteran community so many years later.

There was a sharp click and whir from somewhere on the floor.

"Yeah," she said, looking up with a smile, "he put himself through undergrad on the GI Bill. I kind of think that's why he hired—"

Too late, Rowan saw the land drone streak across the floor and directly under Vivian's foot. He took a giant step and leaned in to catch her as she pitched forward with a shriek. Rowan received her entire weight in one flailing mass, grabbed for what he could, and tried to keep her from hitting the floor.

Moments later, he found himself staring down into her gray eyes as she clung to his shoulders, panting. It was only then that he realized while one arm was wrapped around her waist, his other hand was firmly clamped on her ass... under her dress. And what a fucking ass. Thick, soft, overflowing his hand, just like he'd pictured.

"Are you all right?"

"I think so?"

Vivian planted her feet and took some of the weight off his arms. But that moved her face closer to his and a little wave of apricot scent floated up to him. Along with the weight shift came the realization that there seemed to be some strappy bits in surprising locations.

"Should I let go?" he asked.

"Ummm…"

The pause lingered, and her lips puckered ever so slightly. He liked the pause. It gave him time to assess what was going on. She had definitely *not* said to let go.

"Vivian," he murmured, adjusting his hold and running his finger along the strap of what he could now tell was a garter belt holding up some thigh-high stockings. She shivered, and her eyes widened with a little gasp. "You appear to be wearing some *very* not suitable for work undergarments."

"No one is supposed to know," she whispered.

"I think maybe it could be our secret?" he suggested.

"Yes, please," she whispered again in the softest baby voice.

The *please* hit him like a sucker punch to the libido. Without thinking twice, he lowered his mouth to hers.

Soft lips, apricot smell, luscious body up against his… Vivian was perfection. He ran a more gentle and exploratory hand over her ass. Lace, silk, and even silkier skin had him longing to go further. She pressed into him, tongue tangling with his. Dear fucking God in heaven, he was going to taste every inch of her and then fuck her on the damn desk.

"Batteries, achieved!" bellowed Doc from somewhere out in the hall.

Vivian leaped away from him with a squeak, her cheeks going bright pink, fingers flying to smooth down her skirt.

"Uh… Papers," she mumbled, staring at him like he could speak English right now.

He looked down at the floor. There were indeed papers there. Right. She had come in with papers.

He bent down to pick them up at the same time she did, and they clunked heads just as Doc walked in.

"Ow!"

"Fuck!"

"Uh… Are you guys OK?" Doc looked like he thought they were insane, which Rowan thought he might possibly be.

Vivian scrambled to pick up the papers while Rowan rubbed his head and tried to make words.

"I found the batteries for the controller," said Doc. "Uh, do either of you want an ice pack?"

"These things." Vivian shoved the pile into his hands. "Everything you need to know."

"OK. Thanks. Uh, I will see you at the gala?"

Her eyes flew to his. "Yes? I mean, yes. Definitely be there. OK. Bye."

11
Vivian

BRAIN TRUST

Vivian sat in the back of the bi-monthly staff meeting and thumbed out a message on the group text thread.

EMERGENCY.

Since Vivian had already seen the agenda and notes that had been handed to Howard pre-meeting, she felt free to zone out. Which was good because her brain had checked out the moment Rowan Valkyrie had kissed her.

WHAT UP, BRUH?

Ashley thought she was hilarious.

I JUST KISSED ROWAN VALKYRIE.

The gif from Loretta was a cartoon character with his eyeballs popping out.

OR HE KISSED ME. I'M NOT ENTIRELY SURE.

Christine's bubble popped next.

GOOD KISSING? BAD KISSING? GOING TO NEED MORE TO APPRO-PRIATELY GAUGE MY MEME.

Vivian stared blankly at Ms. Branch. The brunette sixty-some-thing partner was in charge of the criminal division. She had hired a new lawyer away from the District Attorney's office and was smug about it.

OK, NO, SERIOUSLY. YOU CAN'T LEAVE US HANGING ON THAT.

Rachel sent a string of serious face emojis to underscore her point.

Best kiss of my life?

Duck, yeah. This is what happens when you fish in the right pool.

Christine had never bothered to adjust her autocorrect's understanding of swear words.

Also, he somehow got under my skirt, and now he knows about my underwear situation.

That resulted in a string of laughing emojis from all of her friends.

I like how she says "somehow."

Ashley's comment bubble warred with Loretta's.

I can tell you how.

More laughing gifs landed on her thread.

OK, OK, so there was making out is what I'm hearing. Not sure what the emergency is. Do you need permission to go back for more? Because Mama Bear over here says go get 'em tiger.

Ashley included a Tony the Tiger meme.

The crowd clapped, and Vivian tucked her phone under her leg to join in, and then had to wait until everyone was distracted again before going back to her phone.

We got interrupted, and I got flustered, but before I rushed out, he asked if he was seeing me at the Gala, and I said yes.

Vivian took a quick crowd check to make sure she hadn't missed any cues. They had opened the folding wall between rooms of the conference space to accommodate everyone, but it was still crowded. Vivian wished she'd managed to skip this meeting, but Howard had insisted, and she'd been too dazed from her run-in with Rowan to object. Her phone ticked as the messages piled up in response.

Great.

Sounds promising.

Clear signal of interest.

STILL NOT SEEING THE PROBLEM.

Vivian heaved an annoyed breath.

WELL, WAIT. I THOUGHT THE GALA WASN'T FOR ANOTHER MONTH. HAVE I BLIPPED THIS? I THOUGHT ASHLEY WAS GOING ON ABOUT EARLY BIRD TICKETS AT YOUR BIRTHDAY.

Loretta's question underscored Vivian's problem.

EXACTLY MY POINT! I DON'T KNOW IF THAT WAS SMALL TALK TO COVER UP NEARLY GETTING CAUGHT OR AN ATTEMPT TO ASK ME OUT. I MEAN, I HAVE TO GO TO THE GALA.

She paused to scan the room again, and Ashley's response came through before she could continue.

YOU'D BETTER BE GOING TO THE GALA. DO NOT FUCK WITH ME, KAYE. YOU HAVE A FIVE-MINUTE TIME SLOT RIGHT AFTER FATHER FRED.

EASE DOWN, RIPLEY. I MEAN, ASHLEY.

Loretta's *Aliens* GIF showed Ripley blasting aliens and carrying a little girl.

Ashley sometimes forgot that Vivian was the one who had brought her on board to plan the gala for the Victory Mission Foundation. Not that Vivian minded. She loved Ashley's passion for her work.

Christine sent a string of question marks.

VIVIAN IS GIVING THE ASK THIS YEAR BECAUSE IT'S THE TEN-YEAR ANNIVERSARY. SHE'S MY ANCHOR.

Ashley's clarification got a thumbs-up from Christine.

BUT I DON'T THINK ROWAN REALIZES THAT.

Vivian wanted to say more but couldn't even think of what GIF to put in to encompass her feelings.

OHHHH. DOES HE EVEN KNOW WHEN THE GALA IS?

Christine's question made Vivian pause. She tried to recall Howard's question from earlier.

UH... NO? I DID GIVE HIM THE PAPERWORK, SO HE'LL FIGURE IT OUT EVENTUALLY. BUT HE PROBABLY DIDN'T REALIZE IT AT THE TIME.

So, I don't know if he thinks... I just don't know what he thinks!

The phone stopped vibrating, but Vivian could see the bouncing dots that indicated that replies were being composed.

You said you talked to his employees — maybe you can get a vibe off them?

Christine was first, but Vivian didn't like the answer. It seemed uncertain and like asking someone's friends if the boy she liked, liked her back.

Barf. No.

Abject rejection from Loretta, which got a thumbs-up from Rachel and Ashley.

OK, I know you all are tired of my polyamory advice. But give me a sec to finish this phone call, and then I have thoughts.

Ashley's text resulted in various groan gifs.

Vivian waited and tried to pay attention to the meeting. Howard's update on their recent estate case that was before the State Supreme Court had everyone's attention, but since she'd done all the work she didn't need the refresher.

OK, so, one of the things I've been enjoying about polyamory is that it advocates for sharing expectations, boundaries, and desires up front. If you want to know what he was thinking, I would recommend going back up there and asking him. It's a lot less crushing to know upfront if you're not on the same page before you've invested a ton in this thing.

Vivian took a deep breath. That still sounded massively intimidating.

"And, of course," said Howard, "I could not do it without my right-hand woman, Vivian Kaye."

Clueing in on her name, Vivian sat upright in her chair and smiled like she knew what was happening.

"Her brief prep has been astounding."

There was a round of applause, but Vivian could tell it came from the other paralegals and secretaries. Belinda was blatantly checking her phone.

"So, as a quick reminder, the person who convinces Vivian to go to law school gets a bonus."

That got a round of laughs. They had all heard Howard make the joke before. Vivian wouldn't have minded going to law school, but she knew it would mean taking out student loans, and that much debt scared her. She could never convince him that law school probably wasn't in the cards for her. Not that she needed the lawyers in the front row to laugh quite so loudly about it.

Howard passed the baton to Mr. Kato, and Vivian looked back at her phone.

I HATE TO ADMIT IT, BUT I'M VOTING WITH ASHLEY. JUST ASK AND MOVE ON ONE WAY OR ANOTHER.

Loretta liked Rachel's message.

Vivian had already confronted Rowan in the elevator and called him an asshole in the basement. How much harder could it be to walk into his office and ask if he was interested in dating her?

OK, BUT YOU CAN'T DO IT UNTIL TOMORROW.

Christine's texts started to pop through in quick succession.

YOU NEED A MINUTE TO CALM DOWN AND THINK ABOUT WHAT YOUR DESIRES ARE.

IF YOU GO BACK UP NOW, YOU'LL END UP NAKED ON HIS DESK, WHICH I'M NOT AGAINST, BUT YOU WON'T GET YOUR QUESTION ANSWERED.

AND LAST BUT NOT LEAST, IF YOU GO TOMORROW, YOU CAN SHOW HIM A DIFFERENT UNDERWEAR SITUATION.

Vivian took a deep breath, feeling more settled. That was a plan. She had a plan. She hearted all of Christine's messages and put her phone down to clap again. The only real trouble was going to be sticking to it because going back up there right now seemed very tempting.

It seemed even more tempting when she got home at the end of the day. It had been a grueling commute.

Her phone rang, and she picked up.

"Hey, Christine," she said.

"Oh, no! You sound depressed. You went back up and talked to him, didn't you?"

"No, I wish I had. Even if he totally turned me down, at least I might have missed the traffic."

"And that should tell anyone all they need to know about Seattle traffic," said Christine.

"Facts," agreed Vivian.

Vivian looked around her apartment as she divested all her work items. She lived in a ludicrously expensive one-bedroom near Roxhill, and theoretically, that meant she was located a mere fifteen minutes from work. That had only ever been true during the pandemic when no one had been on the road. Today, it had taken nearly an hour due to accidents and the interminable construction on the waterfront.

"But you are still going to go talk to him?" asked Christine.

"Well, to be perfectly honest, I would like to do less talking and more kissing," said Vivian.

There was no way that seven hundred square feet should be so depressingly empty, but her apartment managed it.

Christine chuckled. "OK, great. I was just calling to check-in. You know, in case there needed to be more pep rallying."

"I'm fully pepped. Or at least I was until I got in the car. Now I'm just tired, depressed, and wondering if my soul got left somewhere on Second Ave."

Vivian wondered what it would be like to go home with Rowan. He was probably a neat freak, but she bet he had expensive sheets.

"Probably," said Christine. "You really like him, don't you?"

"I… I really do, Christine. What if he says the kissing was just an oopsie? Like, sorry you tripped and landed on my face, but let's not do that again."

Christine laughed. "I don't think he is going to say that. I saw him at the donut shop. He was into you."

"Really? You swear?"

"He was standing too close, and he stopped breathing when you said boobs."

"He did? Are you sure? Because he didn't look at them once, and I really shoved them at him."

"He kept a lock on your face. It was impressive. But I'm pretty sure he really *wanted* to look at your boobs, so I think you've got a good shot tomorrow."

"Thanks. I guess maybe I did need extra pepping."

"Hey, everyone needs a cheer squad. Plus, you spend a lot of time pepping up everyone else, and sometimes that makes people think you don't need it. I just figured… Maybe that means you need it extra."

"I wish you were here so I could hug you."

"I'll collect on that next time," said Christine, and Vivian heard the smile in her voice.

They talked for a few more minutes. Vivian felt better when she hung up the phone, but staring into her fridge depressed her all over again. She gave up and ordered DoorDash while she changed into her sweats. Vivian was on the way out to the living room when her eyes landed on her father's flag in the case with all his medals. She knew she wouldn't have been living with him at her age. But there would have been holidays, random messages, and the ability to call whenever she wanted. She was tired of meals for one. She wanted what everyone else had—a family.

12

Rowan

TUESDAY

The morning had been torture. The night had been torture. Everything was torture. He had no idea if he should call Vivian or if he was supposed to play it cool. He wanted to go down to the twenty-third floor, grab Vivian, kiss her, and then possibly cave-man carry her off to his house. That was normal, right?

"Hey," said Doc, popping in the door.

"What's up, Doc?" said Rowan, then sighed when Doc completely missed the reference.

"I had an idea about the land dro—"

"OK," said Mark, walking in the door and past Doc as if he wasn't there. "I know I was joking the other day, but I've thought about it, and I think Jenny is right—you need someone who can kick your ass."

"What?" Rowan blinked at his VP in confusion. He felt like he'd missed about three steps in the conversation.

"That's Vivian. She can take you to the mat," said Mark confidently.

"I held my own," objected Rowan.

"Yeah, yeah, sure you did. Point is you should ask her to the gala."

"The gala isn't for another month," snapped Rowan.

"Oh, that's not soon enough," Mark said, and Rowan glared at him.

Having now read the paperwork Vivian had given him, Rowan was aware of that fact. He was also aware that now, having asked her, that it had gotten all weird. The caveman solution genuinely looked like a better option.

The office door opened again, and Teddy came in looking nervous. "Boss, you got a second?"

"Yeah, Teddy, what's up?"

Teddy looked nervously at Mark and Doc, who looked at him in puzzled confusion.

"Uh... OK, I'm here. I'm doing it. Just going to say it. When I played poker with Vivian on Friday, I was really impressed. She's really got her shit together, and she's smart. And it was pretty clear that she is single and definitely *not* looking for a lawyer."

"Where are you going with this, Teddy?" asked Rowan, trying not to growl. If Teddy wanted to ask Vivian out, Rowan would be punching something.

"And I know it's none of my business, and maybe you're not in the relationship zone, but I have to say maybe... It was just that in the elevator yesterday..." He paused and looked desperately at Doc and Mark, who stared blankly back, apparently still mystified by what Teddy was trying to do. "She was giving you flirty eyes. Those were definitely *signals*. I think you should ask her to the gala thing."

"What is going on right now?" asked Rowan, looking at Mark.

"I think Teddy and Mark are trying to talk you into asking out the same girl," said Doc.

Teddy looked at Mark in surprise and then held out his hand for a fist bump.

"But he can't go to the gala with that girl," said Doc.

"What? Why not?" demanded Mark, pausing mid-fist bump.

"Well, he already asked that pretty girl that he head-butted."

"Oh, God," said Rowan, face-palming himself.

"You head-butted a girl?" asked Mark, looking like Rowan had lost his mind.

"She dropped her paperwork, and we both bent over to pick them up."

"I did offer them an ice pack," said Doc anxiously. "But then Rowan asked if they were seeing each other at the gala, and she said yes. It was a definite, you know, agreement to be seen." Doc looked like this topped his list of coolest things Rowan had ever done.

Rowan groaned.

"You can't ask out random girls," protested Teddy. "We like Vivian."

"It *was* Vivian!" snapped Rowan. "And who is we? Did everyone take a poll?"

"Yes," said Teddy. "And we like Vivian."

"Well, if that was Vivian, then she said yes," said Doc.

"Hoo-rah," said Teddy. "Now, if you could stop yelling at her for about two seconds, you might have a shot."

"I don't yell!" yelled Rowan, then took a breath. "OK, well, thank you all for your opinions, but I will handle my own life. Can you get back to work now?"

"Is it safe to come in?" asked Forest poking his head into the office. "Or is Rowan going to yell about not yelling some more?"

Rowan glared at his dark-haired middle brother.

"Olly!" chorused Teddy, Mark, and Doc, holding out their hands for the toddler on Forest's hip. Oliver took a plastic ring out of his mouth and chortled in delight at being greeted with that much enthusiasm.

"I'm chopped liver," said Forest, looking at Rowan.

"That's OK," said Rowan. "Apparently, they all took a poll and decided who I should date."

"Cool. Tell them to take a poll for me," said Forest, handing Olly over to Mark. "Here are all the things." Forest set down what looked like an entire luggage set. Rowan remembered their childhood and was pretty sure that Asher's diaper bag had been an old gym bag that Rowan had found at the Goodwill. He was bemused by Forest's insistence on having designer everything. Not that Forest didn't look good, but it seemed like a lot.

"Are we invading Russia? I thought it was just for the afternoon?" asked Rowan, looking skeptically at the barrage of bags.

"I just want to make sure you've got everything," said Forest.

"I've carried less on a three-day patrol," said Mark, eyeing the pile.

"I just..." Forest hesitated, "like to anticipate the contingencies."

Rowan translated that to mean that Forest had anxiety and control issues and seriously needed a vacation.

"Half the office are Marines, and what we can't improvise, Doc can invent," said Rowan reassuringly.

"And, of course, if shit gets seriously FUBAR'd," said Mark, extracting Oliver from Forest's arms, "Rowan will just buy whatever it is we need."

"That is one-hundred percent accurate," agreed Rowan.

"Unca Roan!!" yelled Olly, paddling his legs in the air and holding out his arms, much to Mark's disappointment.

"Olly is going to be fine," said Rowan, grinning and grabbing his nephew, who threw his arms around Rowan's neck and hugged him tightly. Rowan hugged him back. A hug from a three-year-old was possibly one of the best things on earth.

"Yeah, of course," said Forest, smiling at Rowan and Olly. "Of course."

After Forest left, Rowan made the rounds of the office with Olly in tow, which was both hilarious and frightening as Rowan had never considered how many things Olly could get into. It was common knowledge that if something needed breaking, all anyone needed to do was give it to a batch of eighteen-year-old recruits, but Rowan now thought that three-year-olds might be the new benchmark.

Olly, on the other hand, was living his best life. Everyone he met was excited to see him, give him candy, and let him play with previously forbidden toys. Then there were the bathroom breaks.

Olly's command of his bladder was not the best, and Rowan had to keep an eye out for the potty dance. Then, it was an all-out race to the restroom, which Olly found hilarious. By the time Rowan's three o'clock meeting rolled around, he was more than happy to hand Olly off to Mark for an hour. No wonder Forest looked exhausted all the time.

Rowan closed off his Zoom call with the promise to have a contract sent over and then went to find Mark and Olly. He entered Mark's office to see his nephew standing on top of the desk, hands on his hips, surveying the office triumphantly. Rowan could see Mark heading back down the corridor, his iPad in one hand and a phone in the other.

"Olly-man, are you supposed to be up there?" asked Rowan.

"Yes," lied Olly instantly.

"No," said Mark, walking in. "I swear I walked out of the room for a second! How is he that fast?"

"I don't know, but you'd better get used to it. You've got one coming your way."

Mark looked around as if checking for eavesdroppers. "Yes, *she* is coming my way."

"I thought you and Jenny agreed not to find out?" asked Rowan, amused.

"Yeah, but I couldn't take it anymore. I called at lunch and asked the doc."

Rowan chuckled as he picked up Olly. "That's good. Jenny called this morning and then called me, freaking out, about how to not tell you."

"What?" Mark looked annoyed.

"Well, she's really bad at keeping secrets from you, but she thought you wanted to be surprised. So she didn't know how to *not* tell you."

Mark grinned. "Last time she bought me a birthday present, she got so excited that she blurted it out after an hour."

"Uh-huh. I seem to recall a *please don't tell me if her ring arrived yet, because I'm dying to show her but it will ruin the surprise* forty-eight-hour period where you called me like fifty-eight times to ask if the ring arrived."

Mark laughed unrepentantly. "And you were such an asshole that you didn't tell me!"

"You asked me not to! Also, your ring was making Melissa even more pissed off that I wasn't proposing, so I was a little annoyed."

Mark made a face. "Thank God you didn't give in to her pressure. I mean… Mel was nice and all, but sheesh, that girl could never figure out that she didn't outrank the United States Marine Corp. Can you imagine if you'd gotten stuck with her?"

He could imagine it. Melissa had been quite detailed. They would have had two kids, a dog, and he would have been on the advancement fast track because she didn't drive domestics.

He wondered what Melissa would think about him now. Her parting shot—that he was a lost cause who was happy being just another Marine—still rankled. There was not one damn thing wrong with being just a Marine. Being a Marine meant you were better than a whole fucking lot of the population. Rowan had told her that he'd had plans for his own company when he got out, but that hadn't meant anything to her. And when he'd decided to pull out all of his retirement funds to help Forest start his business, she'd exploded in fury—screaming that he was throwing away *her* future on Forest. Rowan looked down at Olly in his arms and smiled. That had been money well-spent. Forest's company had been able to hit the ground running, and he had paid back every penny with plenty of interest.

"Yeah, well, this time I told Jenny to go ahead and tell you, so act surprised when you get home."

"Nah, I'll just call her now," said Mark with a shrug.

Rowan took Olly back to his office, but he couldn't help looking over his shoulder at Mark, who was now happily talking to his wife. Mark and Jenny were each other's permanent hype team. They loved making each other happy. Rowan envied that, and his thoughts turned back to Vivian.

His moment with Vivian had been electric, but she was so much younger than him. Should he be focusing on someone like her? Someone who probably wasn't looking for something serious? If he wanted any shot at a family, maybe he needed to put his energy toward someone who was on the same page. The idea of that made Rowan depressed.

He looked down at Olly again.

"Olly-man, do you need cousins?"

"Yes!"

"Do you even know what cousins are?"

"No!"

"That's right. Besides, we still have Uncle Ash. He'll probably give you cousins."

"Yay!"

Olly was the best yes man ever.

Rowan hugged his nephew and decided that not every second of his life had to be on plan. Besides, what was wrong with a fling? He'd been dreaming about this life for so long and Vivian made him feel like it was finally coming true.

13

Vivian

VALKYRIE SECURITY

The guys at the security desk had said that Rowan was still in the building, so gathering her courage, Vivian hit up instead of down on the elevator. The lobby area of Valkyrie Security was dimmed, but a few office lights were on. The door between the lobby and offices was propped open, and she walked cautiously toward Rowan's office. She needed to know. Had that kiss been a one-off? Had he really meant to ask her out? Her gala attendance was mandatory, but she wouldn't mind having a date. Although, this would probably dictate her dress choices and absolutely her underwear selection. And also whether or not she went home and spent too much money on alcohol and ice cream tonight.

But she had picked out her lingerie today for confidence, and if she didn't at least let Rowan get a glimpse of it, then it was a wasted effort. She had worn what was supposed to be a breezy casual shirtdress that buttoned up the front, and flats. All of the excitement was underneath.

She could see that the light was on in Rowan's office. Vivian's heart seemed to battering against her ribcage in an attempt to fly away. She hadn't felt this nervous to talk to a boy since high school.

Oh, dear, sweet baby Jesus.

Rowan lay on the floor holding a toddler. Vivian watched in ovary-melting shock as Rowan tossed the little boy into the air, caught him, and brought him down for a raspberry on the tummy. The little boy squealed with delight.

"A-gin!"

Up in the air and back down for another tummy tuba.

More shrieks of laughter. And that made Rowan laugh nearly as much as the little boy. They shared the same hazel eyes that crinkled the same way when they laughed.

Vivian hadn't given much thought to Ashley's train station theory previously, but she was now pretty sure she had just pulled into baby town.

"Lady!" exclaimed the little boy, spotting her, and Rowan looked up, letting the toddler sit on his chest.

"Hi," he said, smiling at her without moving. She thought it was the first time she'd seen him look genuinely relaxed and happy. His carpet was littered with toy tanks and a few Cheerios.

"Hi. Sorry if I'm interrupting. I didn't realize you were in a crucial meeting with a VIP client," said Vivian, smiling back. Hadn't she told Christine no on step-kids? Why was this the most adorable thing ever? It was cuter than puppy videos, but this should be a red flag, right?

"Well, Oliver is the *most* important client," said Rowan, laughing. "But you're not interrupting."

"Unca Roan!" exclaimed the little boy, grabbing Rowan's face with both pudgy hands. "A-gin!"

Oh. Uncle. And it was green flags all the way down the track.

"Again?! I'm starting to think you're destined for the paratroopers."

Vivian chuckled. In the distance, she heard the ding of the elevator and the sound of hurrying feet.

"That's going to be Forest," said Rowan without moving from the floor. He tossed the little boy up in the air again as the door burst open.

"I'm here. I'm here. Sorry, sorry."

The man looked to be in his thirties and with dark, disheveled hair as if he'd run all the way up from the parking garage. Vivian recognized the piercing green-flecked eyes that Rowan shared with Oliver, but the slightly frantic edge was not something she associated with the Valkyrie aura.

"Daddy!" chirped the little boy.

"Breathe, Forest," ordered Rowan, using what Vivian thought of as his commanding voice, and Forest automatically inhaled. "We're fine," said Rowan more softly.

"Sorry," said Forest again. "I didn't mean to be late."

"Everything's fine," said Rowan. "Olly is training for the paratroopers, and I am getting my arm workout for the day."

Forest snorted, then he spotted Vivian and looked embarrassed.

"Hi. Sorry. I'm Forest Valkyrie. The small one is my son. The big one is my brother."

"Nice to meet you," said Vivian, holding out her hand. "Vivian Kaye."

"Vivian is my building rep," said Rowan, without moving from the floor. Oliver was now driving a tank over his chest. "She works downstairs at Hoskins, Branch, and Kato."

"Oh, they handled Olly's citizenship after Vera passed," said Forest.

"Olly's mom was from Australia," said Rowan by way of explanation, and Vivian nodded.

"Nice guy named…" Forest hesitated, seeming to search his memory. "Grant Ichikawa."

"Oh, yeah. Grant's great," agreed Vivian. Grant was one of the nicer lawyers at the firm.

"I didn't know they did other stuff," said Rowan. "I thought they all did Estate Planning like everyone else in the damn building."

"That's Howard's specialty," said Vivian. "We have civil and criminal divisions, too."

"Estate planning," said Forest, dropping into one of the chairs that Rowan had pushed up against the wall. He looked exhausted.

"I'm going to have to figure that out at some point."

"You don't have a will?" asked Rowan, surprised.

"Like you do," said Forest sourly.

"I've had a will since I was eighteen and entered the service," said Rowan. "I had to assign death benefits."

"You never said anything!"

"You were twelve, and Ash was nine, and you were already freaking out about me leaving. I didn't need to add an *oh by the way if I die you'll get a bunch of money and don't worry I've put it in a trust so Mom doesn't blow it all on her shit boyfriends.*"

Vivian blinked at the casual description of their childhood. It seemed to explain a few things about how seriously Rowan took himself.

"But, but," said Forest. "I don't even know how to get a will." The panic was evident in his eyes. It was as if Rowan had just assigned him a new and insurmountable task.

"Forest, it's fine. I'm in a high-risk profession. It just makes sense. You're in real estate development and construction."

"An elevator could break and I could plummet to my death or an I-beam could drop on me on the next site visit!"

"Then you should probably get one," agreed Rowan soothingly. "But there's no rush."

"I'll tell you what," said Vivian, feeling sorry for Forest, who had anxiety rolling off him in waves. "If you worked with Grant before, then you're already a client. I'll email him now, and tomorrow, he'll send you a questionnaire and some stuff to fill out, and then we can draw up a will for you to approve or modify."

"Questionnaire?" asked Forest.

"So that we can get a sense of how you want your assets divided. That kind of thing. And who would get custody of Oliver."

"Rowan would take Olly, of course," said Forest as if it were obvious. Then he blinked at Rowan. "You would, wouldn't you?"

"Yes, of course," said Rowan. He pretended to eat the tank

Oliver drove over his face and Olly chuckled. "Although, I might have to fight Uncle Ash for you. Yes, I would." Vivian tried not to melt over his growly but sweet baby-talk voice.

Vivian took out her phone and stepped around Rowan to lean against his desk while she typed.

"I'm sure Ash would be fine," said Forest. "But I don't really think he's ready for kids. And obviously we can't let Mom have him."

Vivian tried not to take that as a statement about Rowan's readiness for kids.

"Well, considering that you're not about to die, I think it's kind of a moot point," said Rowan, sounding amused as the tank drove up his face.

"There," said Vivian, hitting send. "Grant will take care of you. You'll barely have to think, I promise."

"Thanks," said Forest, looking like he genuinely meant it. "I've been meaning to get to that, but I didn't even know where to start."

"Amazing what happens when you ask for help," said Rowan, in what Vivian thought was slightly too pointed of a commentary.

"Help is nice, but sometimes it's just faster and easier to do it myself," said Forest. "I don't want to spend forever explaining what I want to someone."

Vivian resonated with that, but she had also learned that attitude wasn't sustainable. Not in her work and not in her personal life. That's why she had the brain trust of girls on a permanent text thread. She didn't know why boys didn't get themselves a brain trust of bros. She looked around the office and then down at the floor and wondered if that was Rowan's entire business model.

"Mm-hmm," said Rowan, and Vivian thought it was a tactical withdrawal from the argument. Olly climbed off Rowan and toddled toward Forest.

"Daddy. Tank!"

"Yes, that is a big tank," agreed Forest, scooping up his son.

"You ready to go home and get some dinner, big man?"

"Nugits!"

"Right," said Forest, looking around. "Where's all his stuff?"

"Piled in a cart by the elevator," said Rowan. "You can wheel it down with you and leave the cart by the elevator when you're done."

"Didn't use any of it, did you?" asked Forest with a sigh.

"Where do you think I got the Cheerios?"

Forest shook his head and hoisted Olly up. "Thanks, Row. I really do appreciate it."

"Any time," said Rowan from the floor. Forest's footsteps receded, and Rowan looked up at her. "Thank you," he said after they heard the elevator door close. "Forest's wound so tight these days sometimes I think he's going to bust a spring. He's hiring a new nanny, but if that doesn't take the edge off, Ash and I will have an intervention."

"It was literally the least I could do," she said.

Vivian realized she had a dopy smile on her face for no good reason and looked for something to say.

"Are you going to lie on the floor all night?"

His head twisted to one side slightly. "I don't know… I kind of like the view."

Her first instinct was to look up and see what had him so fascinated, and then Vivian realized that *she* was what was up for him.

"Rowan Valkyrie," she said, trying to pretend she wasn't smiling, "can you see up my skirt?"

A cocky grin spread over his face.

"Yes, but not nearly as far as I'd like," he said, and Vivian bit her lip trying to suppress a giggle.

14
Vivian

THE DESK SET

Putting out a hand, Rowan drew a finger along the seam at the back of her ankle. Vivian shivered at his touch, goosebumps forming on her skin. Her navy blue shirt dress had a forties vibe, and the seamed stockings worked with the look. She didn't think anyone else had thought about how far up the seam went.

"I wasn't sure what I was supposed to do," he said softly. "I didn't know if I should call you."

"I wasn't sure either. I meant to come up earlier, but it was kind of a circus today. I could have called, but I didn't want to... *just* call," Vivian finished lamely.

"Mm. And what *do* you want?" Rowan asked, his finger traveling up the back of her calf. It was one damn finger and her stomach did a triple backflip. A hot flush warmed her cheeks.

"Well," said Vivian, breathlessly. Her fingers fidgeted with her skirt, and very slowly, she gathered up the fabric, lifting the hem higher. "I know yesterday you said you could keep a secret."

The grin on his face stretched even wider.

"I can," he promised.

"I thought maybe..." She inched her hemline even higher. "You might be interested in other... secrets." Vivian knew that wasn't what she came to ask, but it seemed like the most pertinent thing to ascertain at the moment.

He flipped over, and then he was on his knees in front of her.

He slid his palms up the back of her legs, grazing over her calves and slowly moving to the back of her thighs. Her skin prickled like a heat wave had hit. He slid one hand to the front of her thigh, and then pop, pop, pop, he undid the bottom three buttons of her dress. The next three buttons he undid with his teeth and tongue.

Vivian made a little meep of excitement. This was way better than she'd even hoped for.

He'd reached the lacy three inches at the top of her stockings that hit just at the plump part of her thighs.

"Well, so far," he purred, dropping kisses on the skin that showed above the edge of the stocking, "I think these are valuable secrets."

"Top Secret Clearance required," she said, squeaking at the end in pleasured shock as he licked her thigh.

"My eyes only," he growled and flicked another few buttons. Her dress split up to her bra, and Rowan inhaled as if the sight of her silk and lace-covered body was the most breathtaking thing he'd ever seen. With his eyes fixed on hers, he trailed kisses across her stomach. She reached up and undid the last two buttons with a shaking hand.

"This is *so* against the employee handbook," she muttered, and Rowan grinned.

"But it'll be worth it."

He pushed her dress open wide and froze, his eyes fixed on her breasts.

"Bows?" he asked, finally tearing his eyes off the cut-out details on her bra to look up to her face.

"Well, I like to think they're a gift," said Vivian. "So they need bows on top of them."

Rowan's chuckle was all the assurance she needed that he agreed. He leaned in and flicked his tongue under the nearest decorative bow detail, teasing her nipple. At the same time, his thumb caressed across the satin-clad place between her thighs. Vivian shivered in a cascade of sensation. His tongue flicking in and out of the cut-outs of the bra was the most divine thing she could have imagined.

There were two ways to wear a garter belt—under or over panties. Over was how they were always shown in pictures, AKA the sexy way. But under was the way that made it possible for panties to come off without disconnecting everything from the stockings, AKA the way that going to the bathroom is possible. Vivian had dithered greatly over her selection but eventually went with the garter belt on top because she wanted to look good. But now she realized that she didn't want to *look* sexy—she wanted to have sex. And her underwear would be challenging to remove. She was being foiled by her own lingerie choices. This was not how things were supposed to go.

His thumb slipped underneath the edge of her panties and made a light little circle.

She let out her air in a little woof of shock, her legs spreading involuntarily. She wanted more of that.

He kissed across her stomach, and Vivian was no longer worried if she had a little roll there, or was extra curvy in her hips, because he definitely wasn't.

Vivian had not thought that she was prone to public location sex. She was a very safe and sane individual. It was just that right now, she wanted to be dangerous with Rowan. Dangerous, dirty, and downright bad. What she wanted was for him to put his mouth on her most intimate parts and make her scream his name, but she was also still worried about the underwear situation.

His kisses trailed onto the satin of her panties, and without missing a beat, he simply moved the fabric off to one side. OK, so he was an improviser who did not let obstacles get in his way. Problem solvvvvvvvvv....

Vivian's thoughts ran out as his tongue caressed her. She exhaled and buried her fingers in his hair. Rolling her hips, she blessed the belly dancing class she'd taken and grabbed the edge of the desk. He alternated between his tongue on her clit, and his fingers inside her, and Vivian found herself rocking gently to the rhythm.

"Ohhhhhhh." It wasn't a word so much as one long sustained moan. "Rowannnn."

She knew her voice had gone all pouty, but she wasn't sure she had control of that anymore. She had no fucking clue what Rowan was doing down there and did not care because it was better than anyone else she'd ever had. He put one of her legs over his shoulder, and she tilted back, panting.

The room seemed to spin, and she felt hot and cold at the same time. She swore to whatever god was out there if Rowan let her come, she would fuck his brains out on this damn desk. She had reached the point where dick sounded really good, but she knew she'd come soon if he just...

"Oh, fucking God, right there! Oh, fuck, Rowan! Please, please, please!"

The heat between her legs seemed unbearable. She didn't know how to beg any harder. His tongue seemed to wrap around her clit, and he pressed in so hard and deep that it felt like everything in her body climaxed at once.

Everything was blurry, and she could barely breathe, let alone think. But, oh, Rowan Valkyrie was in for it once she could figure out how to move again.

15

Rowan

THE HR POLICE

Rowan looked down at Vivian sprawled across his desk and couldn't help but growl at the delicious sight of her. She was flushed pink from her orgasm and panting. He'd never known he'd had a desk fetish previously, but right at the moment fucking her on his desk was the sexiest thing he could imagine.

He leaned over her, and she twined her arms around his neck.

"Ms. Kaye," he whispered, putting a kiss on her neck.

"Yes, Mr. Valkyrie?" she asked, using the pouty little baby voice that made him sweat. He kissed higher on her neck and then licked up the crest of her ear. She shivered underneath him, and he sucked at her earlobe, which made her moan.

"You'd better clear your schedule for the rest of the night. I have some… desk work that needs your assistance."

"I am here to help," she said breathlessly.

He leaned in, intending to put a kiss on her luscious mouth. Then, out in the lobby, the elevator dinged.

They both froze. Vivian's eyes were enormous.

"Did you leave the lobby door open?" he hissed.

"It was open when I got here!" she whispered back.

Then he realized he'd told Mark to leave it open for Forest, so of course, it had been open.

"Top-notch security for everyone but ourselves," he growled, standing up and yanking Vivian to her feet.

"Shit, shit, shit," whispered Vivian, trying to rebutton her dress. Rowan could hear the tip-tap of high heels across the lobby floor and realized that Vivian wasn't going to make it. He reached out, yanked the handle of the wardrobe, and flung open the door. He grabbed Vivian by the waist and shoved her bodily inside.

"Well, hello," the woman from Vivian's office purred as he closed the wardrobe door and turned around.

"Uh, hi?" said Rowan, running his hand over his face and through his hair in what he hoped was a casual manner. Belinda looked around the office, appearing to notice the tanks and cheerios.

"Brittany, was it?"

Rowan supposed she was pretty. Perfect makeup and sleek hair matched her sophisticated outfit. Rowan thought she looked boring.

"Belinda," she said, annoyance flashing across her face.

"Sorry. Is there something I can help you or Howard with?"

"I thought I'd pop up and offer a touch more about the gala. I just wanted to say that if you don't want to attend, I *can* get you out of it. I know you didn't seem thrilled to be backed into buying a table. I can make a few calls and find someone to take the spot."

"It's fine," said Rowan. "I really don't do things I don't want to do."

"Oh, I'm sure. But Vivian can be… Well, for an assistant, she sometimes comes across as a bit like she thinks she's in charge of something. I know that can be unpleasant."

"Vivian's been perfectly welcoming."

So fucking welcoming.

"Well…" Belinda hesitated and then took a step closer. "Well, I also wanted to make sure that she hadn't been too welcoming?"

"Too welcoming?" repeated Rowan, now thoroughly put off by Belinda. What had been a funny double entendre in his head sounded sleazy coming out of Belinda's mouth. He'd wanted to get rid of her before, but now he actively disliked her.

"Well, I know it's frustrating, as a paralegal, to be associating with a lot of high-power individuals, knowing that she's never going to be one of us, but it's completely against the employee guidelines to date clients. And I'm not saying that she would try anything like that with you. Although, of course, I understand her temptation."

She brushed a hand along his arm, and Rowan tried not to make his step away too obviously quick.

"But," continued Belinda, apparently oblivious to his discomfort, "I just thought someone with your assets might appreciate a word of warning."

Rowan paused and considered how to respond, knowing full well that Vivian was listening to every word, but his pause went on too long.

"As I was saying, Vivian and Howard are a little obsessed with the gala, but I do promise there will be quality people there."

He was annoyed that he felt trapped into being polite to this woman.

"I wasn't concerned, actually, but thanks, I guess. I have confidence in Howard." He kept his tone clipped and terse, hoping she would take the hint.

Belinda laughed.

"Oh, of course. Howard is such a charming old fossil, and he dotes on Vivian because of the whole military thing, but he doesn't quite see that times have changed. You can't just grow someone into a position. They really ought to have a proper education to start out."

Rowan felt his teeth grit.

"I can't say I agree with that," said Rowan. "Mentorship and growth through training and experience are core parts of the military ethos."

"Oh," said Belinda, taking a step back.

"But thanks for the tip. Anyway, do you mind heading down on the elevator without me? I'm going to lock some things up and arm the security system before heading down."

"No, of course not," she said. "I guess I'll see you at the gala?"

"Uh, yeah, sure. The team will be there."

"Great," said Belinda. "See you then." She smiled icily and turned on her heel.

He waited until he heard the elevator doors close and opened the wardrobe. Vivian had fully rebuttoned but still looked pink. Then he got to her face and realized she was tinted red by fury.

He held out a hand, which she took as she stumbled out into the office.

"I..." She pointed toward the now absent Belinda. "I do not..." She vibrated in sheer anger.

"Look, this happened all the time in the military."

She took her hand away like he was on fire and leaned back, one hand going to her hip.

"I'm sorry, but what the fuck are you talking about?"

He knew exactly where he'd gone wrong, but, damn, he loved it when she swore. Tough-talking Vivian was precious.

"No. Sorry," Rowan said, trying not to laugh. "No. To clarify. Co-workers undermining each other happened. That part. That's the part I was referring to—officers trying to take credit for enlisted efforts."

The angry glare diminished by about five watts, but she still looked flushed.

"I'm not enlisted," said Vivian. "And when it comes to the gala, I'm the fucking general. Also, I'm not a gold digger! I'm not frustrated by associating with high-powered people or whatever she said. She only thinks people are jealous of her!"

"Viv," he said, trying to sound soothing and not condescending, "she came up here and basically spent the entire time talking about you. Someone's jealous, but it isn't you."

"Yes, that was weird. What the hell was this?"

"Um..." Rowan felt awkward saying it, but he finally shrugged and made the statement. "She was hitting on me and trying to eliminate you as competition."

"I…" She looked like he'd announced Belinda had been intending to go to the moon. "That's insane."

"Are you saying I'm not worth hitting on?" he asked, sliding an arm around her waist and pulling her close. "I think my feelings are hurt."

"Suck it up, Marine," said Vivian, adjusting his collar. "I'm going home with you. I'm sure your feelings will get over it."

"Yes, ma'am," he said, grinning.

She tugged at his collar again, her lips puckering in a pout.

"She ruined my after-glow."

"She ruined my shot at desk sex," he said sadly.

"Yeah, you should try that," said Vivian, smirking. "It was great. Ten out of ten. Would definitely recommend."

He shook his head, and Vivian giggled and went up on tip-toe to kiss him.

By the time he pulled into his garage and waited for Vivian to pull in after him, Rowan had been given time to consider if this was his best idea. But as he opened the door to her Mini-Cooper, she swung one leg out, revealing the damn garter belt, and any doubts he might have had vanished. Good idea or bad plan, it didn't matter. He wanted Vivian.

She took his hand, and he could see he wasn't the only one who had been having second thoughts.

"You can change your mind," he said and held his breath.

16

Rowan

COUNTER OFFER

"Yes, I can change my mind," said Vivian, as if she was slightly offended that he thought she needed the reminder. "But I haven't. I'm just wondering if there's going to be food."

"Before, after, or during?" he asked, trying to figure out what he would serve in each scenario. Vivian giggled, and he swung her car door closed as he leaned down to kiss her. Her lips were so soft that he almost forgot that they'd been speaking about something.

"I have food. But I will order you whatever you want," Rowan said, trying to answer her immediate needs.

"It *is* Tuesday," she said.

He stared at her blankly, unsure of what Tuesday had to do with anything.

"So, I'm asking for tacos."

"Ah. Sorry. I'm not opposed to tacos," he said, taking out his phone. "But I think somewhere along the way, I didn't get the memo. I got back from Afghanistan, and suddenly, everyone knew what Tuesday was for. There was a tidal taco shift in society, and no one told me." He punched in what he wanted and then handed her the phone.

"The Lego movie probably came out. It nationalized the awareness of Tuesday's taco compatibility."

Rowan chuckled. "Possibly. I never saw it. Give me just a second."

He opened the door to the house and turned on the lights, checking the pathways to the livable portion of the house. She followed behind him, putting in her meal selection.

"Just hit order when you're done."

"OK, here is... Oh, you live in a construction zone."

"Yeah, sorry. They say it will be done next month, and the parts that are done are comfortable. We just have to navigate through the mess."

"OK, but here's your phone."

"Oh, hold onto it for a second." He walked through, secured any loose material, and pinned back the hanging clear tarp for her. She came after him, still holding out his phone. "You can put it on the counter. I'm just going to take my jacket off."

"Rowan!" she protested, laughing.

"What?"

"You can't leave your phone with a girl!"

"Why not?"

"They'll go through it!"

"And see what? My email thread on contracting, or the fifty million photos of my nephew? Or the drunk text from Teddy telling me the company should buy a horse? I saved that one for the company Christmas party."

Vivian laughed harder.

"Girls will look for photos of other girls."

"Yeah, I'm old enough and just that single that I don't do naughty things with my phone." He hung up his jacket and shoved the phone in his back pocket.

"What? Nothing naughty? Nothing at all?" She looked skeptical. "All that time being deployed, and it never occurred to you to send naked anything to anyone?"

"Operational security says destroy all evidence after the mission is complete."

And the last time Rowan had done any sexting was when he was with Melissa, and he'd deleted every photo of her he could find.

"A reasonable policy," agreed Vivian, still looking amused.

He couldn't believe that he'd just admitted to how single and old he actually was. Shouldn't he be trying to minimize that? On the other hand, she ought to know what she was in for. He was a dumb jarhead who got lucky and knew how to manage people. He would never be that cool.

"I am going to go turn on the front door lights and turn off the security system on the gate for the delivery guy. I will be right back."

He walked toward the front door and had just finished punching in the code when his phone chirped. He took it out and saw a text from Vivian. Confused, he opened it and immediately gasped at the photo of Vivian sitting on his kitchen island with her top unbuttoned. The granite had never looked so good.

"Vivian!" he yelled down the hall, kicking off his shoes.

"Your phone needed some love!" she yelled back.

He turned on the sound system from his phone and walked back into the kitchen, unbuttoning his shirt as Marvin Gaye started to play.

"What can I say? I'm a little bit naughty." She had removed her shoes, and her stocking-clad feet kicked playfully as she unbuttoned a few more buttons on her dress.

"I think I like naughty girls," he said.

"Are you going to spank me?" she asked innocently, but her eyes sparkled with mischief as she nibbled at one of her fingertips.

"Baby, I will bend you over whatever you want."

It was like she couldn't stop the giggle that burst out of her, and it made her breasts bounce. If delight could be personified, it would look like Vivian.

"Come here," he growled, burying one hand in her hair and pulling her close. Her lips were fire against his. Soft, hot, and divine. In contrast, her cool fingers finished unbuttoning his shirt and pushed it off his shoulders, trailing gorgeous shivering lines down his chest.

He returned the favor until she was as naked as she had been on his desk. Her lingerie was more extensive than he usually dealt with, but having had a previous look, he was pretty sure he knew how to get her out of it. First up was the garter belt. The little clips went ping, and with a simple slide of his hand, more of her silky thighs became available. She gave a little moan as he used his teeth to drag her bra straps off her shoulders. He was a little torn on the bra. The damn bow cutouts over her nipples made him crazy, but he wanted all of her with nothing in the way. He pushed her dress off, then reached around and undid the bra.

"Rowan?" she moaned as he tossed her bra over his shoulder.

"Mm," he murmured between kisses.

"I think you're giving me a furniture fetish. I really want…"

Her hands fumbled for his belt buckle.

"Mm," he said, pulling back and grabbing her hand to stop her before she sent his pants toward the floor at warp speed. She looked up at him, tensing at his unexpected halt. He reached back and pulled out first his phone and then his pistol, set them down on the counter.

"My lingerie is less fun," he said. "And doesn't like being dropped."

"Forgot about that," she said breathlessly. Then she glanced at the gun. "Beretta? Just couldn't make the switch to the M18?" Her roguish expression told him she knew damn well he would have an opinion about the Marines switching the standard sidearm.

"Shut your filthy mouth," he growled, pulling her off the counter. He silenced her giggle with a kiss as he worked her panties off. The little wisp of silk and lace slid down and onto the floor, and he was about to put her back on the counter when he pulled back and looked down into her beautiful gray eyes. Her lips were plump from his kisses, and he couldn't wait to taste them again, but she had said…

He flicked one hand and made a resounding smack against her

ass. She gave a gasp and pressed herself against him.

"Naughty girl," he whispered as she sank her teeth into his chest in tiny nibbles.

"Do it again," she whispered back.

One more smack on her ass made her wriggle against him and him rock hard. It was possible he shared her furniture fetish. He put his hands around her waist and lifted her back onto the island. She made a little surprised noise.

"Cold," she said to his questioning noise. She fumbled for his belt again, and this time, he let her continue. He hadn't been aware at the time it had been installed, but this portion of the counter was precisely the right height. He would have to ask Forest how to send the installers a tip—they'd been very insistent about having the correct counter levels.

He groaned as she pushed his pants and then his boxers off his hips. A quick assist to free his legs, and they were both buck ass naked in his kitchen. It wasn't the weirdest place he'd ever had sex, but he suspected it was about to skyrocket into his top ten favorites.

Vivian's arms wrapped around his neck, luring him in closer. Then she grazed his leg with her foot, bringing it up along his thigh in a sensual, insistent point of contact. He sank into her kiss again as she wrapped her legs around his waist.

She tried to pull him into her, and he resisted for no other reason than he liked to feel the strength of her legs.

"Rowan!" she complained as he cupped her breast, teasing the nipple with his fingers and her pussy with his cock.

"Rowan," she moaned.

Finally, he gave in and rocked his hips forward, pushing inside her.

"Oh, fuck me," gasped Vivian, and Rowan couldn't help laughing, although it was breathless.

"Yes, ma'am," he said, although he didn't think she'd meant it as an order.

Her head fell back as he thrust into her again, arching and holding herself up with her hands on his shoulders. It was a goddamn gorgeous view, and she felt even better.

He ran his hand down her torso. From the glorious handful of her breasts, her tiny waist, and soft belly that flowed into the hips and legs that were wrapped around him, she curved in all the right places. He took a firmer grip on her hips, which made her moan and cling to him tighter.

He felt lost in the sensation of being with her. The sound of her voice. The sensation of being inside her. The heat of her skin against his. He curled his hand around the back of her neck, bringing her closer so he could taste her lips again. With each thrust, it was as if they moved nearer to finding their own unique rhythm until they moved together in a perfect synchronization of push and pull, and they were both gasping at the rising sense of urgency.

Her eyes closed, her bottom lip quivering as she made the tiniest whimper.

"Rowan, please," she whispered, her tone fragile with longing.

Nothing was better than this. Vivian was another word for heaven.

He thrust harder, and she gasped. "Yes! Oh, please, yes!"

Her fingers dug into his shoulders, and she arched, her legs spreading wider, silently inviting him to take her. He gave up and gave in, driving into her until she reached up and her hand clenched into his hair.

"Oh, God, yes!"

He came a moment later, pleasure searing down his spine, muscles tightening across his chest.

She nuzzled into his neck, panting, and he held her tight. He felt hot, empty, and gloriously electrified all at once.

His phone had three alerts in a row, dinging with what felt like overly loud insistence, and Vivian squeaked in panic and clung to him tighter.

"I am not getting in a cupboard!"

"Doors are locked," he said, trying to keep from laughing. "You're not going anywhere."

He grabbed his phone while maintaining his hold on Vivian. He had no intention of letting her go.

"That was the app, a text, and another text, all telling me that tacos are on the porch. No emergency. Just food."

Vivian giggled breathlessly and buried her face in the crook of his neck. He put his face into her hair and inhaled, wanting to memorize the scent of her and the feeling of her in his arms.

17
Vivian

ROWAN'S PLACE

Vivian blinked and tried to figure out what was wrong with her curtains. Probably nothing. She wouldn't know because she wasn't actually looking at her window. Because she was in Rowan's bedroom. For the sixth morning in a row. His window curtains were a gorgeous green velvet. Everything that wasn't under construction was lusciously textured and vibrant. She was used to the rich people she'd met living in beige boxes, but Rowan said he'd lived too long in desert camo to have a beige house.

She'd tried going home at some point over the weekend, and then he'd asked why, and she hadn't been able to come up with a reason other than feeling like it was polite. Then he'd said late-night driving was unsafe, and that was a reasonable point, so, obviously, she'd had to stay over again.

She rolled over and snuggled into his chest. He made the rumbly happy noise that made her smile and then wrapped his arms around her. If they stayed here long enough, she would start to sweat. The man put out more heat than a small volcano, but she didn't have to worry about that because what she was going to do was nibble on his chest a little, and then he would sex her up until she got all sweaty for different reasons.

She didn't understand how, for years now, she'd been totally fine not starting and ending her day with an orgasm. Orgasms were clearly the better way to bookend a day. What had she even been doing with her time before now?

Stealthily, Vivian kissed his collarbone, then followed along the ridge to the hard muscle of his shoulder, where she opened her mouth, preparing to give it a little bite.

"Do you think I can't see what you're doing?" he murmured quietly.

"Who, me?"

"You are *such* a naughty girl," he growled, and under the covers, he gave her a little spank. She'd initially been joking about needing to be spanked, but damn it, now she craved it.

"Nope, I'm a good girl." She kissed his shoulder to prove her point. There was scar there and a matching one in his side, not that he talked about how he got them. He called them Recon Souvenirs. She gave the scar a little kiss and then worked her way down a few inches.

Then she nibbled.

"Bad girl," he reiterated with another smack.

"I *could* be good," she offered, looping her leg over his hip and kissing down onto his chest, but she ended with a long caress of her tongue. "If you make me."

With a sharp twist, Rowan rolled her onto her back and pinned her arms above her head on the mattress. She looked up into his tawny hazel eyes, so full of all the colors, and smiled.

"Good morning, Mr. Valkyrie."

"Good morning, Ms. Kaye," he said, smiling back at her.

He kissed her gently at first, soft and tender, while his hands held her tight and his hips ground against hers. She groaned as she felt the length of him press into her. They moved together, and soon she was gasping between his kisses. His hands moved over her body, making every thrust twice as intense. He changed his rhythm, and Vivian felt her toes start to curl and her body clench.

"Rowan," she gasped, digging her fingers into his sides.

His only response was a non-verbal growl that made her arch

and shiver.

"Oh, God, Rowan!"

He finished right after she did, and they lay tangled together. Vivian smooshed herself against him, wishing they could spend the day that way. Finally, he pushed away from her and got out of bed with a groan. She pouted and watched his ass. She loved looking at him.

"I think I like the weekend schedule better," he said, looking over his shoulder at her.

"In bed until brunch is better," agreed Vivian. "I guess Mondays are always going to suck."

"Baby, if that sucked, I will get back in that bed and do the damn job right."

Vivian laughed and pulled the sheet up to her nose.

"Poor choice of words," she said. "Mondays are not as much fun as the weekend, and we do not have time for you to get back in bed!"

He shook his head and laughed as he headed for the bathroom.

Eventually, when Rowan was already dressed, Vivian got up and headed for the shower. The rest of the building might be a construction zone, but the bathroom, kitchen, and den were gorgeous. She also had to admit that having someone make breakfast for her was another perk she did not know she'd been missing. Rowan had been embarrassed to admit that he subscribed to a local caterer who did custom meal prep, which amused Vivian since most of the people she knew in his tax bracket didn't bother to cook, period. He had all the rich guy toys but a very budget-conscious attitude about the rest of his life, which strangely put Vivian at ease. She hadn't realized she was uncomfortable with partners who didn't plan things, but dating Rowan was a sharp contrast to her last three boyfriends. Rowan made it easy to discern all the ways she hadn't been compatible with them. Haphazard spending. Lack of goal setting. And a disinterest in their families. Rowan was the opposite of all of them, and the more time she spent with Rowan, the more she realized what she'd been missing.

He frowned at his phone and reached for the honey jar. There had been a series of pings, and Vivian couldn't tell if that meant there was a work emergency or if his brother Forest had sent more cute baby pics. She had begun to think that Forest was personally trying to talk her ovaries into forgetting their birth control pill by sending pic after pic of what Valkyrie babies looked like.

Rowan dolloped a blob of honey on his oats and looked up. "OK, I know you're doing the gala thing, so maybe this is too much. Feel free to tell me to take my thoughts someplace else, but you did say to be more community-oriented, and I have an idea."

"Send it," said Vivian, and then realized that, for once, she wouldn't have to explain that little piece of military-speak that was permanently embedded in her vocabulary. What a relief that she didn't have to translate for Rowan.

"Halloween Fair in the lobby. The businesses can each do a booth. Kids can trick-or-treat. Everyone can invite clients and their kids."

"Forest doesn't know where to take Olly for trick-or-treating?"

"Damn it, baby. Stop being psychic."

Vivian chuckled and tried not to relish his use of the word *baby*. "It's still a good idea. I'll suggest that to Howard." For all she knew, he used *baby* on all the women he knew. "I'll have to outsource most of the work because, yeah, I can't do two events and a job at once."

Rowan grimaced. "I shouldn't have said anything. I'm not trying to come up with more projects for you to do."

"I'll just make it someone else's project," said Vivian with a shrug. "What kind of booth are you guys going to do?"

Rowan looked guilty. "Can we do nerf guns?"

Vivian burst out laughing. "It's literally your idea. If you want to create a Halloween event so you can have a giant obstacle course to play Nerf guns with your brothers and give your nephew someplace to trick-or-treat, that's fine with me. I'll have to make Howard do a wine garden booth so I can loll about and watch."

"Now you're talking. And we can pitch in on the planning. I've got guys who could be enhancing building relations. If they can plan an op, they can plan an event."

"If you're serious about it, maybe I'll text Howard now." She looked around and realized she'd left her phone in the bedroom. She made the quick dash upstairs and back down, but was still mid-text when she heard a sharp ding that she thought was the toaster oven.

"Is that my bagel?" she called as she entered the kitchen. Then she looked up and realized Rowan was on the phone. He continued talking as he opened the toaster oven, plopped the bagel onto a plate for her, and pushed the avocado spread her direction.

"Yeah, Mark. I'm just finishing breakfast. I'll be in shortly."

Vivian froze.

"Yeah, OK," said Rowan.

He hung up, turned to her, and paused. "You look weird."

"I'm not telling anyone at work about us," she blurted out.

"OK," he said evenly.

"After Belinda's bratty little HR spiel, I thought it would be better not to."

"OK," he said again.

"I am telling, you know, real people."

"Just not work people?"

"Right. We haven't talked about... uh... anything. But you were on the phone with Mark. I just thought maybe I should tell you where I was at."

"Um... Mark is always going to know."

"Well, he's your best friend, right? So, of course. I thought maybe we should be discreet at work for a while." Vivian felt nervous. She didn't want him to think this was some kind of casual situationship, but she also didn't want to take everything public yet. That was too much pressure.

"Yeah, that makes total sense," he said with a sharp nod.

"OK," she said. He looked fine, but Vivian still felt a nervous churning in the pit of her stomach.

18
Rowan

CLOUD EIGHT POINT FIVE

Rowan stared at another email about the warehouse renovation. The exploratory dig had indeed found a propane tank, but it was smaller than they had thought from the sonar, and it appeared defunct and previously remediated to 1960s standards. The project manager thought they would lose an extra week but was hopeful they could get back on schedule in the winter when the jobs slowed down and they'd be able to pull additional work crews. So basically, it was the best possible version of bad news.

And Rowan ought to care about all of that, but all he could think was that Vivian wasn't telling anyone about him. Which wasn't fair. She had only said that she was being discreet at work. That made total sense. Who wanted to take a new relationship public in front of work acquaintances? But he couldn't help feeling like it was a sign that she wasn't serious about him. Only he wasn't supposed to be being serious anyway. It was supposed to be a fling. Right?

His intercom buzzed.

"Hello, sir, your brother, Asher, is here to see you. Are you available?"

"Um, yeah, of course."

Moments later, Ash came in. Rowan wondered if Ash grew his sandy hair long just to drive Rowan nuts. Half the time, he didn't even tie it back properly. It was practically down to his shoulders. With his lanky frame and bespoke suits, it gave him a rogue businessman look.

"Hey," said Ash, dropping into the guest chair and propping his feet up on Rowan's desk.

Rowan eyed the feet, and Ash grinned impudently, waiting for a comment.

"Hey," said Rowan, deciding not to rise to the bait. "What brings you all the way downtown?"

"Forest hired a nanny."

"Oh, thank God," said Rowan.

"Yeah, maybe," said Ash. "He called me last night and told me he had to pick up his temp nanny and wanted me to stay with Olly at the house while he went to get her."

"OK," said Rowan. "I'm feeling like there's something you're worried about in there."

"Remember when Forest was living overseas, and every pic on his socials was some girl with extra piercings and tattoos?"

"Yes? Wild child was his type. I've been relieved he grew out of that."

"Yeah, the temporary nanny has purple hair and a nose ring. And even though that is *not* my type, I still thought she was fire on the smoking hot yoga instructor scale. And definitely not wearing a bra."

"That is exactly who Forest would *not* want as a nanny," said Rowan, frowning. "I looked at his ad for the position, and his requirements were... extensive."

"I saw it too. He wants a PhD in child-rearing or something. It was ridiculous. I'm not saying get some rando off the street, but some of his stuff was absurd."

"Well, there's no rule that you can't have a PhD and purple hair, and Forest has always been uptight as fuck about Olly's care, so maybe there's something we don't know?"

"Maybe," said Ash, "but I'm just officially telling you that I thought it was weird."

"And what am I supposed to do about it?" asked Rowan with a laugh.

"Uh... pump him for information next time you talk." Asher scooped up a pyramid of bulldog clips off Rowan's desk and began to daisy-chain them together.

"You talk to him as much as I do," said Rowan.

"Isn't he handling your house and warehouse remodel?"

"His people are," said Rowan with a shrug. "They're doing a solid job, and I know he's checking in on them, but he's the CEO. I think the days of him personally overseeing anything are long gone."

"Oh," said Ash, looking disappointed. "I guess I just pictured him out there building things."

"He has over two hundred employees and triple that in subcontractors," said Rowan.

"Oh," said Ash, now looking uncomfortable. "I only have three people working for me." Rowan tried not to laugh. The Valkyrie competitive streak was a mile wide.

"And yet your net worth is about double both of ours," said Rowan.

"It pays to invest. Speaking of which, want to toss in on one of my projects?"

"What's the stake?" asked Rowan.

"Mmm, like a quarter mil if you can make it. You can do less, but for that amount, you'd be a primary stakeholder and tripling your money in a year."

"I'm trying to renovate a warehouse," said Rowan. "I can't just move a quarter million around!"

"Well, think about it. I swear it's going to go big, though. You should definitely put in something."

"Research is not predictable," said Rowan, quoting Ash back at himself. Ash stuck out his tongue. "You can't really know how long it will take to get money back, can you?"

"I've been doing this for nearly a decade," said Ash. "I'm getting better at predicting who is on the fast track. I'll send you the prospectus for what's coming up."

"And I will look at it because the last time I invested in you, I got to retire from the Marines and start my own company."

"You're not investing in me," snapped Ash, sounding annoyed. "You're investing in technology start-ups."

"That you, with your nearly a decade of experience, are vetting."

Ash sighed grumpily.

"What's up, bud?" asked Rowan, scrutinizing his baby brother. Asher hesitated, clacking the one of the bulldog clips to bite the air, but didn't look up.

"Like I said, I've been doing this for a while. I have piles of research on why I pick the projects I do, but a lot of people act like I'm some Magic Eight Ball. Which is fine if I pick winners, but I don't always. Not because of a failure in the metrics but because sometimes... shit happens. However, if I act goofy or say... break up with my girlfriend, there are rumors that I've lost my touch."

"It's a lot of pressure being a Magic Eight Ball."

"Yeah, and it's the kind of thing that can snowball. One wrong pick, act too funny, and suddenly, I can't get investors. No investors on this project means no investors on the next one. Everyone says Asher's lost his touch. Boom. Whole house of cards comes tumbling down."

"If you retired right now, are your finances secure?" asked Rowan.

"Yes, but that's not the point!"

"The point is that you love what you do, but half of what you're doing is sales, and that depends on a public persona that took a hit when you broke up with your perfect heiress girlfriend."

"She wasn't perfect," growled Asher.

Rowan debated whether or not to keep his mouth shut. If it were anyone else, he probably would, but he hadn't liked Emma, and he didn't want her making a comeback.

"Far from perfect," agreed Rowan, and Ash looked surprised. "She was a snob. She never liked Forest or me."

Rowan knew his opinion counted for a lot with both his brothers, and he tried not to take advantage of that, but this felt worth it.

Ash was silent, and then he tossed the clips angrily back on the desk. "Sorry. I wish you'd said something."

Rowan grabbed up his jacket and took it to the wardrobe to give himself something to do.

"We hadn't been seeing much of each other, and it didn't seem like you wanted to hear it. But these days we're all in the same city. And with Olly around... I don't know. Breakup aside, I liked hanging out with you guys the other night. The whole point of locating Valkyrie here was that I would be closer to the two of you. What do you think about doing the holidays together this year?"

He adjusted the row of shoulder holsters, giving himself the time to straighten his face. The wardrobe now made him think of pink and flustered Vivian and that made him grin like an idiot.

"Can we invite Mom?"

"Sure," said Rowan, turning back to Ash with a shrug. Of the three of them, Asher seemed to be the one who still held out hope that their mother might someday behave like an adult. "She won't come, but we can invite her."

Ash sighed, then smiled. "It would be kind of awesome to watch Olly open his presents. Let's make Forest host Christmas."

"OK, I'll do Thanksgiving," said Rowan.

"That leaves me New Year's. This is going to be great!"

"We'll see what Forest thinks," said Rowan, chuckling as he went back to his desk.

There was a sharp knock on the office door and Mark leaned in, peering at Rowan over the top of his clear-framed glasses.

"So?" demanded Mark. "Hey, Ash."

"So, what?" asked Rowan, and Mark groaned as if Rowan was being intentionally obtuse.

"Come on! That was Viv on the phone this morning, wasn't it?"

"Viv?" demanded Asher, looking between Mark and Rowan. Mark ignored him and focused on Rowan.

"So, was that like... we bumped into each other at the bagel place or let me feed you the bagels from my cupboard?"

Ash gave a chuckle. "Yes. Inquiring minds want to know. What type of bagel are we dealing with?"

"Oh, for fuck's sake," muttered Rowan.

"Come on! You know all my dirt," protested Ash.

"And all of mine," said Mark.

"You have no dirt," said Rowan. "Either of you."

"All my past dirt," amended Mark.

"I might have dirt," said Ash. "You don't know. Who is Viv?"

"Vivian Kaye," said Mark. "Paralegal. Works downstairs. Told Rowan off in the elevator. It was great. She's great."

Rowan knew Vivian was great. She was amazing. He wanted to shout it from the rooftops, but she specifically did not want that.

"Soooooo?" prodded Mark. "Jenny will be waterboarding one of us if I don't come home with details."

"Fine," growled Rowan. "Vivian stayed over. Can we not make a thing out of this?"

Because Vivian clearly wasn't ready to make a thing out of it. Never mind that waking up with her had been the first morning since moving into his stupid building that it had felt like a home.

"Who's making a thing of it?" said Mark, exchanging looks with Ash. "I mean, you date so much that it's just another day of the week."

Ash snort-laughed, and Mark grinned.

"This is why I don't bring dates anywhere near any of you," said Rowan sourly. And because usually that much testosterone in one place scared reasonable women away.

"Whatever," said Mark dismissively. "Vivian likes us."

"That's a good sign," said Ash, trying to balance the clips on top of each other.

"What do you mean?" asked Rowan.

Ash looked up in surprise. "Well, didn't we just establish that having a relationship with someone who doesn't like your family is a bad idea? So if she's down with your crew, then she's gotta be pretty cool."

"Yes, but we're trying not to blab this all over the building, OK? She has to work here," said Rowan, looking between Mark and Ash.

"Yeah, of course," said Mark. "But I'm not the whole building, and Ash doesn't know anyone here. So we're good. I'm just saying that dating Vivian was my idea, so I want credit."

"Uh, what now?" demanded Teddy, stopping mid-way through the hall and peering around Mark. "Did this guy just say dating Vivian was his idea? Hey, Ash."

"Hey, Teddy. He did say that," said Ash.

"Uh, no," said Teddy, looking offended. "It was totally my idea. Also, this conversation does imply that he is actually dating Vivian."

"Yeah," said Ash, "she stayed at his place last night."

"What? Way to go!"

Teddy gave a fist pump of enthusiasm, and Rowan glared at him.

"I mean, way to go, sir?"

"Does discreet mean nothing to any of you?" demanded Rowan.

"Who am I going to tell?" asked Teddy.

"Besides everyone," murmured Mark.

"I'm serious," said Rowan. "She's worried about repercussions at work. So, for Vivian's sake, could you all not behave like the Marine Corps gossip train?"

"Oh, yeah. Of course," said Teddy, sounding contrite. "But still…" He ended on a massive grin and then sidled out of the doorway. Ash laughed, and Mark looked like he wanted to.

"Glad I have so much privacy," muttered Rowan, shaking his head.

"You can have all the privacy you want," said Mark. "As long as you tell us everything." He added that parting shot as he followed Teddy down the hall, which made Ash laugh again.

Then they both blinked as Doc's land drone zipped past the doorway.

"Did a remote control car just go down the hall?" asked Ash.

"That is a land drone," said Rowan.

Moments later Doc went pelting past the door after the vehicle.

"It's still in the testing phase."

"You really did it, didn't you?" asked Ash laughing.

"Did what?" asked Rowan.

"I remember when you were going over resumes. I thought you had the weirdest criteria. You kept keying in on the oddest things and talking about unit cohesion. But you've gone to a great deal of trouble to create a team that you want to hang out with all day long."

"Yeah," said Rowan, in surprise. "Of course."

"And this girl is friends with your crew?"

"Well, that might be pushing the parameters of friendship since she took them for four hundred dollars at poker. Which, come to think of it, I believe she used to pay for your breakup donuts."

Ash's grin stretched from ear to ear. "Yeah, OK."

"OK, what?" asked Rowan.

"Nothing. I'm going to go. You'll call Forest about the holidays?"

"Sure, sounds good," said Rowan, suspicious of his brother's dangling conversational thread.

"Great," said Ash, standing up. "See you later."

"Yeah, later," said Rowan.

19
Vivian

LEADERSHIP ROLE

Vivian managed to make it into the conference room and dropped her enormous folder of gala stuff onto the table in front of Ashley. Ashley looked up from her phone, her natural curls bouncing in luscious spirals that Vivian envied. It was so orderly. Vivian was well aware of the amount of effort Ashley put into her hair, including the small sacrifices to the rain gods. However, Vivian suspected that even if she put in that much effort and sacrificed the UW mascot, she'd still end up with hair that looked like a creature had built a nest in it.

"OK," said Vivian. "Give me a sec to grab my tea, and then we'll get down to business."

"You're the client," said Ashley, with a grin. "I am at your disposal. But you know we need to preface any work talk with what is going on with you and Rowan Valkyrie."

Vivian winced. "Shhhhhhh." She waved her arms frantically and looked desperately out into the hall to make sure no one was around to hear. Ashley looked at her like she was insane.

"Belinda made a big deal recently about staff not dating clients," she whispered, gently closing the door. Vivian didn't want to say exactly when Belinda had brought it up. Hiding in Rowan's wardrobe was a ridiculous story that she did not plan to share until everyone was already drunk.

"He's not a client, is he?" Ashley whispered back.

"Not exactly, but a building tenant is probably close enough that Belinda could make a stink about it. And knowing Belinda, she definitely would."

"That would prevent literally anyone in your company from dating anyone else in the building. That's ridiculous."

"Yes, and I'm sure I could fight it, but the point is that I don't want to have to fight right now. It's only been a couple of weeks. Not even that." Twelve days. Twelve glorious days.

"And you've spent practically every night over at his place, haven't you?" demanded Ashley. "Bet you get a drawer in his dresser real soon."

Vivian hesitated.

"Oh, my God," Ashley crowed, getting louder again. "You already got one."

"Yesterday," said Vivian guiltily. "He said my lingerie needed dedicated space."

Ashley rocked back in her chair, laughing. "It's funny because it's true."

"Oh, hush," said Vivian, checking the hallway again through the glass sidelight as Ashley giggled again. Vivian realized there was bottled water on the side table and grabbed one instead of going for tea.

"I can't wait to meet this guy. He's coming to the gala, right?"

"Yeah," said Vivian, dropping tiredly into one of the conference table chairs with the water. She adjusted the height of the chair. She sometimes wondered if midnight elves went around altering the conference room chairs to the oddest measurements.

"Although, he doesn't really get why we can't go together," she added as she sank a few inches closer to the floor.

She also got the feeling that Rowan didn't understand her role at the Victory Mission, but she was at a loss as to how to explain it to him. Rowan listened intently when she talked, but he frequently looked perplexed. *Event Committee Chair* apparently meant nothing, and the entire nonprofit world appeared to be a mystery to him. He seemed to exist in a very for-profit space.

"Uh, 'cause I need your ass to be working," said Ashley.

"That he gets and supports. He just doesn't actually get what I'm doing." Vivian shrugged.

"Well, I expect he'll get it when he shows up," said Ashley. "Trying to explain the moving parts of an event to someone is hard until they see it happen. Although, switching to work talk for a moment…"

Ashley paused, and Vivian suddenly felt nervous. Ashley was usually a straight shooter. Hesitation meant she thought it was a sensitive topic.

"So, I guess the search for a new Executive Director at the Victory Mission is not going well? Or at least that's the impression I got from Father Fred and Kandie?"

Kandace was the Board President, and Father Fred was the current Executive Director. As a founding member of the Victory Mission, he had served well, but she knew he was just plain tired and wanted to retire into his true passion of volunteerism.

"It's hard to find a candidate who understands the non-profit world and can speak to the military," said Vivian. "And we've found a few we like, but we can't be as competitive in pay as some bigger nonprofits."

"Well, that is because you only have ten full-time employees and three part-time staff."

"And a ton of volunteers and programs to manage," Vivian pointed out.

"You're small," said Ashley.

"We're efficient, and we could grow with the right leadership."

"You're punching above your weight class."

"You're goddamn right we are," said Vivian proudly.

"Yes, but that makes it extra hard to find a qualified director, and none of you want to settle for someone who will do the job but won't really get the mission."

"We shouldn't have to," said Vivian grumpily.

"Yeah," said Ashley, nodding. "Which is why I think you'd be perfect for the job."

Vivian laughed. "What?"

"You have a degree in Communication. You have nearly a decade of experience in fundraising, and you know and understand the military."

"I'm a paralegal," said Vivian.

"For the top law firm in the State. You've written briefs for the State Supreme Court. You have years of experience in Estate Planning, which is exactly the donor base the Mission needs to talk to, and you've brought in half the board."

"I've contributed to briefs," said Vivian. "Howard had the final say. I don't have any leadership experience."

Ashley laughed. "Vivian, you are my girl. Don't go all imposter syndrome on me. You lead all the damn time."

There was a soft knock on the door.

"No, I don't," said Vivian, confident that she didn't.

She glanced out the side light and saw Courtney at the door. She waved to the assistant, and Courtney opened the door.

"Vivian," said Courtney, looking embarrassed. "I can't find Howard, and I don't know what to do."

"Oh, no," said Vivian, soothingly. "What's wrong?"

"I just talked to Ms. Branch, and she gave me a whole list of files to pull for a seminar she's speaking at, and on the list is one of the briefs you just filed on that Supreme Court case."

"Oh, right," said Vivian, remembering Ms. Branch had mentioned it the week before.

"But I don't know if she wants the whole decision or just what you filed, and she wanted me to get a statement from Howard."

"She's doing an annual impact report on this year's rulings and wants to brag on Howard's work and do a little plug for the firm. What she really needs is an overview and then probably a quotable from Howard. I'll write up the quote for Howard's approval, and then you can ask Etta to write the overview. Tell her she's got about two hundred words."

"How is Etta supposed to get the entire case down to two hundred words?" asked Courtney, looking alarmed.

"She won't, but if I tell her she's got four hundred, it will come back at six. Tell Ms. Branch I'll run the quote from Howard under his nose tomorrow, and she should have it by Friday."

"OK, thanks!" said Courtney, looking relieved.

"No problem."

Courtney disappeared, shutting the door gently behind her.

"I'm sorry, what were you saying about not leading?" asked Ashley. "I got distracted by you telling someone what to do."

"That's not Executive Director leadership. Being a director isn't just staff. It's budgets and networking and development and grants."

"All of which I have watched you handle while working on the gala," said Ashley. "I think you should at least mention to Father Fred that you're interested."

"I can't tell Chappie that," said Vivian.

"Why not?" asked Ashley seriously.

"Because he would say what a good idea it was," said Vivian.

"Yes, because it is."

"No, because he loves me and thinks I can do anything. He and Howard get along great in that regard."

Ashley chuckled.

"But he doesn't have a say in the hiring. The board does that. And I don't think I'm a serious enough candidate."

"Well, I won't argue with you right now," said Ashley. "I will just say that you should think about it."

"I appreciate your belief in me," said Vivian. "But I have to be realistic."

"Like you're being realistic about Mr. Hotstuff Security Guy who makes you smile every time you say his name?"

"It's only been a few weeks," protested Vivian. "Falling in love right now would be ridiculous."

"Bitch, please," said Ashley. "You were in love at the donut shop. Why are you fighting this?"

Vivian sighed. "Because he makes me so, so, so happy, Ashley and that is scary."

Ashley's smile was gleefully smug. "I hear that, but at least allow me to cheer you on. I love happy on you. It's your look."

The door opened abruptly without a knock, and Vivian looked up.

"Viv," said Trent Michaels, unconsciously running a hand over his coiffed blonde locks. "Howard's missing again, and he's locked down his schedule."

"I'm in a meeting. And he's not missing. He's having lunch with his wife."

There was a visible eye-roll. "Well, be a sweetie and change his Tuesday with me to two-thirty."

"I'll look at the schedule and see what's available," said Vivian. "And ask Howard what he wants to do."

"Nooooo," said Trent, wagging his finger at Vivian. "We all know you can do it, and Howard will do whatever is on his calendar. So just fix it for me! There's a good girl."

He shut the door before Vivian could reply.

"His calendar is locked down because certain people kept getting the secretaries to change it without asking," said Vivian, turning back to Ashley. "And now they bug me instead."

"You have to get out of here," said Ashley. "Seriously. Think about what I said."

"I'll think about it," said Vivian. And she would because it wasn't like she had come up with any other career ideas. She just didn't think the Board would take her any more seriously than Trent did.

20
Rowan

UNDERCOVER

Vivian was on the phone again. The closer they got to the gala, the more Vivian lived with it in her hand. Rowan wasn't sure why throwing a party was so complicated.

"OK, well, we've run into this before," she said, walking by on her way to the kitchen. "It's an insurance issue. We can add a rider, but honestly, the venue should cover it."

There was silence while Vivian listened. Rowan poured them both a glass of wine, leaned back on the couch and eyed the plastic-draped dining room through the archway. The house had inched closer to done, but they weren't out of the plastic yet and Thanksgiving loomed ominously on the calendar. He was also worried about what to tell his brothers about Vivian. He wanted her at Thanksgiving, but his hesitant initiation of the topic had been interrupted by a gala phone call. Melissa had always insisted on going to her family's house for the few holidays he was home, but Vivian hadn't mentioned the holidays, or any future plans with him at all. He was trying not to let that bother him, but it really did.

Rowan's phone chirped, and he looked down to see a video of Olly and a woman who must be the new nanny, Chloe. They were jumping in a mud puddle in the backyard, wearing big rubber boots. He could hear Forest laughing in the audio. Olly looked elated. Chloe looked up, her purple hair flashing out from under the hood of an old military poncho. She was prettier than he'd expected, and her grin was as big as Olly's.

Rowan didn't know what to think about that. The last time Rowan had tried to take Olly out in the rain, Forest had refused, saying that Olly would get sick. Apparently, Chloe possessed secret magic rain-dancing powers.

Ash's response popped in after the video.

Aw! I remember when Rowan would do that with me.

Rowan laughed. Being eight years older than Ash meant remembering a lot of his brother's childhood markers.

I'll still hang out in puddles with you, bud. I mean, we'll probably have to do push-ups, but...

And I remember doing exactly what I'm doing now. Staying inside as the only sane brother.

Ash's laughing emoji popped up instantly on both Rowan's and Forest's text.

"Well, yes, I appreciate that she wants that, but no, I really will not be telling a bunch of veterans who have concealed carry permits that they can't carry legal firearms at our event."

Rowan nearly choked on his sip of wine. Vivian looked up and winked at him.

"Wait, she said, what? Who is this person? Seriously, is she one of those people who find Bob threatening?"

Rowan was now thoroughly confused. He didn't think Vivian had ever mentioned Bob before. He shook his head and went back to the family text thread. He hesitated over his next message but plunged ahead.

Looks like Chloe is working out.

He could see Forest's response bubbles percolating. Then they stopped. Then they restarted.

She's been a big help.

"No, don't call Chappie. That would be a disaster. Do not let a former combat chaplain start talking to some neo-liberal hippie woke wench. He'll have her recruited in no time. His brainwashing is way more powerful than hers. Just have her call me if she won't fall in line."

Rowan hadn't met Chappie yet, but the former Army Chaplain sounded hilarious.

Another text came through on a different thread. It was Ash.

OK, I'M PRO OLLY PUDDLE JUMPING, BUT WTF? IS THIS CHLOE CHICK SLIPPING FOREST ANTI-ANXIETY MEDS IN HIS RED BULL OR SOMETHING?

WORKS FOR ME. AND APPARENTLY FOR FOREST. GLAD HE'S EASING BACK.

YEAH... BUT...

The message came with a monkey scratching his head and Rowan gave it a thumbs up. He agreed with Ash that Forest seemed to be reacting uniquely to Chloe, but he wasn't about to throw up any roadblocks. Whatever Chloe was doing, Rowan wanted her to keep doing it.

Vivian hung up and dropped onto the couch beside him with a loud *ugh*, flopping her limbs out in exhaustion.

"You going to make it, baby?"

"No. I mean, probably yes. We somehow manage it every year. But I've got to get people out of the habit of calling me. Most of the time, they already know what the answers are. They're just scared to do it without backup."

Rowan grunted in acknowledgment. "Yeah, that's tough. You need it while they're learning, but there comes a point where you need them to stand on their own."

"They have Ashley now, but they keep calling me!"

He handed her a glass of wine, and she took a long sip and worked herself around until she leaned against his chest. "Well, work in progress, I guess," she said after another drink.

"Who's Bob, by the way?" he asked wrapping an arm around her.

"What?" Vivian tilted her head back until she looked up at him from his chest.

"You asked if she was one of those people who was scared of Bob?"

Vivian burst out laughing and her wine bounced precariously on her stomach.

"Bob is the dummy. You know, the punching dummy? The pink man on a pole that people use in martial arts classes. He's just a head and torso. We call him Bob."

"OK... Bob I can get with. But why would anyone be scared of Bob?"

"No idea. But one time I took a yoga class with the girls at Christine's gym and the instructor thought Bob was bringing negative energy into class with his threatening expression, so she put a scarf over his head."

"I..." Rowan found he was literally speechless. Vivian pointed up at him and laughed.

"Yes! Your face! Oh, God! That's the face I made!" She laughed hard enough that tears leaked out the corners of her eyes. "I could not go back to that class!"

"I don't think I would have made it through class in the first place," he said.

Vivian's chuckles subsided. "It was a good workout, but it was... OK, you can't repeat this anywhere. I'm as liberal, feminist, and allied as I can be. But I firmly believe that there needs to be some amount of... aggression, balls to the wall, fuck you mother fucker attitude to get things done."

"If you're expecting an argument then you've come to the wrong place."

"Intensity and competition make things fun."

"Again... Not going to argue."

"There is a time and place for being quiet and peaceful, and then there are times for mosh pits. You cannot and should not make every place a Zen garden. And frankly, the people who feel threatened by an inanimate object because they think it represents violence are not my people, and I don't understand them. Also, they're pussies."

"Hoo-rah, baby," he said, laughing, as he brushed her hair out of her face.

"The last part is the part you can't repeat," she said, looking up at him.

"I actually got that," he said.

"Non-profit people don't like it when I say stuff like that. It's what makes Victory Mission kind of a step-child in the non-profit world. I think it's why we've been having such a hard time finding a new Executive Director."

She always said *we* about the Victory Mission. He thought it was cute that she took her volunteering so seriously.

"Cultural conflict," he agreed. "Military attitudes do not always translate well into the civilian sphere."

Vivian made an agreeing noise, but her phone chirped and pulled her attention away from him.

"Your Halloween thing seems to be coming along," she said, scrolling through a text. "That will be a nice fun thing for us the end of the month."

"Will it?" he asked.

She looked up in confusion.

"Seems like at work there's just you and me. No us."

Vivian sighed deeply. "Yeah, well, work also has Belinda who literally made a little speech at the last staff meeting about how everyone needed to be careful of liability with regards to romantic entanglements with clients."

"I'm not a client. At best I'm contracted to Howard personally since he owns the building."

"And since he's been pushing me to do more tenant management that line is getting even blurrier. Look, I just need to tell Howard and ask how he wants to handle it at work."

"I don't really like having my relationship dictated by Howard."

"It's not!"

"I can't kiss you in the elevator, so yeah, it kind of is. It's been almost a month. I understand wanting to be discreet, but it's starting to feel like we're hiding."

Vivian wrinkled her nose. "Yeah. I know."

"And we're not even going to the gala together."

"Well, even if we were out, we still wouldn't be," said Vivian. "Unless you want to show up and volunteer your cute little tushy for some work hours."

"Which I wouldn't mind doing if you thought it was worthwhile, but we're not even sitting together."

"I have to present! So I have to be at the front table! Once the speeches are all done then I will be all yours. I promise!"

"Uh-huh." Rowan wasn't sure what he wanted. He'd told himself this was a fling, but every time she said *Mr. Valkyrie* in public it rubbed him like sand paper. Every time she said it in the bedroom, it made him hot as hell, but that was probably a personal kink not a relationship issue. If it was a fling, it didn't matter who she did or didn't tell. He needed to leave it alone, but he kept picking at it like a scab.

Vivian looked like she was about to say something, but her phone dinged again.

"Oh, for fuck's sake," she muttered shaking her head at the message and promptly dropping her phone onto the coffee table.

"The event venue has exploded?"

"Charles Tate Senior is re-doing his will for the fourteenth time. Seriously, he's been dinking with it for a month. It's never getting signed because he keeps making adjustments. And then his son talks him out of the changes."

"Ah, Chucky. Such a winner," said Rowan, lifting his glass.

"More like such a fucking clowndick," said Vivian and Rowan nearly spit wine onto her face. "I'm serious. Every time his father tries to leave money to anyone else Chucky whines more than a dog.

Someone needs to get him a fresh cup of suck it the fuck up—he is not owed that money in any way. That guy is such a waste of space that he makes me think he should have been a blowjob."

"Baby!" laughed Rowan, laughing so hard that it made her head bounce.

Vivian giggled. "Too much?"

"Oh, my God. Mark needs to hear that one," Rowan said, reaching for his phone. He'd had to add an office slack channel just for Vivian's quotables and now *Who said it – Vivian or Drill Sergeant?* was a favorite polling question.

"I've got more. Because, believe me, when it comes to Chucky, I could keep going."

Moments later, a text from Mark popped through.

"Mark says you missed out on your calling as a drill instructor."

Vivian laughed. "It never would have worked out. I don't like push-ups."

"No one likes push-ups."

"Yes, but I'm very competitive so I would have had to do more so that no one would be able to show me up. And then I would have been mad that I was doing push-ups."

"The push-ups that you gave yourself?"

"Yes, exactly."

"I am dating a very strange woman."

"Well, you saw my hair and you still decided to go for it. So… I mean… I don't know what you thought you were getting."

"A strange girl with fantastic lingerie. The filthy mouth is a bonus."

Vivian giggled and looked up at him. "I really will tell Howard about us. I'm sorry it's been taking so long."

"It's your workplace. Sorry I'm pushing."

"No, I get it. You are not the sneaky link kind of guy."

"I literally don't know what that is."

"You like to be upfront about your life. You don't mind being private, but you don't like sneaking around."

"Yes," said Rowan, feeling relieved that she understood. Although, he suspected that she probably wasn't being technically accurate about the definition of *sneaky link*.

"I'll tell Howard. It won't change where I'm sitting at the gala, but we will be able to dance and feed each other dessert or whatever."

"Are you just setting me up to feed you chocolate?" Rowan asked, suddenly suspicious.

"Mmm… Maybe?" she asked with a grin. "Is that going to be a problem?"

"Never," said Rowan, leaning down to kiss her.

21
Vivian

OUT IN THE OPEN

"OK," said Howard, scanning his email, "I think that catches us up. Have you got anything?"

What she had was a relationship. That she hadn't expected to have. And didn't know how to talk about it.

Vivian glanced at her notes. "No, I don't think so."

But she could tell that Rowan was starting to have a problem with it. Not just starting. He *did* have a problem with it.

"OK, well, then I am going to leave early. Trent will have to suck eggs."

Vivian always found Howard's non-swearing cute. She thought it was due to his religious upbringing but couldn't understand how the military hadn't rid him of the habit.

"Sounds good," she said, standing up. She was halfway to the door before her courage caught up with her.

"Um, actually," she said, turning back around. Then she stopped.

"What's up, Viv?" asked Howard, looking concerned.

"I…" She swallowed. "I am dating Rowan Valkyrie."

"Oh, thank God," said Howard. "For a minute there I thought you were going to tell me you were quitting."

"No, I'm not quitting."

"And I am very appreciative of that. You're helping me coast into retirement. Meanwhile, Valkyrie? I mean… OK. I just thought…"

"You thought what?"

Howard scratched his head and then nodded. "No, that makes sense."

"Does it?"

"Well, I'm a little surprised. He's a bit older than you. But after chatting with him more this last month I can see how you're temperamentally similar. That's nice! I'm assuming it's nice or you wouldn't be telling me."

"Well, I'm telling you because Belinda keeps making snide comments about not dating clients and I didn't want it to become an issue."

"Well, first of all, he's not a Hoskins, Branch, and Kato client. And secondly, and more awkwardly, I believe Belinda has her eye on your boyfriend. She also keeps suggesting that I make her his liaison. And while I haven't talked to HR, I feel quite strongly that the legal standing for banning two adults who happen to work in the same building from dating is quite weak. I think if we tried to enforce that you would probably sue my pants off."

"Well, I would probably quit at minimum," said Vivian. "And go to work for that nice lawyer woman who keeps offering me a job. You know, Alison something or other."

"You mean my daughter?"

"Oh, yes, right. That's the one."

Howard mockingly clutched at his chest. "Stabbed in the back by two of my favorite girls."

"That's your front," said Vivian and Howard laughed.

"Yes, stabbed in the back from the front. Very tricky. Viv, you weren't really worried about telling me, were you?"

"Not you, exactly. More like making it public and awkward and having to fight for it and then having to retract when we break up."

"I take it you've been seeing each other long enough that you're willing to make it public and don't think you're breaking up?"

He stopped talking and waited for her to speak. It was his special lawyer skill. Vivian knew it, and she still fell for it.

"It's been a month. If we're breaking up, he's going to have to do it because I'm crazy about him."

"Aww! Excellent!"

"OK, so... if you see us arriving at work together, it's because we're two adults in a relationship who care enough about the environment to share a car."

"Carpooling is the environmentally kind thing to do," agreed Howard. "And now he can be your date to the gala tomorrow night!"

"Well, he can be my date after I finish the ask," said Vivian. "Up until then I'm on the clock. But afterwards, yes, I will be changing my seat to the one next to his."

"Ha! This is great. Wait until I tell Nadine."

"Well, glad I could be the hot topic over dinner," said Vivian with a smile. Howard delighted in being able to bring his wife intel like other people delighted in gifts. Gossip was their love language.

She turned to go back to her desk and then glanced at her phone as an email alert popped up.

"Did we have another appointment with Charles Tate Sr.? His assistant just sent me something."

"I'm taking him the latest draft of his will right now. We're golfing. He will sign it, or I will donk him over the head with a golf club."

Vivian snorted.

"Sounds good. I'll let the assistant know that you're handling the matter directly with Senior and that we don't need another meeting."

"Great. Now I'm going to hustle out of here before someone comes in and wants me to do work."

Vivian returned to her desk and dealt with all the immediate fires in her inbox before texting Rowan.

HOWARD SAID THAT LEGALLY HE DOESN'T SEE HOW HE COULD POSSIBLY STOP INDIVIDUALS FROM DATING OTHER PEOPLE IN THE BUILDING AND AGREES THAT US CARPOOLING IS THE ENVIRONMENTALLY FRIENDLY THING TO DO.

She got back a laughing emoji.

GREAT. THEN I WILL PICK YOU UP IN AN HOUR FOR LUNCH. MEET ME AT THE ELEVATORS.

Vivian stared at the text and then looked around the office, wishing she had someone to make eye contact with. She had a date with the handsome Rowan Valkyrie, and they would kiss and hold hands and probably feed each other French fries. Her fantasy was completely junior high-rated, and Vivian did not care. Rowan made her as giggly and silly as when she'd been thirteen.

At one hour on the dot, she went out to the elevator, carrying her jacket and purse and was slightly disappointed that there was no one around to witness her going off on a lunch date. The doors slid open, revealing Rowan's broad-shouldered frame leaning against the back wall, and Vivian sighed at the sight of him.

"Ready?" he asked, raising an eyebrow.

"Yes," she said, trying to keep herself from beaming like an idiot.

She stepped in and glanced up at the security camera and waved. Then she went on tip-toe and kissed Rowan. He looked down at her in surprise.

"I figured if I was telling Howard, I should tell Barb too," she said.

Rowan laughed and pulled her close to kiss her more affectionately.

"OK," she said, pushing away from him a moment later and straightening her skirt. "We're telling Barb. Not giving everyone on the security team a peep show."

"Yes, ma'am," said Rowan, with a cocky grin, which was his way of saying that he wouldn't be arguing with her.

Lunch was even better than her fantasy since he took her to Matt's in the Market. They cozied up at a corner table next to the enormous arched windows that looked out on the world-famous Pike Place Market sign, indulged in lunchtime cocktails, and ended with the candy bar square dessert. The weather had blessed them with a sparkling, crisp fall day. The sun bounced off the damp cobblestones below the restaurant and the yells of the fish monger could be distantly heard as they finished their lunch. If this was what openly dating Rowan was going to be, Vivian knew two things—she needed to work out more, and it was going to be heavenly.

Then, they walked through the lobby holding hands. The security desk personnel pointedly did not look their way. Which was security guard-ese for saying *nothing to see here, move along*. They managed to be the only ones on the elevator again, and Vivian wished for once that there wasn't a security camera because she really wanted to do something naughty to Rowan. It was probably the cocktail talking, but she really wanted to put her hands in inappropriate places.

"Oh," said Rowan, as the elevator slowed. "I should come in and talk to Howard for a minute. He left me a voicemail. Something about security for a wedding?"

The doors opened, and Vivian led Rowan through the side entrance that ran behind the front desk and was a shortcut to Howard's office. It was a simple PIN code entry, and she saw Rowan clock her PIN number and sighed. She mentioned switching up the code to Susan, the office manager, the previous month, but she would have to push for it again.

"He has an Indian-American client who is setting up a trust for their daughter's wedding and they're trying to budget. We have numbers on standard American weddings. Well, I mean, standard rich people weddings. But Indian weddings are a whole other proposition."

"So, you're planning people's weddings now? I'm confused."

Vivian laughed. "No, we're advising on how much they should realistically save or invest for the future."

"I'm still confused. I feel like that would be an accountant thing, not a lawyer thing."

"Estate planning overlaps with multiple disciplines."

She waved at Stephen from HR, who was passing at the mouth

of the hallway. They waved back too enthusiastically. So now announcing to everyone that she was dating Rowan was taken care of. Even if she hadn't been, it still would have been handled.

They arrived at Vivian's desk, and she dropped her purse and jacket in her cubicle and then went to Howard's door.

"Hm," she said, feigning disappointment. "Looks like Howard isn't in."

"Well," said Rowan with a shrug, "I will make up something and email him."

"Gosh. I just hate to have wasted your time."

One of his eyebrows went up. "You knew he wouldn't be in," he said accusingly.

"Did I? Prove it." She pressed herself against him and trailed her fingers up his lapel.

"I will subpoena your face," he said, wrapping his arms around her waist.

Vivian giggled and kissed him. She'd been aiming for only a little naughty, but somehow between his hands on her waist and the way his thigh felt pressed between hers, she found herself, kissing him harder. Her tongue tangled with his and they stumbled backward against the wall.

He pressed his face into her neck, leaving a trail of hot kisses that had her gasping. She pulled back and stared at Rowan.

"Uh… Want to make out in the supply room?" she suggested, pointing to the door down the hall.

"Yes, ma'am."

"OK," said Vivian, kissing him again as they stumbled sideways.

They paused outside the door. She had to admit that she probably shouldn't have had that cocktail because she was probably going to be doing more than making out.

His hand was all the way up her skirt, and he'd take a very commanding handhold on her ass when Vivian heard someone call her name.

"Shit," gasped Vivian, untangling herself. Rowan blinked at her in confusion as she reached behind him, opened the door to the supply closet and shoved him inside.

"Hey Courtney," said Vivian, leaning in what she hoped was a casual way against the supply room door.

"Vivian! Oh, thank goodness. I thought I saw you come this way," said Courtney, clenching her hands nervously together. "I just talked to Charles Tate Senior's assistant. Apparently, Mr. Tate got back from golfing and had a cardiac event."

"What?!" gasped Vivian in shock.

"That's what the assistant said. But apparently, on his way into the ambulance, he told the assistant to tell Howard. Which... I don't want to sound callous, but I don't know what we're supposed to do with this information."

"He and Howard were golfing earlier this afternoon. So they must have just seen each other. Um... Well, I'll text Howard and let him know, but in the meantime, you can run the grave illness protocol and set up a card for Howard to sign and arrange for flowers. Probably we can wait until Monday, but let's see if we can get an update before we send anything. We'll want to make sure we send the appropriate message."

"Oh! OK," said Courtney, looking relieved to have actionable steps to take. "Thanks!"

She hurried away, and Vivian slowly released her hold on the door handle.

"Yes, we are *so* out in the open," said Rowan, straightening his tie as he came out.

"I was supposed to let Courtney catch me with my skirt up around my ears?" demanded Vivian. "If you want out in the open then we're probably going to have to stop making out in public spaces."

"And now I'm torn," said Rowan.

"I am also conflicted, but I'm just saying..."

"Right," agreed Rowan, his eyes twinkling as he leaned down to kiss her cheek. "We need to behave *appropriately*. Got it." Then he leaned even closer. "But tonight, I will not be appropriate," he whispered in her ear.

"Thank you, Mr. Valkyrie," said Vivian, primly.

"Mm-hmm. See you later, Ms. Kaye," said Rowan, walking toward the elevator.

Vivian watched him leave with a smile and then turned to go back to her desk, only to find Belinda standing square in the hall and watching her with narrowed eyes.

"Really, Vivian," said Belinda. "Why don't you just throw yourself at him? It's so obvious he's not going to go for someone like you. I mean, you might get him for a night or two, but long-term? It's a lost cause. Who would take you seriously?"

Vivian wanted to respond, but it felt like her tongue was stuck to the roof of her mouth. Belinda shook her head in the most sadly condescending manner and stalked off. Vivian wanted to scream something after her. Probably something with a lot of profanity, but instead, she stood there, silently trying not to cry. The very worst part about Belinda was that every single time, she somehow managed to say the thing that would hurt the most.

22
Vivian

THE GALA BEGINS

Vivian arrived three hours before event time in her sweats, her hair carefully pinned up in a scarf. She parked her Mini-Cooper, stuffed to the windows with supplies in the fire lane in front of the building, and got out. With her gown in a garment bag over her shoulder, Vivian stopped to survey the venue's exterior.

The Performing Arts Center was a little older and therefore not on the top tier list of event venues for Seattle, but it did have ample parking and a recent remodel had freshened up on the inside. The outside still had a seventies vibe with a jutting portico and heavy swooping concrete planters that had been filled with native grasses. But the portico offered a covered walkway up to the front doors, making a red-carpet effect possible. Overall, Vivian was pleased with the venue, particularly for the price.

Vivian arrived at the Arts Center as the staff began to roll out the Astroturf. The theme was garden party, and the fake grass was vibrantly green against the shades of gray cement. The tall planters also had the enormous six-foot-tall poppy flowers the event committee had spent a weekend crafting. Vivian almost clapped her hands in glee.

"I know!" exclaimed Ashley, coming through the tall glass doors. "It looks just like we envisioned it, right?"

Behind Ashley, Vivian could see the floral window decals going on. The front of the building was encased in floor-to-ceiling windows, and once the sun set—which at this time of the year would be around six—the lights would shine through the colored flowers.

"It really does!"

"Did you bring the lanterns?"

"In the car."

"Great! I'll round up someone to bring a handtruck out and we'll get them unloaded.

Vivian and Ashley worked through the remaining time. The servers had finished setting up the pre-function cocktail bars, and Vivian was glaring at her checklist when she heard a cheerful voice boom from the entryway.

"How we doing?" exclaimed Father Fred. "Because it looks like we're doing awesome!"

"I think we're on target," said Vivian.

"Then you should probably go get ready, Cinderella," said Father Fred. "Can't have you wooing donors in your sweats. Or anyone else, for that matter. Are you bringing a date this year?"

She should have seen it coming. Father Fred asked her that every year.

"Um..."

His head swiveled back like he was robo-priest. "Yes?" he said, raising an eyebrow and a smile beginning to grow.

"Well, I can't sit with him until after, but... he did get a table."

"We like tables," said Chappie. "But do we like *him?* What kind of person is he?"

"Retired Marine Force Recon," Vivian blurted out. She realized suddenly that she'd never had to run any of her boyfriends by her father and maybe that's why she had the flop sweats over telling Chappie and Howard. She'd never practiced introducing anyone who mattered to anyone who had come to matter.

"Well," said Chappie, rocking back on his heels. "That's a driven individual. We like that too. Family? Religion?"

"Two brothers and a nephew, and I don't really know? You

know Marines."

"Yes, the Corps is rather their religion. We can work with that. How does he treat you?"

"With respect and care," snapped Vivian. How did he think her boyfriends treated her?

"Excellent." He looked inordinately pleased.

"Oh, you and Howard!" exclaimed Vivian in exasperation.

"Yes," agreed Chappie, nodding. "Howard and I generally see eye to eye on a great many things."

"I'm going to get changed now. You can go find Howard and gossip all you want."

"Thank you. I believe that I will."

Vivian went upstairs to the tiny office that was their assigned changing area. She carefully unzipped her garment bag and stared at the one-shouldered red satin gown she'd selected in the hopes of knocking Rowan's socks off.

She was only mid-way through make-up and hair when she heard guests start to arrive. Ashley came in to shimmy into her black tux pantsuit. Vivian watched enviously as Ashley went Skims-free into narrow pants and a well-tailored jacket.

"What?" asked Ashley, laughing as she buttoned herself up and carefully settled her headset back over her hair.

"You look so streamlined," said Vivian. "I always feel like Miss Frizzle, and, while I am rocking this corset, I sometimes wish I was a little less hourglass-shaped."

"And I look awesome AF, but still, just once, I'd like to be described as curvy. Do you know how hard it is for a Black girl to hear *why you gotta white girl ass* in high school?"

Vivian grimaced. "Oh, God. Why are boys so mean?"

"That was from my aunts," said Ashley bitterly.

"You're beautiful exactly the way you are!"

Vivian blushed as she realized she had nearly yelled her angry compliment.

"And you will throw hands on that?" asked Ashley, laughing.

"Yes, probably," said Vivian. "We do not bring our girls down. There is only up."

"Well, that *is* why you're my girl," said Ashley. "Fortunately, my Mom has the same attitude, so I managed to make it to adulthood as the well-adjusted weirdo that I am."

"Uh, I think you mean the well-adjusted weirdo we know and love," said Vivian.

There was a rise in voices, and Vivian went to peer out the window down at the lobby.

"The doors to the dining room have opened," said Ashley, assuredly.

"Yeah," said Vivian vaguely as she spotted the Valkyrie crew. It was possible that she was crazy, but she could have sworn Rowan was walking in slow-mo. The suit was black and fit him in all the right places. Damn, her man was fine.

"Ohhhhhhhh," said Ashley, peering over her shoulder. "That is a boy squad I could get with."

"I think they get mad if you call them a boy squad," said Vivian.

"What are they then?"

"A boy squad," said Vivian. "But you can't say it to their faces."

"OK, but which ones can I have?"

"That one is married, and that one is mine," said Vivian, pointing out Mark and Rowan. "After that, have fun. But I like Teddy a lot. And Tyrique is really sweet, although he can't play poker."

"I can't play poker either," said Ashley.

"Well, then, you're a perfect match."

Ashley chuckled. "OK, finish getting pretty, and I'll—"

"Oh, shitballs," said Vivian. "He's talking to Chappie. What do you want to bet Chappie says something monumentally embarrassing? Like how he remembers when I had bangs or got my period or something?"

"Those are the two most embarrassing moments of your life?"

asked Ashley, looking startled.

"Well, Dad told literally everyone, and those bangs shall live in infamy."

"Well, I understand, but still... *Those* are the top two? Those are the ones that make you cringe at three in the morning and wish the universe had turned out differently?"

"No, that's asking out Brian Swanson and the fifth-grade fart. But Chappie doesn't know about those."

"OK, whew. I was kind of feeling like one of us wasn't living our life right. OK, well, I'll go see if I can't separate them. Do you want me to tell Rowan to meet you back by the backstage area so he can get a look at the dress?"

"Yes, please!"

"OK, but no making out because I only have one makeup remover wipe left, and I won't know which one of you to use it on."

Vivian chuckled as Ashley left but hurried to finish her makeup and wiggle into her dress. She turned to look at herself in the mirror.

Tonight was the night. Vivian felt an unmistakable flutter of nerves. She'd been telling everyone that she was trying to keep things lowkey for work, but the truth was that publicly stating that she was with Rowan meant that everyone would know how broken-hearted she was when things went south.

She had never wanted anyone like she wanted Rowan. But she also couldn't help feeling like they were on unequal footing. If everyone saw them together, would they think he was dating down or, even worse, that she was just arm candy? Or even worse than worse, what if *Rowan* thought of her as this month's entertainment?

Vivian ran a hand over her waist and hip, smoothing the fabric, and stood a little straighter. If this dress couldn't make Rowan fall at her feet, then she didn't know what could.

23

Rowan

THE GALA

"Woah," said Mark, looking at the front entryway as Rowan handed the keys to the valet. Jenny had elected not to come—she said she felt like a whale and refused to even attempt to find a dress. Which meant Mark was Rowan's date. Despite Vivian saying that she'd told Howard, Rowan still felt like it was a sign that she wasn't serious about him. As a result, he'd banned everyone from bringing a date and just brought the work team.

"Holy crap," said Tyrique as he and Teddy exited Delacroix's Range Rover with Jake and José.

"Yeah," said Teddy. "I know Viv said the attire was black tie, but somehow I was picturing some sort of mess hall situation. This is…"

They all stared at the glowing interior through the translucent flowers on the window. It was already filled with well-dressed guests. Rowan didn't want to admit it, but he hadn't expected this either.

"Is it bad if I say it looks like *Alice in Wonderland?*" asked Delacroix quietly.

There was silence while they all considered that. Rowan hadn't seen *Alice in Wonderland* in a couple of decades and only vaguely remembered that there had been giant flowers. Still, he was fully aware that Alice fell under the Disney Princess arena, which could be problematic for younger men to admit to knowing anything about.

"That's what it looks like to me," said Rowan confidently, and a chorus of nods followed.

Having decided that knowing what Wonderland looked like was acceptable to their masculine identities, Rowan led them toward the front door, where a photographer was waiting to snap red-carpet pics of the guests arriving. The guys were enthusiastic about this, and he quickly found himself pulled into a Valkyrie group shot. After that, there were a variety of poses. Anyone who thought girls hogged the camera had never been out with a group of young men who felt confident in their fashion choices. When they started flashing the hardware a little too much, Rowan corralled them and forced them through the door.

Rowan paused at the edge of the party, surveying before diving in.

"OK," said Teddy, who was sometimes a vocal processor. "Multiple points of entry. Cover points behind the big cement columns. That's nice. No visible threats. Don't know if anyone's checked the staff."

"We're not working," murmured Rowan, even though Teddy's monologue echoed his own thoughts.

"I know you're right, but I don't know how to turn it off," said Teddy, sounding concerned.

"We don't. But we keep the threat assessments on the inside when it's not our party," said Mark.

"We *are* all carrying, right?" asked Tyrique, nervously touching the outside of his jacket as if reassuring himself that his gun was still there.

Rowan realized that attending this kind of party as guests instead of working as security was causing more anxiety for his team than he had thought it would. He should have prepared them better.

"Yes, of course," said Rowan, trying to reassure and correct simultaneously. "But, again, that is an *inside-the-head* thought."

"I just wanted to make sure," said Tyrique, sounding embarrassed.

"I wore my dress 1911," said Teddy. "With the pearl grips."

"Ooh!" exclaimed Mark. Rowan gave him a look, and Mark raised his hands and grinned.

Mark knew what Rowan was thinking, but as always, he was the half-step between Rowan, who had to be proper, and the team, who were sometimes too green to keep themselves out of trouble.

"Gentlemen, if one of you takes out a gun right now, I will be *very* displeased," said Rowan, trying not to laugh.

"I was just saying that I dressed for the occasion," said Teddy. "It's Viv's big night."

"And I'm sure she will appreciate the effort," said Rowan, thinking she actually would, "but probably no one else will."

"And what are you carrying?" Mark asked, refusing to be cowed.

"A Walther PPK," admitted Rowan.

"James Bond," said Jake. "Classic."

"If I'm going to be fancy, then I should be fancy," said Rowan, and that got a chuckle. "Now, ask Mark what he's carrying."

"Just my standard fancy dress munitions. A Glock 19, a pocket knife, and a vintage derringer that Jenny got me on my ankle."

"That's true love," said Tyrique.

"It is, but I don't think we can say it's normal," said Rowan. "So, for one night, let's all pretend like we're reasonable people and keep our guns to ourselves."

"Well, we'll do our best," said Mark. "But it's very difficult."

Rowan took a quick glance at the crew and saw with relief that they looked more relaxed. Once again, he and Mark had turned their stupid banter into something that helped. Rowan shook his head and moved into the fray. Waiters circled through the crowd with appetizers, but most people seemed to congregate near a long table with a smattering of *hors d'oeuvres* and the two bars. Rowan began to recall snatches of conversation from Vivian's many phone calls. Balancing the budget against staffing considerations, which appetizers to select, all the myriad details that had seemed like silly things to worry about became solid concerns as he realized that a third bar would have cut down on the lines but had been nixed due to budgetary concerns.

The guys split up, double teaming the bars to see who would get to the front of the line first and then switching to the winner. Rowan briefly saw Howard, who waved at him cheerfully over the crowd, and Rowan felt a knot in his neck that he hadn't been aware of begin to ease. Howard adored Vivian, so if he was still smiling at Rowan, then it seemed their relationship really did have his approval.

The doors into the dining room opened, and the crowd began to trickle through them. As if on cue, Rowan's team reassembled. They hung back, as usual, to wait for the group to clear. A priest was circling through the guests, seeming to herd them toward the doors.

"Welcome," said a smiling, round-faced priest coming toward them. "I don't think we've met." He had thinning gray hair, but Rowan couldn't help noticing that there didn't seem to be any paunch around his middle, and he still walked with the firm tread of someone who knew how to go the distance without falling out.

"You must be Chappie," said Rowan, and the priest's head cocked to one side as if assessing.

"Well, these days, most people call me Father Fred," he said with a smile. "Not many people remember when I had more combat boots than collars. You must be Vivian's Marine."

"Ha!" said Mark, then seemed to realize he'd said it out loud. "I mean, yes, sir, he is."

Father Fred grinned.

"Rowan Valkyrie," said Rowan, holding out his hand.

"Good to meet you," said Father Fred, shaking his hand with a firm grip. Rowan found himself being scrutinized in a way that he hadn't experienced in a very long time. He was being held against an invisible yardstick, and he would be up the proverbial shit creek if he didn't measure up.

"Viv's upstairs getting dressed," said Father Fred. "As usual, she worked until the very last minute."

"Um, Chappie?" asked Tyrique, leaning in. "Viv said that if any of the guys wanted to donate, we could give it to you when we got here."

"Yes, of course," said Father Fred, looking surprised.

"Oh, good," said Tyrique, reaching in his pocket. "It's been making me nervous." He handed the envelope to the priest with a sigh of relief.

"You didn't have to do that," said Rowan, worried that the guys had been pressured because of his relationship with Vivian.

"Yeah, we know. But Teddy looked up the Victory Mission when Viv told him about it, and we all had a look," said Jake. At six-foot-five, with a Virginia accent, Jake's baritone voice always sounded like it was coming from on high. "Some of the guys who aren't here tonight wanted to pitch in."

"I'm sure she'll really appreciate that," said Rowan. He felt touched that they'd made the effort but also a little embarrassed that he hadn't bothered to look up the Victory Mission too. He had been focused on the party, not the cause.

"Well, I think everyone's had too many Monsters and a dark night or two," said Tyrique, now more embarrassed than ever. "If there's someone out there who could help, then that's pretty worthwhile."

"Ugh. Monsters," said Father Fred. "That takes me back. Although, I've always been more of a coffee drinker myself."

"Did you know," began José, "that the red can of Folger's can hold nearly a pound of explo—"

Rowan cleared his throat sharply.

"Stuff," finished José. "It's watertight and holds a lot of stuff."

"Actually, we got over a pound in one," said Father Fred. "And we blew up a cow."

There was a squeak from Teddy as he tried to keep himself from laughing. Beside Rowan, Mark's shoulders shook in silent guffaws.

"We felt bad about it," said Father Fred, looking sadly reflective. "It was an accident. The cow wasn't supposed to be there. And we did pay for it. I still think of burgers every time I see that red canister. But you're more Monster drinkers, are you? I'm getting too old for that kind of thing, but I've had more than my share of Ultra Golden Pineapple."

"Peachy Keen," said Tyrique.

"Papillion," said Delacroix.

There was a chorus of Monster Energy Drink flavors, and Rowan vividly recalled each one.

"Nitro Super Dry," Rowan said. "And that is why we don't stock it at work."

"Ultra Violet," said Mark with a wistful sigh.

"And how much caffeine do we drink now?" asked Rowan, looking sternly at the team.

"Four hundred milligrams a day," said Jake dutifully.

"That's right. Four hundred is our limit as per the USDA," said Rowan. "And Teddy, I see you crossing your fingers."

"Well, I mean, the USDA says lots of stuff is bad for you. But what do they really know?"

Father Fred chuckled. "Well, we do know that disrupted sleep affects depression rates, and caffeine can impact sleep. So maybe we want to keep our addiction under control just a little?"

"Four hundred is still four point six Monsters," said José. "I did the math."

"That's not too bad," said Teddy thoughtfully.

Father Fred met Rowan's gaze, and Rowan could see laughter bubbling beneath the surface.

"So you didn't leave the military so much as take it with you?" asked Father Fred.

"Um, yes," said Rowan. "Yes. That would appear to be the case." Father Fred chuckled.

"Hello," said a Black woman in a sharp-looking tuxedo pantsuit. She wore a headset, and Rowan thought he recognized her from the donut shop.

"Hello, Ashley," said Father Fred. "Did you need me for

something?"

"No, we're still in the mingling phase. However, Vivian suggested that Rowan might want to meet her in the backstage prep area."

The team was tactfully quiet, but he could sense a lot of mugging behind him.

"Thanks," said Rowan. "I'd love to."

"Right this way," said Ashley, making a polite gesture.

"Mark, I'll meet you at the table?"

"Whatever," said Mark with a shrug. "We are not working this party. You do you. Or, you know, whatever Viv wants."

Ashley chuckled. "He'll meet you at the table. Viv's got to be at the front to keep things on schedule. Although we'll be lucky if she remembers to eat."

"Take away her phone," said Mark. "That's what I always do with him." He jerked his thumb at Rowan.

"Good call," she said with a smile. "Rowan?"

He followed her and realized that they were in the awkward zone of knowing about each other without actually knowing each other.

"Everything is going all right?" he asked as they walked. "She wasn't panicked when she left and seemed to think everything was under control."

Ashley laughed. "Vivian doesn't panic even when it's *not* under control. But I think we're all good. Pre-event donations are up, and that always bodes well. I think this might be our best year yet."

"Good to hear," said Rowan, not that he had really expected anything else.

Ashley led him to a back hallway area that had been curtained off with black fabric.

"Just wait here," said Ashley with a smile. "She'll be down in a minute."

"Thanks," he said. She disappeared, and Rowan set himself to being patient. Boredom was a skill the military instilled with careful training and brute strength.

But he hadn't been standing for more than thirty seconds when he saw Belinda approaching. She wore a sweeping blue gown that emphasized her long legs and smiled as she approached him.

Rowan tensed, uncertainly. Women—at least a certain segment of women—liked a man in uniform. He'd become adept over the years at spotting the ones who liked the dress blues but weren't particular about which man was underneath. But being the owner of his own company put him in an entirely new environment and he still wasn't sure how to react to the predators in this new jungle. His training said to always be polite, but that hadn't worked out so well last time

"I thought I saw you come this way."

Rowan had no idea how to respond.

24
Vivian

EMERGENCY CALLS

Vivian looked in the mirror one last time. The dress was devastating. The bow on one shoulder prevented it from going totally Jessica Rabbit, but she expected Rowan's eyes to pop like a cartoon just a little bit. Her hair was… as perfect as she could get it. Some things were just never going to happen without the aid of a professional. But overall, she thought she looked damn hot.

She carefully left the office and walked down the short hallway. Negotiating the stairs in her gown took a little bit of effort. There was a lot of skirt. She ended up hitching it up and sort of tip-toeing down so she wouldn't trip and kill herself. She reached the bottom and took a moment to compose herself. She didn't want to look discombobulated when she saw Rowan.

Vivian stepped out into the hall and approached the curtain, hoping that Rowan was waiting for her. She reached for the curtain, preparing to make her entrance, and stopped as she heard a woman's voice.

"Well," purred Belinda, "what do you think?"

Vivian stood behind the curtain and hesitated. She wanted to go out and tell Belinda exactly where to get off. But if she went out there, she would have to stand up and say she was dating Rowan. Was this the time? She generally avoided squaring off against Belinda directly. Vivian didn't have the power that Belinda did and she also found it silly to be so at odds with the other woman. On the other hand, Victory Mission and the gala belonged to her. Belinda could go fuck herself.

"Not a bad little shindig, right? Vivian is such a good assistant. She really did hire the right event planner. These galas have really become one of *the* fundraisers to be at."

Vivian took a deep breath and gathered her skirt, intending to go out and smile politely at Belinda until she went away.

"I have to admit I don't really go to many fundraisers," said Rowan. "But yeah, it seems great."

Vivian stopped. *It seemed great?* That was worse than an insult. It was the *it's fine* of compliments.

"Well, the firm likes to align itself with quality talent," said Belinda, and Vivian wrinkled her nose.

What was Belinda playing at? Those had almost sounded like compliments.

"Someday, Vivian might grow up into quite a little manager. I don't think she's picked her direction in life yet, though."

"I'm not sure I can offer an opinion on that," said Rowan. Vivian glared at where she thought Rowan was through the curtain. What did that even mean?

"Really?" asked Belinda with a laugh. "You seemed pretty close with her last week when I saw you in the hall. I mean, I completely understand. She's adorable. But maybe you're right—it's better not to get involved in the inner workings of the twenty-something mind. Who knows what you'll find?"

Rowan let out a surprised bark of laughter and Vivian ground her teeth.

"Anyway," said Belinda. Her voice had the same perfect pitch as when she delivered her closing argument. "When you're ready to have someone who can carry a conversation, maybe you should give me a call."

"Belinda, I don't think—" said Rowan, his tone was politely firm, but it didn't negate the laugh from a moment earlier.

"I get it. You're the kind of person who likes to keep things discreet and tidy. So do I. See you around, Rowan."

Vivian peeped through the curtains in time to see Belinda caress his arm as she left, hips swaying gently. Rowan watched her as she walked away.

Vivian opened the curtains and stepped out. She felt flushed. Rowan shook his head as if in disbelief at Belinda and turned around. Vivian waited. If he said she looked great, she would punch him in the face. Instead, he didn't say anything.

"Viv," he began, a slow smile curling the corner of his mouth. "I don't know what to say."

"Let me guess, you can't really offer an opinion," said Vivian.

"What?"

"I told *everyone* we were dating," she said angrily, trying to fight through the block of tears that seemed to be clogging her throat. "You said that's what you wanted."

"You didn't tell Belinda," he growled. It was a tone she'd never heard from him before—aggressive and sharp.

"I told everyone who matters," she snapped. "But I guess you wouldn't want to investigate the inner workings of my mind to find that out."

"What?" He looked equal parts confused and angry.

"Well, us twenty-somethings aren't very bright."

His phone began to ring, and he looked at it impatiently and swiped it off.

"Oh, that doesn't apply to you and you know it!"

"Who else does it apply it to?" she demanded.

"All the idiots on my payroll. They have about six highly trained brain cells between them. You are not in the same category."

"Gee, thanks so much for the sterling endorsement," retorted Vivian.

"Viv, I don't know what you want from me."

She wanted him to take her seriously. She wanted him to love her. She wanted him to say it out loud.

His phone beeped a text, and he glanced at it.

"9-1-1," he muttered.

Then the phone rang again, and he picked it up this time.

"Forest," he said. "Is Olly OK?"

Vivian couldn't hear what Forest said in response but she could hear the tone—it was sheer panic.

"Wait? What? Forest, talk slower."

Rowan was silent as he listened to Forest.

"Rowan," said Vivian hesitantly. She didn't have much time before the gala started.

"OK, the process server came to the door. But with what? What did he give you?"

Vivian hesitated. Legally speaking it was an absolute fact that process servers did not bring good news.

"Vera's parents served you with custody papers—" said Rowan.

Vivian was still furious at Rowan, but she felt her heart racing for poor Forest. He'd said his partner had passed. If Olly's grandparents were suing for custody, Forest was probably freaking out. He needed a lawyer immediately.

"No, that is a terrible idea," said Rowan, firmly.

"Rowan!" Vivian grabbed at his arm, but he shook her off.

"Forest, don't hang up. Just give me a second. No one is taking Olly anywhere."

"Yes, I am listening but wait. Forest, just wait. Do not put Olly in the car and drive to Canada. That is not what you need to do."

"He needs to call—" Vivian began, but Rowan turned away from her.

"No, don't hang up."

Rowan made a frustrated, angry noise and stared at his phone. Then, he began texting furiously.

"Rowan, Forest needs to—"

"Vivian, please," Rowan snapped, holding up his hand like she was one of his underlings.

"I'm trying to tell you—" She grabbed his arm. "He needs an attorney and I can help."

Rowan paused and glanced at her. "You're right. Find him one and text me the information."

"I need—"

"I don't have time for this."

Vivian picked her words carefully. "No, you don't. You need—"

"Vivian, you are brilliant, but you don't have the experience for this kind of thing. Forest doesn't need advice from the girl I'm— Mexico? What the fuck."

He cut off, and Vivian stared at him. He wasn't even looking at her—instead, he continued to type on his phone.

"Right," said Vivian, feeling the sharp burn of humiliation. "Right. I'm just the twenty-something *assistant* you're fucking."

"That is not what I said," he said, biting off the words—still without looking up.

"Maybe this *is* a lost cause," she said, shaking her head. His head snapped up and he swung around to face her.

"I'm sorry is my family interfering with your party?" he snarled. "You know nothing about the kind of responsibilities that come with—"

"With being an adult? Yeah, thanks, Mr. Valkyrie, but save the speeches."

"Hey, Viv!" Ashley yelled before pulling open the curtain, but then she froze. Her hand went to her headset, as her eyes swiveled back and forth between the two of them. "They're about ready for you at the front table."

"No problem," said Vivian. She looked back at Rowan. "What I was going to say, if you'd let me finish, is that Forest should call Grant Ichikawa, the lawyer that handled Olly's citizenship. Not that I would know anything about the law since I'm just a paralegal."

"Viv?" Ashley looked like she wanted to be anywhere else.

Vivian gave it a beat, but Rowan didn't speak.

"Yeah, Ashley. Looks like I'm done here. If you'll excuse me, I have a speech of my own to give." She turned away, swallowing tears, and marched into the ballroom.

25

Rowan

THE BURDEN

Rowan stared at his phone. His brothers were his responsibility. They always had been. He needed to go get Forest right now. But Vivian…

No. Family first. He would deal with his own emergency second.

He walked back out to the foyer, but hesitated at the entrance to the ballroom. He was supposed to help Forest, but Vivian was in there.

Mark popped out and glared at him.

"Rowan," hissed Mark, grabbing him by the arm, "what did you do?"

Rowan looked blankly at Mark. Mark shook his head and pulled Rowan through the doors into the ballroom, then pushed him toward a table.

It was like he couldn't form proper thoughts. It had been like this the first time he'd been in combat. None of his thoughts led to anything. They just smashed, incomplete, into the image of Vivian's anguished face as she left.

"Vivian just walked right by us without saying a word. Did you do something stupid?"

"Yes," said Rowan. Incredibly, epically, earth-shatteringly stupid.

Mark looked like he had thoughts on the subject, but waiters were placing dinner plates on the table, and the number of listening ears seemed to have quadrupled.

Dinner might have looked appetizing under other circumstances, but Rowan pushed it away. He needed to talk to Vivian. He could see her at the front table, sitting with rigid precision and not eating either. He tensed, debating throwing caution to the wind and going up there, when his phone vibrated in his hand, and Rowan saw a jumbled message from Forest. Forest's panic was clear from the number of typos. His heart wrenched. Rowan wanted to fix things for his baby brother, but he needed Forest to calm down and think. The phone would be faster than driving over there. He composed a quick reply.

Do NOT go to Canada. Text Grant Ichikawa. He is your lawyer. He's familiar with Olly's citizenship, and you're already a client.

Why had he said that to her? The expression on her face... Vivian wasn't a fling. He'd been lying to himself to even pretend otherwise. She was fucking everything, and he'd all but told her she was irrelevant. If someone else had made her look that hurt, he would have punched them.

He could see Forest replying, but then the bouncing dots stopped.

Rowan took a deep breath, trying to get his body under control. He was having an adrenaline reaction, but that didn't make it better. He was too hot, his skin was clammy, and he felt like puking. He needed to do something. He needed to help Forest, but right now, all he wanted to do was find Vivian.

I think I'm having a heart attack. My fingers are tingling.

Rowan felt like replying that he felt the same, but didn't.

You're probably having a panic attack. Sit down. Breathe.

Rowan tried to take his own advice. He could feel the rest of the team giving him side-eye. He needed to keep it together, but he felt like he'd downed three Monsters in a row. What seemed like hours later, the lights dimmed, and Father Fred took the stage.

"Good evening!" Father Fred exclaimed, beaming at the crowd.

"You have no idea what a delight it is to see so many new faces. The Victory Mission is celebrating ten years of service, and I always love seeing the faces that have become like family to me. It also elates me to see new friends in this hall."

I TEXTED GRANT. HE SAYS THEY CAN'T SHOW UP AND TAKE HIM SINCE I HAVE LEGAL CUSTODY AND I ALREADY HAVE THE CITIZENSHIP TAKEN CARE OF. HE SAYS OLLY ISN'T GOING ANYWHERE WITHOUT A COURT ORDER, AND HE WILL LOOK AT THE PAPERS ON MONDAY.

Rowan breathed a sigh of relief. There was a wave of laughter from the audience, and Rowan realized he'd missed a portion of the speech.

CHLOE ALSO SAYS I'M HAVING A PANIC ATTACK AND THAT I HAVE TO GO MEDITATE NOW TO STIMULATE MY VAGUS NERVE.

Rowan felt an unexpected wave of gratitude toward the purple-haired nanny. Thank God Forest had someone in his corner who could talk some sense into him.

LISTEN TO CHLOE.

Like Rowan should have listened to Vivian.

He looked back at the priest and tried to assess if he could get Vivian away from the table without being noticed, but with a sinking heart he realized she wasn't at the front table anymore. The large screen at the back of the stage faded into an old photo showing four vets, each representing a branch of the military.

"For those who don't know me, I'm Father Fred Murkowski, one of the founding members of the Victory Mission and current Executive Director. I started out as an Army Chaplain with nothing but a divinity degree and a willing spirit to go with the job. After I got out, I entered the priesthood. However, I discovered along the way that a little piece of my heart still wears Army green, so with the Archbishop's blessing, I continued to look for ways to serve my fellow veterans. And as I was looking for that place where I could be of the most service, I ran into a Marine I'd met while I was enlisted—Vincent Kaye. He told me to come along to meet up with some other friends who liked to help out at some group meetings. That's where it started.

Twelve years ago, there were four of us—me, Chris, Ann, and Vince. We were sitting around Vince's kitchen table, his daughter Vivian was... I'm not entirely sure." Father Fred looked toward the side of the stage. "I think you were making Wonder Woman and G.I. Joe defeat the Barbie hordes?"

Rowan froze as the crowd chuckled. From the side of the stage, Vivian nodded.

"But while she was conquering the universe, we were mourning the loss of another friend to suicide. We were hosting a weekly meeting space. We were tagging in with AA meetings. We were doing all the work, but it didn't feel like enough. We weren't making the impact we knew we needed to. And then Vince said the magic words. *This is a mission. We cannot stop, but I don't know how to go forward.* And I think it was Ann—although she swears it was me—but someone said it, *we need to ask for help.* It took us another two years of talking to non-profits, of talking to other vets, of a lot of shut doors in our faces, but when we finally founded the Victory Mission it was one of the proudest days of my life. There are only three of us now. We lost Vince to cancer eight years ago. However, we have been fortunate that his daughter Vivian picked up where Vince left off. I know that most of you know her. She has been with Victory Mission since the beginning and remembers more about the organization than I do. She has volunteered, organized, helped us grow, and sometimes poked us into action when we needed it. Please welcome Vivian Kaye to the stage. She is going to share a little about our mission and Vince's vision."

"Oh, Jesus," swore Rowan under his breath, as there was a wave of applause from the audience. Rowan realized with searing clarity how off his statement to Vivian had been. She knew nothing about adult responsibilities? What the hell had he been thinking?

Mark looked at him sharply.

"What?" Mark hissed.

"I am an asshole," Rowan hissed back.

She'd never volunteered information on her father, and he hadn't wanted to pry. He'd been trying to keep his distance because he didn't need to invest in a fling. He'd periodically wondered about her mastery of military jargon and talented use of profanity, but he'd never stopped to question it. He hadn't investigated why she fit so well into his life because he'd been afraid he'd find all the ways she didn't fit.

"Yeah?" agreed Mark.

Rowan shook his head in frustration. Vivian stood at the podium, looking regal and composed. The dress, which had left him speechless before everything had gone sideways, matched the dramatic red paper poppies on the dais.

"My father, Captain Vincent Kaye of the United States Marine Corps," she paused to let the deafening *hoo-rah* from the audience die down, "lost men in combat, and that wounded him, but it killed him to lose friends Stateside after his retirement. This," she pointed to the screen which changed to a group of statistic, "is the population of the United States. The percentage of deaths by suicide is 1.7%. That doesn't sound like a lot, does it? But that number means that each year, approximately fifty-thousand people die by suicide. It is the eleventh-highest cause of death in our country. But here is what those numbers don't show." The slide changed to a bar graph. "Veterans are about eight percent of the overall population, but they account for nearly fourteen percent of the suicides. Veterans are one and a half times more likely to commit suicide. If you're a female veteran, you are two and a half times more likely to commit suicide than a civilian."

The room was deathly quiet.

"When I was little, I didn't know why Dad spent so much time with his phone beside him. He was a volunteer on a suicide hotline. I didn't know why we spent Saturday mornings with Chappie, Aunt

Ann, and Uncle Chris. We went to support at meetings. One time, I got mad because I wanted to go to a birthday party, and he said, *nope, we have to show up.* And I said, *Dad, those people don't care.* And he said, *but I do. You don't have to be the biggest or the strongest to help someone lift a burden, but you have to show up."*

The slide behind Vivian changed again, and Rowan shifted uncomfortably in his seat. He should have asked. He should have wanted to know everything about Vivian. He should have wanted to know why she cared about veterans.

"This is the number of veterans served by the Victory Mission in the last ten years. And this," she pointed at the screen as a new number appeared, "this is *our* suicide rate. That's point five percent. We are so far below the civilian population suicide rate that people now call us to ask how they can copy us. This is the number that Dad would be the most proud of.

Eight years ago, when I lost him to cancer, I went through the usual things—funeral, grieving, all the rituals. But those of you who have lost someone, you know that eventually, everyone goes home, and you are all by yourself. I thought I was doing OK. Not great. What nineteen-year-old does great on their own? But I was making it. And then his birthday rolled around and..." Her voice cracked, and she looked off for a moment, blinking. "It was not a good day for me. Then I got the mail, and inside was a postcard. It wasn't much. Just a note to say Dad and I were remembered. Then Chappie called. Then Aunt Ann. And Uncle Chris stopped by with a burger to make sure I got dinner. They weren't big gestures. They were just people showing up to help lift the burden a tiny bit. Dad once said that his military family never let him down. Well, that kindness has been extended to me as well, and I have done my best to carry his legacy forward. Dad would be *so* proud of this number." She pointed at the screen again.

Rowan wanted to put his face into his hands. He wanted to wrap his arms around her. What the fuck was wrong with him? Why had he said that shit? She'd tried to tell him what she was doing with the Victory Mission and the gala, and all he'd heard was that she was throwing a party. It was a cute thing for a twenty-something to do. When did Vivian ever do anything cute or half-assed?

"Although I'm pretty sure Dad would also demand to know why it isn't zero. Because if it's not zero, then we haven't achieved total victory. And I'm told that in the entire history of the universe the Marines have never lost."

There was another echoing *hoo-rah* and then a wave of laughter. Tyrique and Teddy pounded on the table with enthusiasm.

"Marines regroup and redefine the mission. One life lost to suicide is too many. Zero is the only acceptable outcome. And I know the Victory Mission could do more, if we had more. So, if you would like to join me in helping to carry the burden, please consider putting something in the envelopes on your table. If that's not an option, please consider donating your time to volunteer with us. Even if you don't feel confident that you can help, I assure you that showing up *is* enough. Thank you."

The applause was thunderous, and Rowan wanted to sink into the floor.

"Are you OK?" asked Mark.

"No," said Rowan, standing up and throwing down his napkin.

"Where are you going?"

"Marines don't lose, but I need to regroup. Do *not* let Vivian leave until I get back."

26

Vivian

DIFFERENT CHANNELS

Vivian waited through the applause and smiled and smiled and smiled some more. She had no idea what she said in response to questions that came her way. She wasn't even sure what the questions were. The only thing she could really focus on was the tall figure that had hurried from the room directly after her speech.

Rowan had left.

Some part of her had been holding out hope that he'd try to apologize. But he'd left.

She wanted to break down and cry. She wanted to scream and throw things at Rowan's stupid head. But he wasn't even there to yell at.

Ashley arrived and gave Vivian the once-over.

"Viv, the photographer wants a picture of you with the board."

Vivian looked at Ashley.

"I know. I'm sorry. I can put them off for a few minutes. Tell me how I can help."

"Gather up the board," said Vivian. "No point in letting one person ruin everything."

"I've got a bottle of wine saved," said Ashley. "Afterwards, we'll talk."

"Afterwards," agreed Vivian.

It took a few minutes, but the board members were extracted from the tables. Dessert service was imminent, so Vivian knew they had a limited window of time. The voices of the guests scraped across her nerves, and she tried not to feel impatient with the Board Members as they lollygagged their way toward the side of the room where the photographer waited.

"Has anyone seen Howard?" asked Ashley, looking at the assembled board.

"I think he took a phone call outside," said Kandie. Vivian was pretty sure Kandie had complimented the speech at least once. Vivian wasn't sure she could take that much goodwill and positive energy right now.

"I'll go get him," said Vivian. Anything would feel less claustrophobic than this enormous ballroom.

"Are you sure?" asked Ashley, looking worried.

"It's fine," said Vivian. "I could use the air."

Vivian walked toward the front entrance. Through the doors, Vivian could see Howard talking on the phone under the projecting front awning. Howard peered along the fire lane that looped in from the street and then continued out to the parking lot as if looking for someone. Out on the road, she could see the Whole Foods sign down the block amid the warm glow of the street lights. Could she just keep walking? The Whole Foods was a bastion of Fair Trade and kombucha. They would have chocolate dark enough to drown her sorrows.

She pushed through the doors and welcomed the damp air with the hint of sprinkles in it.

"Viv, Viv, Viv."

Vivian paused and looked back.

Mark wasn't quite jogging to catch up with her, but it was close. "Don't leave yet," he said.

Vivian rounded on him angrily. "I'm not leaving! I have a job to do. This is my place. I'm not the one who ought..." Tears sprang unbidden to her eyes, and she blinked them back furiously. She would not ruin her makeup and event pictures over *him*. "And anyway, why not? Huh? Why not? *He* already left!"

"He's coming back," said Mark.

"Ha! Yeah, right. Where did he go?"

"Uh..." Mark looked like she'd asked him the formula for nuclear fission. "I don't actually know, but he said he was coming back."

Vivian shook her head. "You know, I have enough people who think I'm a useless idiot in my everyday life. I don't need to date someone who feels the same."

Mark sucked in air like she'd punched him in the gut, and he leaned further away from her.

"Uh... He didn't actually say that, did he?"

"There only so many ways to take being called an inexperienced twenty-something assistant that he's fucking," snapped Vivian.

She turned and headed back toward Howard, ignoring the haze of damp sprinkles in the air, even though it gave her goosebumps.

Howard was still on the phone, standing near the edge of the curb. His head swiveled to look the length of driveway, then he turned back toward the entrance. He wasn't a demonstrative person. His gestures were usually contained and economical, but at the moment Howard's free hand waved in an impatient pinwheel of anger.

"See," said Mark, pointing past Howard, "Rowan is coming back."

On the far side of the street, Rowan walked briskly toward the Center, but as she watched Rowan pointed toward the driveway and yelled something at Mark.

A large black vehicle pulled into the drive from the street. Vivian noted that it was an SUV and driving oddly slow. Maybe they were lost? Or maybe they were the person Howard had been looking for? The window was rolling down even though the rain was picking up. Rowan was halfway across the street and sprinting fast, running straight for Howard.

"Cover Vivian!"

That was a weird thing to say. Why was Rowan yelling that?

She felt Mark grab her, heaving her into the air, and then the world went sideways. She saw something flash from the car window. Multiple flashes. And Rowan tackled Howard.

Everything was gray. Vivian finally realized the gray lumps were rocks. Something was pressing on her and it wasn't until he moved that she realized it was Mark. She put one hand out and touched a heavy concrete planter. She remembered then that there were planters evenly spaced in front of the Arts Center and full of native species plantings. They had seemed overly thick and substantial when she'd first seen them. She and Ashley had shoved giant paper flowers in them to try to make them more festive.

As she watched, a little scrap of tissue paper drifted down in front of her. It was a vibrant red. It must have come from the poppy flowers they'd made. Why was it in shreds?

Mark was really heavy. Something had gone bang. Something had been so loud that now everything seemed quiet. But it wasn't really quiet. Mark was yelling. Shouldn't she be able to understand what he was saying?

Was everything going really slow or really fast?

Tires had squealed. There had been several of the bangs. Then, more bangs. Then tires had squealed, and now there was yelling. Something had come out of the window. An arm, and it had been holding…

It was as if her brain had taken everything in on separate channels and now wanted to reshuffle it into the proper order.

The air smelled like rain and fireworks. Her hair was wet from the drizzling rain. It would start frizzing and curling soon, and all her hard work and product would be wasted.

She felt Mark move away from her and looked up in time to see Teddy go running by with his gun out.

The thing coming out of the window had been a gun. It had been pointed at Howard. And Rowan had been running to get him.

"Rowan," she gasped, trying to sit up.

"Stay down, Viv," ordered Mark, pushing on her back. He had a gun out, too. He snuck a look over the planter.

"Howard," she said, trying to get up again.

"No, Viv," said Mark, pushing her down again.

"Medic!" She heard Teddy's voice clearly. "We need a medic!"

Her breath started to come in gasps. Medics were only needed if someone was wounded.

"Let me up. Rowan and Howard—"

"Tyrique!" Mark yelled. And suddenly, there was Tyrique in front of her.

"I've got EMT incoming. Three volunteer medics want permission to advance and José and Jake are on cover. Delacroix is on crowd control." Tyrique's usual smile had been replaced by a severe expression she didn't recognize.

"Medics can advance. Get Vivian inside. Protect and cover. I'm going for Rowan."

"Yes, sir. Vivian." Tyrique grabbed her and pulled her to her feet. She could see that her gown was torn at the hem.

"No, I want to go to Rowan and Howard," said Vivian.

"Carry her if you have to," said Mark.

"Vivian, Rowan needs you to come with me," said Tyrique, putting his hand around the back of her elbow and steering her toward the building.

"Teddy said medic," protested Vivian, trying to pull away.

"But you're not a medic," said Tyrique. Somehow, they were nearly to the entryway. Two more Valkyrie employees were stationed inside the door with their guns drawn. Tyrique walked Vivian inside but didn't stop. He walked her through the foyer and back into the ballroom, where the dance floor and tables had been cleared. Everyone had been pushed to the back of the space, and Vivian realized that someone had gotten the crowd to put maximum distance between themselves and the street.

"They shot at Howard," said Vivian. "At Howard."

"OK," said Tyrique.

"Rowan was running," she whispered. "But I don't know what happened. Mark picked me up. I didn't see what happened to them."

"Yes," said Tyrique.

"Teddy didn't say who the medic was for." Tears were starting to form. She could tell by the stark prickle and sudden thickness in her nose that they wouldn't be attractive tears—they would be blobby and gross. She was about to completely lose it right here in front of everybody.

"When I get an update, I will let you know," said Tyrique, and she realized that he didn't know if Rowan had been shot or not either. Tyrique was doing his job and holding it together, but he was scared, too.

If Tyrique could function in the dark, she could. She had to. Vivian swallowed hard and pulled herself up as tall as she could. If he could do it, so could she.

"What are we supposed to do now?" she asked.

"Assess the threat. Call for medical personnel and reinforcements."

"They did that," said Vivian nodding.

"Then right now, we're at *wait and keep bystanders calm,*" said Tyrique. "When the team has cleared the threat, they will let us know."

She looked toward the doors again. She knew that she had no skills to help them, but every inch of her wanted to go back out front. She looked back at Tyrique. She had to stay on mission.

"The team," repeated Vivian, nodding to show that she understood. Rowan's people would do things. Probably reassuring and important security things. She just wasn't one of them.

She looked around the crowded ballroom and saw nothing but a sea of scared faces. Guests and staff were huddled together, looking lost.

"The security team is handling security. Shit. Who's handling the staff and guests?"

Tyrique stared blankly at her. "We don't…"

"Ashley!" Vivian swiveled and bellowed, scanning the crowd for her friend.

"Over here," said Ashley.

Vivian finally spotted Ashley fanning a woman who was slumped on the floor.

"Drunk or medical?" demanded Vivian.

"Trying to run in Spanx," said Ashley.

"Kandie, Debra," Vivian snapped her fingers and pointed to two of the board members. "Take her to the restroom in the kitchen. Get her the air she needs. Ashley, has anyone communicated with the staff?"

Ashley shook her head and pulled her headset back on.

"Pretty sure the band is hiding in the kitchen," said Father Fred, joining them.

"Great," said Vivian. "They can stay there until we're cleared to leave. Ashley, how many headsets do you have? Can you give them to the Valkyrie team?"

Ashley put her hand up to her headset protectively. "Um… Do I have to?"

"Please?" asked Tyrique, and Ashley sighed and pressed the button on her radio.

"Annie, can you come to the ballroom? Bring all the headsets."

27
Rowan

AFTERMATH

Tyrique appeared with a headset and handed it to Mark. Rowan had no idea where he'd gotten it and didn't ask. Now was not the time. Rule number one was not to interfere with the operators. There would be plenty of time for questions later.

Mark shoved him down to sit on the edge of one of the planters, which meant he had to watch the medics work on Howard. The medics—who were, in fact, a cardiothoracic surgeon, a Ranger Combat medic, and a veteran medic who was now a trauma nurse—also didn't need an audience or interference, but since no one had handed him a headset, he knew that he'd been officially benched. The trauma nurse stepped away and pulled off her gloves, dropping them on the pavement before pulling on a second set from a bag of medical supplies that had come from sources unknown. Rowan suspected the Ranger medic's car, but couldn't confirm that. The white rubber gloves looked incongruous against the nurse's sequined gown.

"Vivian?" Rowan demanded looking away from the medics, when Mark paused in his conversation with Tyrique.

"Inside and taking command," said Tyrique.

"I'm online," said Mark into his headset. "Give me the sit-rep."

The nurse began to paw at his arm.

"Ma'am, I am fine!" said Rowan sharply.

"I'll tell you when you're fine," said the nurse. "Now shut up, and let me look at it." With a quick snap, she pulled a pocket knife out of her stylish beaded purse and cut a larger hole in his suit jacket to look at his arm.

"This is not necessary," Rowan objected, although he realized it had now reached the pointless stage. There wasn't anything that he absolutely had to be doing, and if she was paying attention to him, then she thought Howard didn't need her.

"Okayyyy," she muttered, tearing the hole wider and pulling at the ragged chunk of flesh on his arm. He was lucky it wasn't worse. It hurt like fuck, and he was pretty sure he'd be covered in bruises tomorrow, but he didn't have any holes in him, and that meant he was a hell of a lot better than Howard.

"Roger that," said Mark, hand to the headset.

Rowan could now hear the wail of sirens. He hoped like hell it was the ambulance.

"Ambulance is inbound," said Mark. "Tyrique, go wave them in."

"Yes, Sir," said Tyrique, jogging toward the street.

"Vivian," repeated Rowan. He didn't know where she was, and he didn't like that. The nurse slapped some shit on his arm. It hurt.

"Roger," said Mark. "Viv wants to know if she can direct the police to the side parking lot or if it's better to come here?"

"Side parking lot. Keep them out of the way of the ambulance," said the Ranger medic without looking up.

"We're going to Harborview," said the surgeon. "Can someone get them on the horn to clear a table?"

"Roger that," said Mark, turning away and beginning to speak rapidly into the headset.

The undulating wail of the ambulance made him want to cover his ears. The nurse stuck a bandage to his arm and then turned back to Howard, stripping off the gloves she had been wearing for Rowan, and grabbing a third set. Rowan wondered how many gloves medics went through on an average shift.

The ambulance screeched to a halt, doors flying open.

The nurse ordered them around. Periodically, the surgeon put in a word that the nurse translated into whatever the fuck EMTs spoke. It seemed like mere moments later that Howard was on the gurney and being loaded into the back.

"We have confirmation from Harborview," said Mark. "They are expecting you."

"Great," said the surgeon, climbing into the back of the ambulance.

"He needs stitches," said the trauma nurse to Tyrique, jerking her thumb at Rowan.

"Yes, Ma'am," said Tyrique. "I'll call Hot Lips."

"Hilarious," said the nurse sourly. "But, seriously, he needs to see someone."

"Hot Lips is our medic," said Tyrique, looking startled. "It's just what we call him."

"Him. Oh. OK. Great," said the nurse, shaking her head as she climbed into the ambulance. For the first time, Rowan realized that Tyrique probably hadn't ever seen M.A.S.H.

The ambulance doors slammed shut, and Rowan took a breath.

"Cops are inbound and getting bitchy about being routed," said Mark.

"Fuck them," said Rowan with a shrug. "The threat is cleared. Ambulance is out. They can come ahead if they want. But fuck their feelings. They can get over it."

Mark nodded and walked away, hand on the headset.

"Where the fuck did we get headsets?" Rowan asked of no one in particular.

"Vivian," said Tyrique, who was texting. He tucked his phone away and looked up. "Your bae is legit. Pretty sure she could run an army if she wanted."

"Only if you give her enough chocolate," said Rowan, feeling in his pocket. The chocolate bars he'd purchased were probably mush now. He'd meant them to be symbolic. He wasn't sure there was enough chocolate in the world to buy his way out of his shit hole, but at the moment, that was the least of his problems.

"OK," said Mark, coming back. "The cops want us to remain here until they can secure the scene."

"It was a drive-by," said Rowan. "They aren't coming back. They were here for Howard and Vivian."

"What?" demanded Tyrique, looking shocked.

"They were parked. I clocked them when I left. Three guys in an SUV. I didn't like the look, so I got the license plate. It's been uploaded to the company drive. But on the way back, I saw Vivian come out to the front, and that's when they started to move."

"They shot at Vivian, too," said Mark. "There's two in that planter that had her name on it."

"I don't think she knows that," said Teddy, walking up briskly. He wore another one of Vivian's headsets and pushed it down around his neck as he approached. "Police are here. Vivian has them bagged, tagged, and doing what they're told already. She's got half of them taking statements from guests so they can leave ASAP and the other half talking to building staff to get whatever security footage they can. Cops say detectives and CSI are *en route*, but our team is to sit tight until detectives say we can go."

"Hot Lips says he'll be here in a few," said Tyrique. "Wants to know how much gear to bring."

"It's just a few stitches," said Rowan, impatiently.

"Got it," said Tyrique, going back to his phone.

"Tell him to come in the back so the cops don't get weird," said Teddy, and Tyrique grunted his recognition of the instructions.

"Meanwhile," said Mark, "can we get back to who the fuck was shooting at Howard and Vivian? Did you get a look at the shooters? All I got was a vague white dude in the driver's seat."

"I didn't get much more," said Rowan.

"You put a clip in the back of the vehicle. Do you think you hit any of them?" asked Mark.

"They didn't stop, so going with no," said Rowan.

He'd popped up after the initial barrage, dumped a clip into the back of the SUV, and gotten squat for his efforts. This was what he got for not carrying his usual sidearm. The Walther PPK was practically decorative.

"That just means you didn't hit the driver," said Teddy, taking out his phone. "I could reach out to some people. See if anyone knows anything about anyone looking for GSW care?"

"You mean illegally, right?" asked Mark.

"No, sir, I was going to call my grandma."

"I just got shot at, shithead. Don't start with me," snapped Mark.

"Yeah, Teddy," said Rowan. "Reach out. Splash some cash around if you think it will help. I'm not sure how on it the police are going to be. Tyrique, call a couple of the guys and get them over to the hospital. We don't know the extent of the threat, and I want someone covering Howard once he makes it out of surgery. If he makes it out of surgery."

"Yes, sir," said Tyrique.

Both Tyrique and Teddy walked away, already on their phones.

"We're going to need someone on Vivian, too," said Mark.

"Yeah," agreed Rowan.

"That could be problematic. Apparently, her boyfriend said some very hurtful things, and she is very angry with him."

"Well, I was working on that, but then all this…" Rowan tried to wave his arm angrily and instantly regretted it as pain sparkles shot up his arm. He took a couple of deep breaths.

"And that," Mark waved at the blood stains on the sidewalk for him, "may readjust the situation but, boy, you need to pull your head out of your ass. I don't know what the fuck would make you say that shit in the first place."

He'd freaked out and tried to protect himself by saying something stupid?

"I listened to Belinda," said Rowan.

"Evil bitch lawyer lady?" asked Mark, looking confused. "Why?"

Rowan groaned. "I don't know! Because I'm an idiot! Can we talk about this… never? I will talk to Vivian. But, no, we're not letting her walk out of here without protection."

"OK," said Mark. "Just making sure we're all on the same page. You're going to grovel, and we'll take you both back to your place once Hot Lips stitches you up."

"I'm not going to grovel," said Rowan.

Mark gave him a look. "Yes, you will. You will get in there and get us back on the field. Olly needs cousins, and little Alyssa wants a playmate."

"Going with Alyssa?"

"We're trying it out," said Mark, putting his hand up to the headset. "Roger that. Police want us to come in. They want to take over the scene, and having a bunch of armed assholes standing around out front is making them nervous."

"Let's go then," said Rowan. He took a deep breath. He wasn't sure why getting shot at was easier than apologizing. But Mark was right. If groveling was what it took, then for Vivian, he'd be on his knees.

28
Vivian

THE POLICE

Vivian was halfway back from checking on the staff in the kitchen when she heard Chappie yelling. Since Chappie never yelled, Vivian picked up her skirt and ran. Jake, from Valkyrie, who seemed to be her assigned minder, went through the door ahead of her. He was an enormous individual, but he moved surprisingly fast.

"Detective Bodge, I am a man of the cloth, but I'm also a damn Captain of the Army, and I will personally pray over the broken nose I'm about to give you!"

Vivian didn't think she'd ever seen Father Fred that red in the face.

"Shit, shit, shit. Jake, stop Chappie!"

Jake put on speed, but Rowan beat him to the priest. With one arm, he hefted Chappie up and walked him back about eight feet, and then a wall of bodies put themselves between Father Fred and the police detective, who looked surprised to find himself blockaded.

"I'm not done talking to him!" barked the detective.

Vivian dropped her skirt and tried to catch her breath before going around the wall of service members. "I think, for the moment, we all might need to take a breather," she said, smiling forcefully. "We don't want Father Fred calling the archdiocese now, do we? I know the Archbishop would hate to disturb the police chief at this late hour."

The detective paused. He was a lean individual who looked too sour for his luxuriously bushy mustache. He'd flashed his badge around when he'd arrived, ogled her boobs, and then ignored her. She'd put Chappie on him because no one ever ignored a priest. Apparently, Chappie hadn't liked the detective's attitude either.

"OK, fine, you know what? I'll talk to you. You were out front when the old guy got shot."

"The old guy," repeated Vivian. "You mean Howard Hoskins, the lawyer? Owner of the Hoskins building. Lead partner at Hoskins, Branch, and Kato. Board Member of the Victory Mission. Veteran of the Navy and victim of the crime. Is that the *old guy* you're referring to?" Vivian could hear the anger lacing her voice. She was aware of all the guests watching the scene and managed not to swear but that was the best she could do.

"Yeah. You know, maybe if you Richie-rich libtards hadn't voted for socialists, there might have been more cops on the street to prevent this kind of crime."

"And maybe if you fascist boys in blue hadn't tried to overthrow the United States government, we might actually want that."

They had both sunk to the bottom of Seattle's political slings and arrows. The city council's policies had led to a downtown city center that was drug-ridden and lawless. But the six Seattle police officers who had attended the January Sixth coup attempt had only deepened the perception that the police couldn't be trusted. Vivian knew she'd gone too far, but she now saw why Father Fred had threatened to punch him. The detective went red in the face and raised his hand, one finger pointing toward Vivian and aiming straight at her chest.

"Touch her, and I will break your arm," said a deep voice, and Vivian didn't have to look around to know that Rowan was behind her. The cop's finger stopped moving as he eyed Rowan.

"Are you threatening a police officer?"

"Are you threatening the victim of a crime?" retorted Rowan.

"Your demeanor is unprofessional," said Vivian, redirecting the police officer's attention back to her, "and your conduct is insulting to myself, Howard Hoskins, and my firm. If you cannot be bothered to perform a thorough investigation, then we will file a complaint and reach out to the Sheriff's Department to investigate both the crime and your response to it. I will be in the green room in five minutes. If you would care to interview me as a witness, then you may meet me there. But until you are out of this building, I expect you to behave in a manner befitting your badge."

Vivian turned on her heel, and the wall of veterans parted as smoothly as a parade pivot, allowing her and her escorts to go through. She didn't have to look back to know that they immediately stepped back into place after she passed. She kept her head up even though she felt like she was only a couple of inches from freaking out.

"Where's Chappie?" she muttered.

"Walking it off," Rowan muttered back. "Mark and Teddy are with him. He'll join us in a minute."

She saw Grant Ichikawa out of the corner of her eye. That meant there were more Hoskins lawyers around. She snapped her fingers at him, and he jumped in surprise but fell into step.

"Grant, I'm going to need you to gather up whatever staff members we have on hand and start shadowing that police detective. The man is a certified twat loogie. I'm not convinced we can trust him not to violate someone's civil liberties just by breathing. I want qualified, professional witnesses observing him every fucking second he's on my turf. Don't interfere in a police investigation. Just make sure we know exactly what he's doing. I'm not going back to Nadine and telling her we let the police screw the pooch on this investigation."

"On it," said Grant and peeled off.

"Jake," she asked, realizing that she hadn't followed up on that thread, "where *is* Nadine?"

"Ashley and I put Mrs. Hoskins in a car to Harborview with Delacroix," said Jake.

"Good." She'd told them to do it and was relieved that it had actually gotten done.

Ashley appeared next to her. "I've pulled the contract with the venue. I'll be able to update you on the insurance and liability status shortly. I recognize that this is not a concern right now, but if anyone asks, you can direct them to me."

"Great, thanks."

Kandace arrived next. Vivian could see the door to the green room—it seemed tantalizingly just out of reach. She wasn't sure when the adrenaline and fumes she was running on would run out, but it seemed like it would be soon.

"Vivian, sweetie, this is a bottle of water. I want you to drink it."

A bottle was shoved into her hand, and Vivian stared at it. She wasn't thirsty.

"Meanwhile, I yelled at the security personnel until they did what I told them and released the security camera footage to the cops."

"OK, great," said Vivian. Vivian had put Kandace in charge of that because Kandie knew how to get her way.

"I saw the footage," said Kandie and her eyes welled up. Vivian stared at her, trying to make Kandie's emotions make sense. Kandie was a bold blonde approaching sixty. Vivian had always appreciated that she channeled her *Bring Me the Manager* energy into positive things. But for once, Kandie looked lost. Kandie abruptly turned to Rowan. "You'll take care of her?"

"Yes, ma'am."

"OK," said Kandie, nodding and brushing tears off her face. "It was just too close. Too close. Thank you. Thank you so much."

Vivian looked from Kandie to Rowan. His face was expressionless, and Vivian didn't know what Kandie was talking about. Kandie abruptly walked off, and Vivian, with nothing better to do, continued toward the green room. Jake opened the door and ushered them inside.

"I'll be outside. I'll send Hot Lips in when he gets here."

"Thanks, Jake," said Rowan.

The door shut behind them, and the silence seemed like a palpable presence. Vivian realized that she was alone in a room with Rowan. She also realized that she wanted very badly to turn around and fling herself into his arms. Instead, she cracked open the water bottle and took a drink. Her hand shook and she put the bottle down after only a tiny sip.

"Did they say anything about Howard?" she asked, her voice husky like she'd been talking too much.

"No. They just put him in the ambulance and left."

"OK," she said, nodding.

She turned around and looked at Rowan directly for the first time. He had a smear of blood on his forehead, and his beautiful suit was now dusty and disheveled, except for the left arm, which was a dark, wet-looking shade of black. In contrast, the fingers on that hand were a dull red. She realized it was because his sleeve was soaked in blood, and her stomach clenched.

"I think maybe you should sit down," he said.

Vivian didn't want to say that if she sat, there was a possibility that she might not get back up again. Curling up into a little fetal ball on the filthy green room couch seemed like a very attractive idea.

"And I think people are counting on me to keep this thing from going off the rails."

"Baby, it's already off the rails."

"There are degrees of off-the-railness here, and we want to stay in the zone where we can at least still see the rails."

"And you can do that while seated."

"You are bleeding out of your cuffs, and you're not sitting down."

Rowan took a deep breath like he was about to launch into an argument, but instead, he looked around, found a folding chair, and sat down.

"Happy?"

"Not anywhere close to it," said Vivian. "They shot Howard!"

Her voice cracked, and Rowan was out of his seat in an instant and pulling her close. She tried to lean into the arm that wasn't injured, but she wasn't sure that he wasn't hurt all over. She felt like one big bruise, but she couldn't tell if that was the truth or if it was just her brain. Maybe it was her heart.

"Viv, baby," murmured Rowan, rocking her as she smushed her face into his chest. She loved being baby-ed. She wanted it so bad. But less than an hour ago, he'd been calling her something else, and Vivian knew that at some point when she had stopped panicking about people nearly dying, that she would remember what he'd said, and she would find it hard to forget again.

"Viv, I need to—"

A knock on the door interrupted him, and Vivian stepped back, blinking away tears. The door opened, and Chappie poked his head in.

"Hey, kiddo! How we doin'?"

"You tell me! Are you going to be punching anyone?"

"Ha! I really did lose my cool there for a minute! He said some very disparaging things about..." He trailed off and glanced at Rowan. Vivian missed whatever message flashed between them, and she looked up at Rowan in confusion.

"Anyway, I did not turn the other cheek, and I will be talking about that in Confession, let me tell you! But it looks like your lawyer friend Belinda," Vivian blinked to hear Belinda described as her friend, "has gotten us a new police detective. So that's good. A Detective Caine. She's in looking at the security footage, and then she'll be over here to talk to you."

"OK," said Vivian. "That's probably good."

"Hey, boss," said Jake, looking over the top of Chappie's head. "Teddy says he's going to step away to splash some cash around."

"What does that mean?" asked Vivian.

"Teddy's taking care of something for me," said Rowan. "Thanks, Jake. Tell him to take José with him."

Jake nodded and disappeared again.

"You just sit tight," said Chappie, smiling at her. "We are under control out here. More or less."

Ashley looked in. "I'm going to start passing out the desserts."

"Good idea," said Vivian tiredly.

"I'll help," said Chappie and left with Ashley.

Vivian looked up at Rowan. "I know that this is not the thing I should be thinking about, but I have to say that it's still on my mind. This will go down in the history of Seattle fundraising events as the single worst event of all time and will be held up in development seminars from now until eternity as a model for what not to do."

"Huh. From the tactical response standpoint, I thought it was going well."

"What?"

"I think you're doing great."

"You're not allowed to say that."

"Why not?"

"Because you think I'm a twenty-something bimbo."

Rowan's face tightened angrily. She didn't know what right he had to be angry since he was the one who had said it first.

"Viv, I said that because—"

"Hi there," said a pleasant voice, and Vivian almost screamed *go away*. Turning around, she plastered a smile on her face and faced the newcomer.

"I'm Detective Caine." The new detective was a Black woman with thick Dutch braids and a film noir-worthy beige trench coat. Detective Bodge hovered behind her, his mustache bristling.

"Hi," said Vivian.

"You're Vivian Kaye?" asked the detective, flipping open her notebook and clicking her pen. "And Rowan Valkyrie?"

"Yes," said Vivian, trying to keep her smile in place. So far, the new detective was leaps ahead of Bodge through the application of simple manners, but Vivian decided to withhold judgment.

"I think I've got the basic gist of events, but I'd like to ask a couple of quick questions just to make sure I've got everyone's locations at the time of the shooting."

"OK," said Vivian.

"Maybe you'd like to sit down," said the detective, taking a seat on the couch.

Rowan pulled one of the chairs forward for her, and Vivian glared at him but sat. He continued to stand next to her. She wasn't sure how to insist that he sit without making a scene.

"So, to recap: you gave what they are calling *the ask,* which is apparently the speech asking for money." Vivian nodded. "Then the intention was to let everyone have time to give and then serve dessert. During this time, Howard Hoskins received a phone call and took it outside."

"Yes, I think so," said Vivian. "I don't know who called, though. When he didn't come back in for pictures, I went out to get him. We wanted one with the entire Board before the dancing started."

Detective Caine nodded. "And you, Mr. Valkyrie? You left right after the ask? Where did you go?"

"I went to the Whole Foods down the block," said Rowan. "I saw the SUV. It was three people in a parked vehicle, and it looked odd. The driver was Caucasian. Due to the reflection on the windshield, I couldn't see much more than that. I took a photo of the license plate, which I will forward to the appropriate person."

The detective nodded. "Mr. Mark Navarro has already sent it. Thanks. But perhaps you can tell me why you happened to step out to the Whole Foods at that time?"

Rowan did not want to share why he had suddenly decided to leave the event. Vivian could see it in every line of his body, but she wanted the answer too.

"I needed to buy chocolate," he said at last. Which was so patently ridiculous that the police detective blinked as if she couldn't comprehend the answer.

Rowan angrily reached into the pocket of his suit jacket and yanked out two bars of Theo chocolate. They were bent and broken, probably from Rowan throwing himself between Howard and a hail of bullets, but the labels were still intact.

"That's my brand," said Vivian.

He looked down at her, and the answer of why he'd had to go to Whole Foods right then was written all over his face.

"Yes, I know," he agreed, holding the bars out to her.

"Thanks," she whispered, taking her apology chocolate out of his hand and clutching it tightly.

"OK," said Detective Caine. "Thanks." She seemed to tick something off in her notebook. "So, you were on your way back and saw the SUV start to move. You yelled at Mr. Navarro to cover Ms. Kaye?"

"Yes," said Rowan.

"Then what happened?"

"I tackled Howard and returned fire."

"CSI will need you to provide the weapon," said Detective Caine.

"Sure," said Rowan with a shrug. "I'll need a receipt."

"Of course. CSI will give an exact total, but can you give your impression of how many times they shot at both targets."

"The majority were at Howard. I thought it was only a couple at Vivian. Mark thought it was at least two."

"Yes," agreed the detective, nodding and making another tick-mark.

"What?" Vivian looked up at Rowan.

"It's fine," said Rowan.

"No. They aimed at Howard. I saw them."

"Yes," agreed Rowan. He hesitated. "And then they aimed at you."

"That's ridiculous. Who would shoot at me? I'm a paralegal."

"And Howard does Estate Planning and Trusts," said Rowan.

"Yes, the most boring field of law possible," said Vivian. "Who would shoot at either of us on purpose?"

"Most drive-bys are drug-related," said Detective Bodge, and Vivian thought Detective Caine's eye twitched slightly.

"I wouldn't know," said Rowan, eyeing Detective Bodge. "But I know that they waited. They didn't move until Howard came out to the street. And if Mark hadn't stopped Vivian, she would have walked right up to Howard. What I don't know is why Howard went all the way to the curb."

"In the video footage," said the detective, "he appears to look around as if he's expecting to see someone."

"I was watching the SUV," said Rowan. "I can't confirm that."

"That's what it looked like to me," said Vivian. "He was mad at whoever he was talking to, but he looked at the street."

The detective nodded and then stood up. "Can I have contact information for both of you? We may have more questions later."

Rowan fished in his pocket, wincing as he attempted to use his injured arm and then pulled out his wallet and provided a business card.

Vivian looked around and realized she didn't have her purse with her. "Um... Chappie—Father Fred—or Ashley have my info. They're giving out desserts. Or I can write it down."

"No, I need to talk to Father Fred anyway," said Detective Caine, waving away Vivian's offer. "He has your home address?"

"Ms. Kaye will be staying with me until the matter is resolved," said Rowan confidently, and Vivian thought about kicking him in the shins. She opened her mouth to correct him, but nothing came out. The detective paused slightly, eyes flicking between the two of them.

"Thanks," she said and walked out the door.

29
Rowan

JARHEAD

"I'm sorry, did I just hear you say I would be staying with you?" demanded Vivian as soon as the door clicked shut. She stood up and turned to face him. He was conscious of how tiny and fragile she seemed on the outside, yet so vibrantly alive—like an eggshell around a dragon.

"Yes. You can't go back to your apartment."

He was also very, very aware of how close he had come to losing her.

"You haven't even apologized. I don't care how wounded and heroic you are—I am going home. Alone. Without you." Vivian poked him in the chest, and he leaned into it. She got confused, and her hand flattened out until it rested on his heart.

It was nice that she thought he was heroic. He wasn't sure about wounded. But he specifically did not like the *without you* part.

"I would like to apologize," said Rowan. "I keep trying to apologize, but we keep getting interrupted. But whether I apologize or not, you are still not going to your apartment."

She gaped at him and instantly removed her hand. It was never a good sign when she was speechless because if he'd learned anything about Vivian, it was that she would rally, and then he was in for it.

"You said I was a lost cause, and I panicked," Rowan continued, which wasn't a great explanation, but it was the truth, and at least he got it out there before she came back with something.

"Well, you said my event was great, and I was just the assistant you were fucking!" She tossed the chocolate bars down in a fury.

"I..." Rowan could see that she was genuinely angry, but he still felt lost. "I never said that."

"You were texting Forest, and you said he didn't need advice from me."

"I don't... I never said fucking. If I said anything, it was dating. And I also apologize for that."

Rowan rubbed his head. Why was there an entire list of things to apologize for? How had he managed to pack so much stupidity into one conversation?

"I was worrying about Olly, and I spoke out of turn. At least Grant said he'd look at the papers and that no one could take Olly away without a fight in court."

"You talked to Grant?"

"No, I texted Forest to text Grant, and he did."

"So, after you said you didn't need my advice, you took my advice?" demanded Vivian icily.

"Yes, because it was good advice. I should have listened to you. But I don't know what is wrong with saying the event was great."

"You didn't mean it! You thought it was lame. Belinda was actually talking it up, and you thought it was lame."

"No, I thought she was lame. I thought the event was great. I didn't get how much went into it until I got here."

"Then why did you call me a child who didn't understand adult responsibilities?" she demanded, her voice rising angrily.

"You said I was a lost cause!" He yelled and tried to wave his injured arm, winced, and grabbed the back of the chair with his good hand.

Vivian took an urgent step forward, tears sparkling in her eyes. "What do I do? Should I get Jake?"

"I'm fine. I just need a couple of stitches. It's fine."

"It's not fine!" Her hands started to shake, and she reached out for him as if unsure what she was supposed to touch. Her hand came to rest on his chest again, and he covered it with his good hand.

"Baby, I'm fine. I'm all right. The medic wouldn't have left me if I wasn't."

Her eyes were huge and her breath was coming too quickly. Planning an entire gala, getting shot at, yelling at cops, nothing made his girl panic except him getting hurt. He needed her to refocus.

"Vivian, I understand that you're mad, and you have every reason to be."

"Yes, I do," she snapped, eyes going to his face. That had worked.

"I don't have an excuse. Also, Marines don't give excuses. It was just... You said I was a lost cause, which is what Melissa said on her way out the door. And you keep not telling people we're dating. All I could see was us ending, and I said some stupid shit to try to..."

"Try to what? Hurt me?" she demanded.

"Yes," he admitted. "So you would hurt *me* less. Only the second it was out of my mouth, I realized I was stupid."

"Who is Melissa?" she asked sourly.

"My ex. We lived together for two years. Technically. I was out of the country a lot. She left because I was too much of a Marine."

"What's wrong with Marines?" Vivian looked offended on behalf of an entire branch of the military, and Rowan tried not to laugh. He rubbed his face tiredly and shoved at his hair.

"I don't know. Also, I didn't want kids, so she said I was a lost cause."

"You don't want kids?" Vivian looked disappointed. It was like all the filters were off her face. He supposed getting shot at had that effect. He was also surprised to find out that he wanted kids more than he thought he had.

"I want kids *now*. But I didn't want them while I was deployed. I want to have kids when I'm here to parent them." With her. He wanted kids with Vivian.

"Oh. That's reasonable," said Vivian, with a shrug. "But who says someone is a lost cause just because your timing doesn't align? I raise my eyebrows at this girl."

Her eyes narrowed at the specter of his ex. Then she looked up at him as if remembering they were still in the middle of a fight.

"I wanted to take it back right then," he said. "Only there were people and talking and bullets. This is not going well. I supposed to make a better speech." He tried to push his hair off his face. It suddenly felt way too long. It practically touched his ears on the sides. He needed a haircut.

"This isn't even a speech. It's just you saying I can't go home and telling me about your shitty ex."

"She *was* shitty, and you absolutely cannot go back to your apartment," he said, reverting to the facts he felt confident in.

"It's my apartment," said Vivian in exasperation. "Where else am I supposed to go?"

"Like I said, you'll go to my place."

"You can't just declare that I'm going to your place."

"Just did. So, yes," said Rowan.

"No!"

"Yes!"

Rowan looked down into her beautiful gray eyes and felt like he was back on the Land Nav course with half a map, one compass, and the sneaking conviction that one of them upside down.

"I love you," he blurted out.

"What?"

"I don't want you to get hurt. Whoever did this knew where you and Howard would be. I'm not letting you go back to your apartment or work until I've caught them."

Vivian stared at him for a long moment then took a deep breath, grabbed him by the tie, and yanked his face down until he was eye-to-eye with her.

"Did you just tell me you loved me?" she demanded in a whisper.

"Yes," he whispered back.

"And then follow it up with a bunch of bullshit?"

"Yes," he agreed. "What should I have followed it up with?"

"Kisses, you dumb jarhead."

"Yes, ma'am."

He crooked his finger under her chin, tilted it to his preferred angle, and brushed his lips across hers. He hadn't known until that moment that the world was wrong, but the moment their lips met, it was like having a bone pushed back into alignment—everything clicked, and his universe started spinning again.

There was a knock on the door, and then it opened without waiting for an invitation.

"Hey, boss," said Hot Lips. "OK, nope, we're fine. I'm leaving."

"Hot Lips is here, boss," said Jake, looking in.

"But I'm leaving."

Jake looked at Hot Lips in confusion. "No, Tyrique said the nurse said he needed stitches."

"But Rowan needs some more… time." Hot Lips glared at Jake, trying to will him into getting the hint. Rowan sighed, and Vivian snorted softly in amusement.

"Vivian, this is Conner Houlihan, our medic."

Vivian gave the Conner the once over. Conner was an unassuming kid about Vivian's age in jeans and a Valkyrie Security polo shirt.

"You do realize that Hot Lips is pejorative and slut shaming?" asked Vivian drily.

"He is a medic, and his last name is Houlihan! We had no choice!" said Rowan.

"It's OK, ma'am," said Hot Lips. "M.A.S.H. was a re-run favorite at our house, and by the end of the series, they'd reclaimed the name. Margaret Houlihan was an independent woman who was not ashamed of having sex. I don't mind being named after her."

"I will accept that answer," said Vivian.

"There was a series called M.A.S.H. – like the Mobile Army Surgical Hospitals?" asked Jake.

"I am so old," said Rowan.

"Not too old to get shot, apparently," said Hot Lips, plunking down his bag. "Jacket off, sir. Let's see what we got." Then he stopped and looked at Vivian. "Unless you need him for more important stuff?"

"No, I think I would rather Rowan stopped bleeding on things," said Vivian, reaching up to help him remove his jacket.

"That is what I'm here for," said Hot Lips.

"And then we're going home," said Rowan. "Assuming the police release us."

"I don't think I can go home until everyone else does," said Vivian.

"Baby," began Rowan.

"No, I'm serious. I'm in charge of this shindig, and as long as my people have to stay, I'm staying."

"We'll see what Chappie says," said Rowan, feeling confident that Father Fred would agree with him.

"Don't think you can use Chappie against me," said Vivian. "He's on my side."

Rowan was fully confident that Father Fred was on Vivian's side, which was also why he felt certain that Father Fred would agree with Rowan. The Chaplain would want to protect Vivian.

"I think the police detective was starting to send people home when I came in," said Hot Lips as he unzipped his bag and pulled out a pair of scissors.

"Your shirt is covered in blood," said Vivian, staring at his sleeve.

"Blood always goes everywhere," said Rowan, reassuringly. "It always looks worse than it is." He didn't want to add that some of it was Howard's blood.

"Ma'am," said Hot Lips, looking around in a show of searching for something. "I don't suppose you could go find me some hot water?"

"Yes, of course," said Vivian. "How much?"

"Two liters," said Hot Lips.

"OK," said Vivian, looking back at Rowan, worry all over her face.

"I'm fine," said Rowan, for what felt like the hundredth time.

"OK. I'll be right back."

She looked down at the chair and then grabbed her chocolate bars, which made him smile. She glared at him before hurrying from the room. Rowan looked at Hot Lips.

"You don't really need hot water, do you?"

"Nope. And no one ever needs hot water when they send expectant fathers out of the room either."

"Yeah, well, the joke's on you. Chances are she'll delegate that action and be back in twenty seconds."

"Chances are that the eight people who tried to give me messages for Vivian will want to talk to her first," said Hot Lips, cutting off Rowan's shirt sleeve. "Getting her out of here is going to be difficult."

Rowan sighed. "Well, you heard her. She's in charge of this shindig."

Hot Lips chuckled. "You couldn't pick out a grunt. You had to get yourself a general."

"Marines aim for the top," said Rowan, thinking that he would carry his general out by force if necessary.

30
Vivian

THE CHIPPED HAM

Vivian woke up with a slow awareness, drifting sluggishly in and out of the reality of warm blankets and the memory of what had happened the previous night. When everything landed all at once, she instinctively put out her hand to find Rowan. He was beside her, putting out enough heat to cook a pizza.

He grunted as her hand clenched possessively on his thigh and rolled toward her. Then he made an unhappy noise as he rolled onto his injured arm, flailed angrily in the blankets, and sat up.

"I am not fucking eating the chipped ham again," he barked and stared aggressively around the room as if daring someone to argue.

Vivian did not know what that meant, but she had been aware that her father had also loathed the Marine Corps creamed chipped ham. He had described it as reconstituted cardboard in puke gravy.

"OK. I was going to order Starbucks," she said, her voice gravelly with sleep.

Rowan looked down at her as if he couldn't remember why she was there. Not the best sign to start off her day. His hair was sticking up, and in the cold light of a Pacific Northwest fall morning, his arm looked nearly purple with bruising.

"Oh, thank God," he said.

"Yeah, Starbucks is a better option than chipped ham."

"No, thank God I'm retired. Although, yes, on the Starbucks."

He looked around the room and then reached for the bedside table, where there was a bottle of painkillers and a bottle of water.

He opened the painkillers in a one-handed movement that spoke of long practice, tossed a couple in his mouth, and chased them with water while Vivian checked her phone.

"Howard made it out of surgery," said Vivian, reading Nadine's text that had apparently come through at three in the morning but hadn't cleared her do-not-disturb setting.

"Yeah," grunted Rowan. "Delacroix texted at some point."

"She says he's still in critical condition and in the ICU. They're all at the hospital."

"We'll go after breakfast," said Rowan. "You want some of these?"

"I don't think so?"

He frowned and then lifted up the covers to inspect her. She looked up at him in disbelief.

"Mmm…" he said, fixating on her hip. "Maybe take one."

"I try not to take drugs unless I think it's really warranted."

"That is so cute. Meanwhile, your hip is bruised, and if you're not sore yet, it's just because you haven't moved."

"And I think I should make up my own mind about my body."

"And I think by the time you realize you hurt, you're already in the hole. It's better to take one to ease you into the day. If you want something not as strong, you can take a couple Motrin."

"Was that some sort of woman joke?"

"What?"

"Motrin?"

He reached into his bedside table drawer and came back with a bottle of Motrin.

"Motrin?" he offered.

She stared at him. He stared back.

"Motrin is for period cramps."

"Motrin is for everything. I once saw a guy hike out five miles on a broken ankle and a bottle of Motrin."

"I feel like this message has not made it out to civilian males. Out here, it's pretty much just for women."

"Well… women and Marines. Seems legit."

Vivian snorted. "Give me four Motrin and the water."

"Going hard," he said, nodding. He handed her the pills and bottle of water. She sat up long enough to swallow and then had serious second thoughts about the painkillers, but she wasn't about to admit it now.

Vivian settled against him, resting her head on his chest, and for a little while, the world returned to warm blankets and safety. Rowan had been adamant about not permitting her to go back to her apartment. He'd said that she could send the guys with her keys and a list of things she wanted, but she would not be going anywhere without protection.

"I'm going to want clothes at some point," said Vivian, and Rowan grunted as if she had woken him up again.

"Baby, it's fine," he said at last, but his eyes remained firmly shut.

"I know you said the guys could get my stuff, but you said I had to make a list. I haven't made a list, and I don't want to make a list."

Vivian didn't want to be a whiner, but at the same time, she also wanted her clothes to magically appear at her wishing.

"What if we just tell them to get everything and bring it here?"

"What everything?"

"Everything, everything."

"Then all my things would be here."

"Yes."

"But then I would just be living here."

"Yes."

Vivian tried to consider that in a realistic way, but all her brain could come up with was that it would be a lot more convenient.

"We've only been going out for a month," she said.

"Mark proposed on his first date with Jenny."

"Mark wanted the housing benefit."

"I think it might have been Jenny, actually, but that doesn't mean it was the wrong decision."

"And I think you took too many pills."

"Too many, or just the right amount?"

Vivian couldn't stop herself from laughing, which was how she knew she would end up moving in with him.

"Fine," she said after a moment. "But only because I'm very attracted to the idea of someone else doing all the moving."

"Great," said Rowan. "Your stuff is in the garage."

Vivian thought about that for a long while. It continued to not make any sense.

"What?"

"Well, last night, I figured that you would want your clothes and, at minimum, a different bra. You're particular about your underwear."

"This is true."

"But I can't keep having the guys clear your apartment every time you want to go home for clothes, and I don't really want them digging through your drawers."

"I also don't want that."

"So, I called this one company we've used before. They move your entire house as is."

"As is?"

"They don't pack things. They box things. So they box your dresser. Your bed. Your closet. Your kitchen. Each drawer gets labeled and put in its own box. And then it gets moved."

"That's genius," said Vivian.

"And it's now in my garage. It arrived around five this morning."

"Did I wake up for that?"

"I barely woke up for it."

"Huh. You know, you would think that would make me more likely to get up and get clothes, but it really doesn't."

"Getting up is for suckers. We'll stay here."

Rowan's phone rang, and he cracked one eyelid and looked at it. Vivian could see his brother's face. With a sigh, Rowan answered.

"Hey, Forest."

"Hey Forest? What the actual fuck?"

"Uh…"

"I turn on the news, and there's Valkyrie Security saving the day at local veteran's charity event."

"Oh, nice name drop. Mark will be pleased."

"Mark will— What the fuck is wrong with you? I was texting you last night. Meanwhile, Rowan Valkyrie, owner of Valkyrie Security, is credited with personally saving Howard Hoskins' life. When did you find time to squeeze me in?"

"You were before all that happened."

"You didn't call me."

"Why would I call you?"

"Mmmm," said Vivian, recognizing his mistake but burying her face in his chest.

"Why—" Forest's voice went up an octave. "Oh, my fucking God. I don't know, maybe because I don't want Grant Ichikawa assuring me that everyone is very shaken up, but not to worry, he'll still make our meeting on Monday, and please do thank my brother on behalf of the firm." She could hear the sarcasm even with the covers half over her head.

"Yeah?" Rowan still sounded confused.

"He's saying you should have told him you were fine so he didn't have to find out from strangers," whispered Vivian.

"Oh. Yeah, sorry. Forgot to text you. But the situation was fluid, and I had to focus on immediate concerns. I am fine."

Forest made an inarticulate noise of frustration that sounded very much like the noise Rowan made when annoyed.

Vivian wondered how many times Rowan had *not* called his brothers after he'd been hurt. Enough that it hadn't even crossed his mind.

"But Grant thought the custody papers weren't going to be a problem?" asked Rowan.

"I emailed them over. He's looking at them. But he literally said *oh, this will be fun* when he saw them, and I don't know what that means."

"He thinks he'll win," translated Vivian quietly.

"It means he thinks he'll win," said Rowan.

"Oh. That is actually reassuring, then. Are you sure you're OK?"

"Yes."

"Like, really sure? Or like that time you were home for six months, sure?"

"Really sure."

"OK."

"Can you call Ash and tell him I'm fine? I'm lying in bed, and I would prefer not to answer more phone calls than I have to."

"Yes, but he doesn't watch news that isn't on Twitter or X or whatever, so he wouldn't call for another hour or whenever local news makes it on there."

"That is an hour I could be sleeping."

"Good point. OK, I'll call him. Go back to sleep."

"I will do that."

They hung up, and Rowan dropped the phone back on the bedside table. There was more warm and fluffy silence, although she could tell from his breathing that he wasn't asleep.

"I—" Whatever Rowan was about to say was cut off when Vivian's phone began to ring. Vivian struggled away from Rowan, floundering in his poofy bedding, and finally grabbed her phone.

Vivian looked at the face and frowned. It was Sunday, wasn't it? It felt like three months had been packed into yesterday. But if it was Sunday, why was Courtney calling?

"Hey, Courtney," she said, picking up.

"Vivian, I'm really, really sorry, and Ms. Branch said not to call you, but I think you would be super pissed if I didn't."

"What's the problem?" asked Vivian.

"Last night, someone broke into the office and trashed Howard's office and your cubicle."

Beside her, Rowan flipped off the covers and sat up.

31

Rowan

PROFESSIONAL TOUCH

"Do you notice anything specific?" asked Detective Caine.

Rowan hadn't wanted to bring Vivian to the office. He thought that, at minimum, it would be upsetting for her, and at most, it could be dangerous. But the police detective, who had called shortly after Courtney, had been insistent. Detective Caine had also banished Rowan to the hall, where he was reduced to glaring through the fractured glass sidelight.

The intruder had gained access through a side door in the company lobby, which made Vivian mutter something about having told Susan to change the code. Obviously, Susan hadn't listened. From there, the company only had security alarms on their documents' vault, so when Howard's office door had been kicked open, no one had known. It wasn't until building security got a repeated alert that the lobby door was open and went to check on it that the intrusion was discovered. As it was a Sunday, they called Susan, the Office Manager. Susan, perhaps unaware of the shooting on Saturday or perhaps not giving a damn, had delegated checking the office to Courtney. Courtney, the only sensible person in the room in Rowan's estimation, appeared to be the first one to connect the dots and call everyone, including the police.

Like Vivian's cubicle, Howard's office looked like it had been hit by a tornado. Every piece of paper had been dumped out of the files and distributed evenly as if someone had thrown them angrily in the air.

"I'd have to go through the papers," Vivian said quietly, as she looked around the office again.

The computer had been thrown down and smashed. The floor to ceiling pane of glass next to the door had also been kicked and broken. The shelf full of awards that Howard called *useless dust catchers* in response to an impressed comment from Rowan had been swept clear. That all seemed like someone was angry, but Rowan couldn't tell if anything had actually been removed. Vivian's desk was similar. Her drawers had all been emptied, but Vivian said that nothing appeared to be missing. Had someone been looking for something and then got frustrated? That seemed to paint the portrait of someone juvenile and stupid.

His phone beeped with a text from Teddy, and Rowan hurried to check it.

GOT A LEAD ON THE CAR. WILL CALL YOU IN A FEW.

Rowan felt relieved that there had been some progress. So far, his best recovery move was successfully getting Vivian to not argue about moving in. Which was no small feat and great for his life, but didn't catch whoever had tried to kill her in the first place.

Vivian frowned and turned in a circle as if trying to take in the entire room.

"This is so pointless," she said, sounding puzzled.

"Criminal acts often feel that way," said Detective Caine soothingly.

Vivian hadn't been upset in that comment. She'd been confused.

Rowan liked this detective better than Bodge, but this morning when they'd arrived together, he thought he'd detected the faintest whiff of condescension. It looked like Detective Caine had filed Vivian under B for Bimbo.

Rowan stepped away from the wall and leaned into the office.

"What do you mean, Viv?" he asked, earning a glare from the Detective.

"Did you talk to Nadine? Did someone try to break into their house too?" asked Vivian, still frowning at the mess.

"Not that we know of. Why do you ask?" Detective Caine's tone moved from victim soothing to alerted interest.

"Well, they smashed things and that's hurtful, but Howard never kept anything really important in the office. None of this is valuable to him. I hate it and I want to fucking punch someone in the face, but he would be less angry than I am. So, if they didn't go to the house then they must have been looking for something that they thought would be here at the office, but..."

Vivian trailed off and scratched her head, dislodging a stray wisp of hair from her bun.

"But what?" asked the Detective.

"Well, going paperless has long been a company initiative. Although it's incredibly difficult in our industry. But since the pandemic we've made massive strides forward as technology has become more legally acceptable. Howard and I both take notes on these tablets." She pointed to a cracked device on the floor. "We plug them in when we leave and they get backed up overnight. Documents get scanned and originals get destroyed or placed in the vault to be kept for the mandated legal period. If we do put something in a file," she pointed to one of the folders from the floor, "it's meant to be temporary. So if it's in a file, it's defacto not that important. I don't understand why someone would break in and go through the files."

"Well, would there be any new paperwork that you didn't know about? When was the last time Howard was in the office?"

"Friday afternoon," said Vivian, slowly. "He left early to go play golf with a client. I left a little bit early too, to finish up some things for the gala, but everything was quiet. There wasn't anything new except for the card for the Tates. But that was on my desk."

Abruptly, Vivian hurried from the office, brushing past Rowan and hurrying to her cubicle. She hesitated at the entrance.

"Can I touch things?"

"We'd rather you didn't," said the Detective following her. "CSI hasn't had a chance to go over it."

"Well, take some photos or something," snapped Vivian. "I need to find something important. Who has gloves? Courtney!" Vivian had an impressive bellow when she wanted one. Mark might be onto something with his idea that Vivian had missed her calling as a drill instructor.

"Yes?" Courtney popped into the hallway like she'd been hovering and waiting for her summons.

"I need some rubber gloves. Go grab some out of the first aid kit in the break room."

"I have some," snapped the Detective, pulling them out of her pocket.

Vivian snatched them up and pulled them on as the detective snapped photos of the cubicle with her phone and made swearing noises under her breath.

Vivian got down on her knees and began to gently lift the drifts of paper, trying to disturb them as little as possible. Rowan admired the way her ass looked in leggings, which was probably the wrong time to be thinking sexy thoughts, but it wasn't his fault that Vivian was so goddamn hot.

"Got it," murmured Vivian, gently pulling out what looked to be the pieces of a torn Hallmark card.

"Hey!" exclaimed Courtney, peering over the cubicle wall. "I picked that card out specially."

"And then someone went and tore it up," said Vivian. She looked around at the other papers on the floor. "They didn't tear anything else up."

"What is it?" asked Detective Caine.

Rowan finally put the pieces together the way Vivian had.

"It's Charles Tate Senior's get well card, isn't it?" he asked.

"Yes, it is," Vivian said, looking up at him grimly.

"Has anyone checked on him?" asked Rowan. "Did he make it

through his cardiac event?"

"There was an email from his assistant this morning," said Courtney, with a gasp. "I saw it when I logged in. Mr. Tate passed away yesterday in the hospital!"

"Email him back. Be polite, but find out what time," said Rowan. "And, if you can, ascertain Chucky's whereabouts both yesterday and today."

"Do you two mind?" snapped Detective Caine. "I will be doing the investigating here!"

"But," said Courtney, "Chucky's an idiot. Why would he do this?"

"Howard went golfing with Charles Tate Senior on Friday. He swore he was going to get Senior to sign the new will. Chucky has been back-steering his father's will revision for the last month. The current version, the version Howard was trying to get signed, reduces Chucky's inheritance to barely a quarter of the estate."

"What happens if that version didn't get signed, or we can't find it?" asked Detective Caine.

"Then it would revert to the previous signed version which leaves Chucky as the executor and outside of specific bequests, he would get everything."

"That sounds like a hell of a lot of motive," said Detective Caine.

"Over two-hundred million dollars-worth of motive," said Vivian, reaching out a hand toward Rowan. He used his good arm to help her off the floor. He suspected the bruise on her hip bothered her more than she would willingly admit.

"But it's kind of a big jump from a torn get-well card to breaking and entering, let alone attempted murder," said Detective Caine, backing up, probably to give Vivian room to leave the cubicle, though it felt like a physical step away from Vivian's theory.

Vivian looked at Rowan. He knew damn well she was getting discounted because of her age and job description and he couldn't fix it for her. On the other hand, they didn't need the Detective's permission to investigate.

"I think we should talk to Nadine," he said. "She'll know if Howard came home directly after golfing and she might know about the will."

"You will do nothing of the kind," said the Detective. "I am investigating and I will speak to the relevant parties. You will stay out of it."

Vivian's hand tightened in his. "Of course," she said using her work voice and smiling at Detective Caine. "You're the professional."

32
Vivian

TARGET PRACTICE

The elevator door had barely closed when Rowan put an arm around her and pulled her into his chest. Vivian let out a woof of air and then realized that she had been holding herself with a rigid tenseness. She burrowed her head into the hollow of his shoulder and leaned into him. She hadn't realized the power of a simple hug to make things feel immeasurably better.

"She was ignoring me."

"I don't think she disbelieved you," said Rowan. "At least not entirely."

"She wasn't going to go talk to Chucky."

"I think she's just going to work her way through all the variables first. It's methodical. And it means that when she gets there, she'll have all the evidence to support it."

"You hope."

"Yes," said Rowan. "That *is* what I'm hoping."

"Meanwhile, Chucky is still out there. What if he tries to hurt Howard again?"

He kissed the top of her head. "Well, that's why we're not waiting for the police."

She looked up at him. "We're not?"

"No. I'm not a cop. I don't have to wait for shit. Were you planning on waiting?" He looked confused.

"Well... no. But I thought you would probably try and talk me out of it."

"Why would I do that?"

"Probably something about it being too dangerous."

"What are you planning on doing?" he asked, looking alarmed.

"I haven't decided yet. I mean, I'm not going to rush over to the Tate's or anything, but something needs to be done."

"Well, I might object to that. I thought we could talk to some people and see if Teddy found the shooter's vehicle yet."

"If Teddy's done what?" Vivian looked up at him in surprise.

"I've got Teddy and the team out looking for the vehicle. He texted and says he's got a line on it. We'll see if he turns up anything."

"Since when?"

"What?

"Since when have they been looking?"

"Since last night. If you want to pursue the enemy you have to move while they're still in disarray. At a minimum we disrupted the plan last night."

"Rowan Valkyrie!"

"What?"

"You are…"

The elevator reached the parking level with the little bounce and he raised his eyebrows waiting for her to finish the sentence.

"Incredibly sexy."

He grinned. "I feel like I'm getting kudos off the hard work of others, but I'll take it. Wait here, please."

Vivian was startled into doing what she was told as Rowan stepped out. She watched him survey the area and walk away. She pushed the *door open* button and leaned out to see what he was doing. He walked around his car, seeming to check his vehicle and then unlocked it and returned.

"OK, let's get you inside."

"Rowan, are you guarding me?"

"Yes, because you are also a target," he said. His head was up, eyes scanning the garage, looking everywhere but at her.

"I don't think I'm a serious target."

"I disagree. In fact, could you call or message Barb? We should let her know that Chucky is a suspect in the attack and that if he makes an appearance, her crew should alert authorities and approach with extreme caution."

"Oh. That's a good idea," said Vivian taking out her phone. She was three texts into her conversation with Barb when she realized that Rowan had diverted her argument about whether or not she really a target.

She finished another text with Barb, which got her up to speed with the building security chief, but it hadn't given her long enough to figure out how or what she felt. It had been a long time since she'd had to answer to anyone about where she was going or why or what the hell she was going to do when she got there.

She tried to remember the last time anyone had even tried. She squinted out the window. There had been that one guy. He'd lasted about three weeks because he had been a jealous freak. This was not the same, but it still felt weird.

But why?

She glanced over at Rowan. Because she was the boss. Except he was also the boss. Technically more of a boss than she was. Except that she was always the boss of herself.

Usually.

"I think we don't need to find Chucky," said Vivian.

"Well, if he's shooting people then, yeah, we do."

"I don't think he is shooting people. I think he hired someone to shoot people. He's effort adverse, but very pro spending money."

"That tracks," agreed Rowan, pulling out onto the roadway as rain drops hit the window with gentle insistent taps. September was always glorious, but October was mixed bag of weather that slowly devolved into the drizzling, spitting, rain and gloom that would last through at least March.

"So, if we don't need to find Chucky, what do we need to do?" he asked.

"We need to find the will," said Vivian. "The will definitely wasn't at the office on Friday. It's possible that Howard dropped it off on Saturday before the gala and then Chucky, if that's who actually searched the office, would have found it. But Howard didn't say anything to me about it at the gala."

"He wouldn't have," said Rowan sounding amused. "You were busy. But from the state of the office, I don't think they found it."

"I agree. But Howard's wife, Nadine, might know what happened to it. The thing is, even if we don't find the will, we still have a signed and dated document of intent that I scanned into files weeks ago. Charles Tate Senior's wife and daughter still have plenty of documentation to fight the old will."

"Not without you and Howard," said Rowan. "It's one signed document that no one else in the firm can speak to. And there is plenty of evidence of him changing his mind. You and Howard are the ones who know what Senior intended. Without you, and that will, Chucky will get the money."

He paused at a stop light, and looked over at her.

"You are making a very grumpy face."

"Yes, because I think you're right and that makes me really mad. Someone needs to punch Chucky in the face. I have thought that since I met him and I'm trying very hard *not* to elevate that to putting a bullet or six into him, but it's is proving very difficult."

"I put your gun in my safe, by the way."

Startled, Vivian turned in her seat to look directly at him.

"What?"

"The movers delivered the gun and your father's flag directly instead of boxing them. Well, they gave them to Jake. And Jake carried them over. I put them in the safe at home."

Vivian felt an intense moment of panic when tears threatened to overwhelm her. She blinked rapidly.

"Um, thanks. I don't like… I wasn't looking forward to figuring out what box that was in."

"I meant to tell you earlier. I forgot. Sorry, I derailed that conversation and now the light's green and we can't hug."

Vivian swiped at her eyes and laughed. "It's fine. I appreciate that people took care of them."

"Did your dad get you the 1911?"

"No, I got the 1911 because I liked it. Not because it's a classic military side-arm, thank you very much."

Rowan chuckled.

"Dad had a Beretta that I liked, but I sold all of his guns after he passed. I don't go shooting enough to justify having eight guns."

"You don't need to justify it. Sometimes you just like having shiny things because they're fun and they make you feel pretty."

Vivian chuckled. "Yes, but as a responsible gun owner, I couldn't keep up with cleaning and or practicing enough to be comfortable using them. I've got one gun that I know, like, and I'm trained on. That's all the gun energy that I have."

"Fair," said Rowan with a shrug. "Want to go shooting sometime?"

"Yes," said Vivian hesitantly.

"That wasn't an enthusiastic yes. We don't have to go."

"I would like to go. I haven't been in a while. But I don't want to be mansplained to while I do it. I want fun date night shooting. Not Mr. Valkyrie telling me how to use my gun."

"Yes, ma'am," he said instantly and nodded. "Fun date night making things go bang and then we go bang."

Vivian laughed and he grinned.

"You're only going to encourage me if you keep laughing."

"I know, but I can't stop!"

"Well, then you know I'm not going to."

Vivian laughed again and then looked around at the traffic.

"Where are we going?"

"You wanted to see Nadine? I'm heading for Harborview while we wait for Teddy to call me back."

"Oh. Great. I can check on Howard and talk to her about the will."

"And I can check building security and update Delacroix. And also make sure there's a rotation roster so Delacroix can get some shut eye. I'm assuming Mark has some sort of plan, but I haven't been fully updated. I'm going to be making calls while you talk to Nadine. If that's OK?"

"Teamwork," said Vivian, with a nod, trying to ignore the fact that he'd added the plan check as an afterthought.

"Teamwork," he agreed, and flashed her a grin.

33
Rowan

THE BOYS

Rowan leaned against the wall and watched through the narrow window in the door to the family lounge as Vivian distributed hugs to Nadine and Howard's daughter. They greeted her with relief and Nadine burst into tears. Vivian didn't seem troubled by this, but hugged Nadine tightly and patted her back.

"Hey boss," said Delacroix, rubbing a tired hand through his hair.

"Hey," said Rowan. "How's it looking here?"

"Mr. Hoskins been bumped up to critical but stable," said Delacroix. "I've communicated with building security. The building already has limited public entrances and security uses a metal detector. No one but staff and immediate family are allowed into the ward, and then only one at a time. Staff use a badged entrance and I've got eyes on the only public entrance. It's not foolproof, but someone would have to work pretty hard to get in. What's the situation out there."

"We've identified a suspect. Charles Tate Junior AKA Chucky. Unfortunately, we think he hired out, so I don't have an identity on the shooters yet. But Teddy's working on the vehicle."

Rowan's phone lit up with an alert and he looked at a message from Barb at the Hoskins Building.

HERE'S THE ASSHOLE YOU'RE LOOKING FOR. IN CASE ANYONE NEEDS TO IDENTIFY HIM.

"And now I'm forwarding you a photo of the suspect."

"Nice," said Delacroix, but the younger man looked tired.

"What's the rotation schedule?" asked Rowan.

"Mark said he'd send someone, but I don't know when."

"I'll check in with him," said Rowan, dialing.

He walked a few feet away, still trying to keep an eye on Vivian and Delacroix. Harborview seemed to be various shades of cream and boring ass gray. It also had a faint aroma of industrial cleanser that always gave Rowan the heebie-jeebies. He knew it meant that staff took cleaning seriously, but somewhere in his various trips to hospitals and medic tents his subconscious had also picked it as the smell of death.

"Hey," said Mark, picking up. "I got your texts. Good progress. How are you doing?"

"Sore," said Rowan. "But I've been worse. I'm at Harborview while Vivian checks on the Hoskins family. Delacroix's looking a little beat."

"I've got Germany coming to replace him in an hour."

"Great."

Rowan was aware that their roster of personnel sounded like a fridge poetry magnet set, but since he rarely had to explain it to anyone, he never bothered to do anything but enjoy it.

"How's Viv?" asked Mark.

"Um… Super in denial about being a target and also hating being guarded so hard, but trying not to say anything about it."

"Yeah, but how'd she take you moving all her stuff?"

"She thought it was convenient. Particularly once I pointed out that her ice cream was now in my freezer."

Mark burst out in a guffaw of laughter. "So, being defacto moved in with you doesn't bother her in the slightest, but you bossing her around and trying to keep her from getting killed, that's a problem."

"That's my girl," said Rowan with a shrug. "The sooner we can get this wrapped up the better."

"OK, I've got Teddy and José at some junkyard. I'm waiting on an update."

"Yeah, I got a text from him, but it was a while ago. I'm starting to worry."

"Yeah, me too," agreed Mark. "I can send out another team, but—"

"He's calling," said Rowan as the phone buzzed in his ear. "I'll patch him in."

Rowan merged Teddy into the call and then put his phone back to his ear.

"Hey, Teddy. Mark's on the line. You're a go."

"I'm not a go. I'm dead in the water because I ran out of cash."

"Where'd you get to?" asked Mark.

"We traced the vehicle to a junkyard out in Issaquah. I can see the damn bullet holes from here—nice grouping, by the way—but the owner's giving us the big fuck you."

"We can call the cops?" suggested Mark.

"Yeah, except we got here because of José's cousin and if we blow shit up for him it's going to blow back on José at Christmas."

"OK, so what we need is to pay the junkyard owner enough to call the cops for himself," said Rowan.

"That's how I'm reading it," said Teddy. "And if we want the names and or security footage of who sold it to him, that's going to be extra."

"How much are we talking?" asked Rowan.

Rowan heard Teddy ask José something in Spanish. There seemed to be some discussion that he couldn't catch. Somehow his Arabic wasn't as handy stateside as Teddy's four years of high school Spanish.

"José thinks two grand and flash more hardware. I say three or the owner is going to tell the cops we were here."

"Yeah, no problem," said Rowan, thinking that it was ridiculous how little money it took change someone's mind. "I've got that in the safe back at work."

"I'll meet you there," said Mark. "I'll drive it out to Teddy. You should stick with Viv."

"You mean I should stick to injured reserve," said Rowan drily.

"I don't know what Mark means, but what I mean is that you're the boss of the company and we're going to need you to bail us out if the cops get annoyed," said Teddy.

All of which was reasonable, but Rowan still felt like he was being benched.

"Mm-hmm," said Rowan. "OK, Mark, give me a couple of minutes to get back over there. I'm going to leave Viv here with the Hoskins and Delacroix."

"Got it. Over and out." Mark's portion of the call went dark.

"Hang tight, Teddy," said Rowan. "The cash cow is on the way."

"Can I start calling Mark that?"

"If it annoys him, then sure."

Teddy chuckled. "You know, I'm definitely going to blow my caffeine allotment for the day, but this is kind of fun. Except for Mr. Hoskins getting shot. Sorry, that probably wasn't cool to say."

"It is fun to use your skills to find bad guys," said Rowan. "Doesn't make us care less about Howard. You can feel two things at once."

"Yeah. Just don't tell Viv I said that."

"She'd probably understand, but no, that's one of the things that stays within the team."

"Thanks, boss," said Teddy. "Over and out."

Rowan hit the red button and turned back to Delacroix.

"Germany will be here in an hour. I have to meet Mark at the office, and I'm going to leave Vivian here. I will talk to her, but let's just keep her here in this nice locked down building until I get back, shall we?"

Delacroix grinned. "Yes, sir."

Rowan knocked lightly on the door before opening it.

"Sorry," he said, looking in at the tearful faces of the family.

"You can come in," said Mrs. Hoskins, trying to smile.

"I don't want to bother you. I just need to borrow Vivian for a moment."

Vivian looked puzzled but stood up and came out of the family lounge.

"You really could come in. Dr. Mendez—the one who brought Howard here and did the surgery—told them what you did. I'm not sure they know what to say to you, but they'd be happy to say thank you."

"I don't know what to say to them either," said Rowan honestly. "I never know. I wish I'd been faster. I hope Howard comes through this."

Vivian opened her mouth, closed it again and then took a breath. "I think this is a longer conversation than the time and location allow."

Rowan shrugged awkwardly. "I don't really... It doesn't matter. But yes, I now have a time crunch. Teddy has a line on the vehicle but needs money. I'm meeting Mark at the office to open the safe."

"Teddy splashed all of his cash around?" asked Vivian, a smile sneaking onto her lips.

"Yes, exactly. It shouldn't take me that long, but I don't see any reason for you to have to go with me."

"OK," said Vivian. "I haven't gotten a chance to ask about the will yet."

"Great. Then I'll meet you back here in an hour or so."

She nodded.

"But uh... do me a favor. Help keep my pulse rate under 100 and don't go anywhere else?"

Her mouth had pinched into a straight line and her chin tilted down.

"I know, I know. You don't think you could possibly be in danger, but I do, so please humor me, and stay here."

"Do as I'm told?" she asked, eyes narrowing.

"Just this once," he said and then wished he hadn't.

"Yes, sir," she growled with a mock salute and went back into the family lounge.

"Hating it so hard," Rowan muttered.

34
Vivian

THE HOME FRONT

"Is everything all right?" asked Nadine as Vivian came back into the lounge. Vivian looked into Nadine's watering eyes and felt horrible. Nadine had been awake all night praying for a miracle. She didn't need Vivian to come in and throw a tantrum because Rowan had woken up extra bossy and over protective. Nadine needed someone to tell her everything would be all right. And Rowan was the one who kept the investigation moving forward while the police had been practically useless. Looking down into Nadine's face Vivian knew she couldn't help Howard or Nadine in any practical immediate way, but she swore she would at least catch Chucky.

"Um, Rowan and I are working on finding the people responsible for the shooting."

"You are? But the police came and talked to me. They said it was a drive-by shooting."

"That was the one with the mustache, right?"

"Yes," admitted Nadine, glancing at her daughter. Nadine was still wearing her gala gown and a Yale sweatshirt that Vivian thought Alison had brought her.

"I told you he was an idiot," muttered Alison. Alison was thirty-four and wore her hair in a sleek bob that Vivian always envied. She had her father's practical streak and her mother's cheekbones.

"Rowan and I think it was related to something Howard and I have been doing at work. Um… With the Tates. Did Howard ever mention them?"

Nadine made a face. "Howard likes Charles. I find him... acceptable in a crowd, but hardly someone I want to spend additional time with. His current wife, Stacy, I think—It's in my phone. I'll look it up. Anyhow, she's nice enough, but rather over-botoxed. The daughter is in college? I try not to think about Chucky."

Alison gave a quiet snort of laughter. "You call Junior, Chucky?"

"It's what your father calls him," said Nadine with a sniff.

"Sorry, that's my fault," said Vivian.

"But," said Alison making a face, "it's just so right."

Vivian felt tears welling up.

"Oh, no, don't you start!" exclaimed Alison, wrapping an arm around her.

"Sorry. But Howard said the same thing."

Alison gave a watery chuckle.

"I don't understand," said Nadine. "What do the Tates have to do with anything? Howard just saw Charles on Friday for golf."

"Yes," said Vivian, carefully. "Did he by any chance bring anything home with him?"

"Yes. He brought Charles' will home. He was ecstatic to finally get it signed."

"OK, but what did he do with it once he got it home?"

"He took it into the library. Where he has his computer and things."

"So, it's still at the house?" asked Vivian.

"As far as I know," said Nadine with a shrug. "Why?"

"Charles Senior died on Saturday. We think this is about the will."

"Chucky," snarled Alison.

Nadine looked between Alison and Vivian. "No. I mean... Chucky's not very pleasant. But we know him. He's been to our house."

"So, he knows where you live?" asked Vivian feeling sick to her stomach.

What if Chucky was at the house right now getting the will? Vivian didn't want to say that out loud.

"One sec," said Vivian and went back to the door.

She looked around and spotted Delacroix who she only knew because he'd been cleaning guns while she'd been cleaning out the other poker players.

"Hey," she hissed. "How long until other people get here?"

"Rowan said an hour," said Delacroix.

"Yeah," said Vivian. "That's how long he thought he'd be too. Thanks."

She was about to go back in when Alison came out.

"We're going to get some coffee. You'll stay with Mom?" she asked Delacroix and he nodded.

Alison grabbed Vivian's arm and pulled her toward the break room across the hall.

"You think Chucky did this, don't you?" whispered Alison and Vivian nodded. "You think he's after that will?"

"Yeah, I do. And I'm more than a little bit worried that he's had all night to find it. Someone searched the office last night. How long do you think it will take for them to go look at the house."

"OK," said Alison. "I've got keys to the house. I'll just tell Mom that I'm going to go get her some clothes and I'll go look for the will. I was going go before you got here, so it won't seem weird."

"No, give me the keys," said Vivian.

Rowan would be so pissed, but considering that half their relationship was arguing, then she was pretty sure she could smooth it over. He had to see that she couldn't allow Alison to risk herself. She couldn't let Chucky get his mitts on the will. And above all, she couldn't wait an entire hour.

"No!" exclaimed Alison.

"Yes! Your mom will freak out if you go and she realizes what's going on."

"She's only going to freak out a fraction less when you go!"

Alison poured herself a cup of coffee, probably to keep her hands busy because she stared blankly at it after she was done.

There was a soft knock on the door and Delacroix leaned in. "The doc is here for another update."

Alison stared at Vivian with a panicked look in her eyes.

"It's going to be good news," Vivian promised.

"He looked me in the eye," said Delacroix. "Usually if it's bad news they avoid eye contact."

"Fingers crossed," said Alison. "Tell Mom, I'll be right there."

Delacroix left and Alison pulled keys out of her pocket. "I'm in the P-1 parking lot, second level. Stall 282. Black beamer."

"I'll be as quick as I can," promised Vivian. "Tell Delacroix I'm staying in here to make a phone call."

Vivian waited until Alison had distracted Delacroix and then slipped quickly down the hallway and into the stairs. She tried to jog down to the parking lot, but her bruises protested. Getting thrown on the rocks and then having Mark land on top of her was more of a thing than she thought it had been originally. Not that she would admit that to Rowan—Mr. Walks Through Bullets himself—that, but she would need more Motrin at some point.

She found Alison's car and got out of the maze of the Harborview campus as quickly as possible. Vivian thought if she moved quickly enough there was half a chance she could even be back at the hospital before Rowan knew she was gone.

Nine minutes later, which was faster than Google's estimate she pulled up to the house. Howard and Nadine lived in a French-Normandy three-story home in Denny-Blaine. The neighborhood was one of the richest in Seattle and Vivian felt a creeping case of classism, a need to keep up with the Joneses, and possibly an impending eating disorder just by visiting. She didn't understand how Howard and his family managed to be as normal as they were. She fumbled through the key ring as she approached the front door. It took her a few tries to find the correct key, but then she was in.

Vivian gently shut the door behind her, and paused in the entryway, flipping the keys around in her hand. She hadn't visited the house that many times—it took her a moment to remember the layout. After a moment's hesitation, she turned left and went down the hall through a rounded archway. The walls were a crisp cream and the wood floors were a dark walnut. She knew that Nadine had used an interior designer, someone flamboyant named Eduardo who split his time between Seattle and Miami. She remembered his visits to the office. And yet, none of the designer's personal color was apparent in the house. She wondered if it had killed his soul a little bit to create such a tastefully vanilla home.

Vivian stood in the doorway to the library that served as Howard's home office. Like the arches, it was also rounded at the top, which meant the door was custom. The furnishings were lovely, but having listened to Rowan making decisions for his house, she realized it was the door that impressed her. She also realized how much better she liked Rowan's eclectic taste and tendency toward color and luxe textures. The quiet-luxury look would never do for him.

Vivian frowned at the room. There wasn't a filing cabinet or any loose piles of papers for the will to get lost in. A wall of books and cabinetry wrapped around a pair of chairs and everything looked cozy rather than functional. The table next to the armchair had a small decorative stone plinth. It looked like the blandly tasteful but meaningless decorative object that got put in showcase houses. She wondered if Howard actually liked that kind of thing, if he even thought about it, or if he just liked that Nadine was happy.

She crossed the room and opened the middle cabinets to reveal a computer and printer-scanner combo. She reached under the edge of the counter and pulled. It telescoped out into a small, but efficient desk. She nudged the mouse and it popped up with the identical log-in as the work computers. That meant that he'd been accessing work files.

Her phone rang and she saw Rowan's face. Taking a deep breath, she picked up. She had known it would be a fight when she left the hospital, but he had to see that this was important.

"Vivian," he said promptly and Vivian tried to stop the delicious shiver that ran down her spine. How did he always do that?

"Hi," she said.

"Delacroix is freaking out because you left him." Rowan had the uber calm tone that told her he was on the far side of the water from tranquil and happy.

"He said it was going to be an hour before anyone else showed up," said Vivian. "I didn't have time."

"Do you have something against being safe?" said Rowan. He sounded exasperated.

"The police are moving too slowly. Chucky isn't going to wait for them. I need to do this for Howard."

"You couldn't wait twenty minutes for an escort?"

Vivian got a sinking feeling.

"It wasn't going to be twenty minutes. Both you and Delacroix said it would be an hour."

"It was an hour under the original plan. We could have changed the plan. I respect your right to make your own decisions, and I also want to find the will. But that was not safe and I wish you would have called me. We could have come up with alternatives together that didn't involve you putting yourself in a risky situation."

She was used to arguing with Rowan, but this wasn't an argument. It was him disagreeing and having valid points about how to accomplish shared goals. He was literally an expert at what he did and she had run off because she felt bossed around. It was entirely possible that she really did have a tiny problem with authority.

"I... Well, shit."

"What?" he demanded his voice intensifying.

"I'm going to have to apologize to you because I was wrong and I really dislike that."

There was an odd clunk out in the hallway and Vivian felt her heartrate pick up.

Rowan let out an annoyed laugh. "I suggest you bring chocolate. It seems to help. Meanwhile, I take it you've made it to Howard's?"

"Yes," she said, looking around the room. Howard didn't have any closets to jump into. What was she supposed to do now?

Chucky walked in, a gun in his hand, and Vivian realized she really was going to have to apologize to Rowan. If she lived through this.

"Hang up," Chucky said softly. He looked even puffier than usual and for some reason he chosen to wear plaid golf pants while committing felonies.

"Well, Courtney, thanks for calling. I'll gather up Howard's things and bring them back to the office on Monday."

"Viv?" Rowan's voice was sharp. "Is he there?"

"Yeah, I hear you, but I need to hang up so I can look at this mess Howard's got going on."

Chucky gestured impatiently with the gun.

"I'm almost there," said Rowan. "Do whatever you have to do. Do not let him take you off the property."

"OK, see you on Monday," said Vivian.

"I love you."

Vivian hung up the phone.

35
Rowan

INFILTRATION

Rowan blasted through the stoplight while tapping the emergency code into his phone. Moments later, Mark rang through on the car's call system.

"You just left," said Mark. "What happened?"

"Vivian went to the Hoskins house. We were on the phone. I think Chucky is there. Get the fucking team to my location now."

"On it."

The line went dead. Rowan cut off three cars and went over a curb as he sailed through another intersection.

He reached Denny-Blaine Park and slowed to check the GPS for the second time. He cruised the block, saw the house, and forced himself to keep driving. Parking down the block, he got out and reached into the back for the bag that was always there.

It was cold, and a drifting fog shrouded everything in damp droplets even though it was nearly noon. The neighborhood was quiet and Rowan didn't see anyone out for a stroll, but he wondered how many people peeping at him through the blinds. He trusted the Ferrari would buy him some time before anyone called the cops. People in expensive cars didn't commit crimes, right?

He yanked open the bag, his hands clammy. Focus on the job, asshole. He knew the steps. He knew what to do. Vivian needed him to keep it together, but the very fact that it was Vivian was making his brain spin.

Rowan had barely strapped on his vest when a silver Ford Leaf sped by him, screeched to a halt, and then backed up.

"I got the code!" yelled Doc, rolling down his window. "What do I do?"

Rowan wanted to say *go find someone helpful*, but didn't.

"What equipment do you have?"

"I was testing the land drone, so I have the land drone. And… lots of tools?"

"Go park," said Rowan. "I can use the land drone."

A black Dodge Viper pulled up and whipped into a spot ahead of Rowan. Tyrique got out as Viper's trunk began to raise.

"I've got side arms, two assault rifles, and three vests."

"Slap one on Doc. We're using the land drone for infil. I only know about Chucky. I don't know who else is in the house."

"Should we be calling the cops?" asked Doc, as he began to unload equipment from the car.

"Mark will take care of that," said Rowan.

A charcoal gray Ford truck sedately rolled down the street and eventually pulled to a stop in front of Doc's car.

"I cruised the residence," said Jake, climbing out. He made descending from the jacked pickup look easy. "There's a Beamer in the drive way, but I didn't see anything else stirring. So, I tried the alley. There is a van and a Porsche parked in back."

"The Porsche is Chucky's," said Rowan. "Delacroix said Viv left in Alison Hoskins BMW. I saw it parked out front. I was on the phone with her when she cut off. She was able to confirm that Chucky was there, but nothing else."

"The van says he's not alone," said Tyrique, as he attempted to strap doc into a bulletproof vest. Doc didn't want to let go of his gear long enough to get his arms through the holes. Rowan thought he'd had an easier time dressing Olly.

"Agreed," said Jake, grabbing one of Doc's arms and forcing it through a hole. Tyrique slapped the Velcro home before Doc could move again. There was a minor struggle over the second arm but they got the job done.

"OK," said Doc, turning around his arms full of land drone. "If they're parked there, then they probably entered from the back. If you can get me to the edge of the property. We can deploy the drone. I've added a telescoping arm that can lift the camera up to window height and a heat vision lens. So either way we can confirm the number of perps. I shouldn't use perps. I'm not that cool. There are probably people. We will see people."

"OK, Jake, you're with Doc. I've got two com sets. Jake gets one. Tyrique gets the other. Doc, you tell Jake whatever you want. Jake, you tell Tyrique what we need to know. You and Doc only advance when Tyrique or I give the go ahead."

"Right," said Jake, putting the com earpiece on and attaching the rest of his set to his belt. Tyrique did the same.

"Oh," said Doc, hoisting the land drone higher in his arms. "We're really doing this. OK."

"Well, they're doing this," said Jake reassuringly. "You and I are just going to take a walk and test the new toy."

"Right," said Doc, fixating on Jake. "Just like other tests. No big deal."

"Right," agreed Jake, leading Doc away.

Rowan watched them go. His arm throbbed, but he didn't have time to pay attention to it. He waited until they were further away before pulling the assault rifle out of Tyrique's trunk.

"Tyrique," said Rowan. "We're going to have this conversation and then you're going to forget it. If Vivian doesn't make it out, then they don't make it out. If that's a problem, I need to know now."

"No, sir," said Tyrique. "Not a problem. But we're going to make sure she's home in time for dinner." He put his hand up to his ear. "Coms are online. Doc and Jake have reached the alley. They're launching Doc's souped up RC car now."

"OK," said Rowan nodding and slamming down the trunk.

"Then let's do this."

It took a few minutes to work their way close to house. Ahead of them, the land drone moved slowly along the base of the house on its chunky wheels.

"Doc says that we've got four individuals in the room on the other side of that wall." Tyrique paused. "Say again." Tyrique's stricken glance at Rowan, said everything that needed to be said.

"Just say it, Tyrique."

"Doc says there's a fifth person lying down and judging from the heat signature…"

"It's a body, not a person," said Rowan. "Got it. We're going to approach the south corner and come in through the French door."

Tyrique nodded. They hurried forward and then paused against the wall. Rowan risked a quick glance through the glass panes of the door. He could see a dining room on the other side and beyond an archway the kitchen. He realized that although the door was closed, that it had previously been kicked open. The handle and lock dangled at an awkward angle.

"Doc says we have movement," whispered Tyrique. "Two individuals leaving the kitchen."

"You don't have to push!" Vivian's voice was faint through the door, but it was still clearly her voice and Rowan breathed out a sigh of relief.

"Doc visually confirms two individuals remaining in the kitchen. Guns on the table. They're going through the fridge." Tyrique whispered.

"This is our window then. We'll go in as quiet as possible and get Vivian."

Tyrique nodded as Rowan swung the door silently open.

"On my signal," said Rowan, readying himself.

36
Vivian

CHUCKY

Vivian's pulse pounded as she hung up the phone. She hadn't even gotten to say *I love you* back. What if the last thing she ever said to Rowan was that she would see him Monday?

"Charles, what are you doing here? What is going on?"

She needed to stall until Rowan came to rescue her. Damn it, that was embarrassing. And so fucking reassuring. Rowan would come for her. She could make it out of this. She wasn't alone.

"Like you don't know," he sneered.

"I don't, actually. Howard's in the hospital. I'm collecting things for work. What are you doing here? Nadine didn't say anything about giving anyone else keys."

She didn't know why, but she wanted him to admit it. She wanted hear him say with his lying mouth that he'd put Howard in the hospital.

"Not dead?" he demanded.

"No," said Vivian. She fought to keep the anger off her face, but then wasn't sure she should bother.

"Joel!" Chucky yelled. "The old man isn't dead!"

"It doesn't matter," said a quiet voice. Behind Chucky, another man appeared. He wore jeans, Asics, and a fleece and looked like any other white guy around Seattle, but Vivian knew she would have avoided him on the street. He had an odd air of menace that she couldn't account for. Then she saw the gun tucked in the front of his waist band. Unlike Chucky's gun, which was a grimy revolver that she doubted had ever been cleaned, Joel's gun was a serviceable black Ruger. She could see the angry phoenix logo on the handle.

"It *does* matter," said Chucky. "He can testify that Dad signed the will."

Joel looked like Chucky was working his last nerve.

"What's his condition?" Joel asked looking past Chucky to Vivian.

"He's in the ICU," said Vivian. "He's in critical condition."

Joel shrugged. "See? Plus, he's old. Odds are he won't make it."

Chucky grunted and looked annoyed.

"You're the secretary chick, right?" asked Joel.

"I'm a paralegal," said Vivian. Joel shrugged again.

"Yeah. You're the girl in the red dress that the other guy picked up." A chill ran down Vivian's spine as she realized Joel meant Mark. Joel had been in the car. "Do you know where Hoskins put the will?"

"I just came to pick up stuff for work," said Vivian.

"She knows," said Chucky, impatiently. "She and Howard worked together. He always said she did all the hard work. So, she knows."

"Just shoot her and we'll keep looking," said Joel. He said it casually. Like he was telling Chucky to take out the trash.

"We *have* been looking and it isn't upstairs. It wasn't at the office. He's put it somewhere. She'll be able to find it."

Joel took a deep breath.

"Joel?" said another, more hesitant voice from out in the hall. "I think Dave's… I think he's dead."

"OK, paralegal," said Joel, gesturing to her. "Come on."

"I'm calling the shots," said Chucky, still glaring at Vivian. The look Joel gave the back of Chucky's head said that he wouldn't be calling anything for very much longer.

"Call them back in the kitchen," said Joel. "Come on."

Chucky came forward and grabbed her arm, pulling her out into the hall. The second man wore work-out pants and a University of Washington sweatshirt. He looked too skinny, his face was pocked mark, and he twitched nervously when he saw her. Vivian didn't know what his problem was, but she was going to go out on a limb and guess drugs.

They trooped down the hall and went into the kitchen. Vivian tried to walk slowly. How much time did Rowan need? How long until Joel got annoyed enough to shoot her?

The kitchen was French Provencial to go with the exterior of the house. The white cabinetry was off-set with touches of oil-rubbed bronze and now splashes of blood. There was a half-mopped trail of blood leading across the travertine tile floor toward the pantry. Through the door way she could see someone's feet. The sight brought her up short and Joel reached back and pulled her all the way into the room.

"Keep an eye on her," Joel ordered and went into the pantry. Kneeling down, by the man's side, he put a hand out. Vivian held her breath as Joel checked for a pulse.

"I checked," said the skinny guy, crossing his arms over chest. Vivian couldn't tell if the gesture was defensive or an attempt to comfort himself.

"You know," said Joel, standing up and looking down at the body, "when you told us about this job, you said there would be minimal security. You didn't say anything about guys with guns."

"It was a charity event," snapped Chucky. "Howard goes every year. He always convinces my dad to write a check. I even went like two years ago or something. There wasn't any security or cops or anything. I keep telling you—I don't know who those guys were."

"Do you know, paralegal?" asked Joel looking up.

"They were guests."

"Do your guests always pack that much heat?" asked Joel, scrutinizing her.

"I think those ones always do, yes. They work for a private

security firm."

"So they just happened to be there? Well, aren't we lucky," said Joel. His voice still hadn't risen. He looked as if all of this were a mild inconvenience.

"Dave's not lucky," said the skinny man quietly.

"Shut up, Eddie," said Joel. "Your talking gives me a headache."

Eddie's mouth pinched shut in a flat line, but he didn't speak again.

"See?" demanded Chucky. "I couldn't have known they were going to be there. Now we just need to make her tell us where the will is."

"She says she doesn't know."

"She knows something."

"Maybe she does and maybe she doesn't and maybe I'm tired of listening to you. So far all you've managed to do is get Dave killed. We aren't any closer to getting that will."

"You haven't come through with anything and I already gave you ten grand," said Chucky, impatiently.

"Which bought you this much of my time, but the meter is running again."

"I paid you for a job," snapped Chucky. "A job that you haven't completed. Hoskins and the girl are still alive and I don't have the will. So as far as I'm concerned, you're not getting another penny until I see results."

Vivian looked around the kitchen, hoping for some inspiration or a weapon. There was a gun on the table but Chucky and Eddie were between it and her. Eddie looked miserable and if she could get him alone, Vivian was pretty sure she could talk him out of whatever this was. But the way Eddie kept his eyes fixed on Joel convinced her that Eddie wasn't the threat in the room. Joel and Chucky continued to argue and Vivian wondered how long it would be until Joel got tired of listening to the whining.

"We don't have to finish searching the upstairs! Make her do it."

He pointed at Vivian.

Vivian might have a better shot of finding the will than these idiots, but she didn't plan to help them. On the other hand, maybe she could hide it if she found it.

"Fine," said Joel. "Eddie, take the paralegal upstairs. Make her finish the family room."

"OK," said Eddie, picking up the gun off the table. He gestured to Vivian with it and Vivian didn't argue. Instead, she went out to the hall and began to climb the stairs.

"You know, Eddie, you could just walk out the front door," she said quietly.

"What?"

"Chucky already paid you, right? You're already in enough trouble. You don't need any more of his stupidity. Just leave."

"Joel has all my money," said Eddie. "He said I wouldn't show up if he paid me up."

They turned at the landing, and Vivian grabbed the handrail for support. The Motrin was wearing off. She turned right and went into the family room. It was an expansive room with tall windows overlooking the street. As she watched, a dark gray pickup truck drove slowly by, but nothing else moved on the road. The cupboards had all been emptied and papers dumped everywhere, but Vivian didn't think there was that much more to do. She picked up one of the paper piles and began to sift through it. Eddie went to stand nervously by the door, where he seemed to be listening for Joel.

"Eddie," she said after a minute, "the will isn't up here. Howard wouldn't ever leave it in some random place in the house. And the fact is that the longer you're here, the more danger you're in. The cops know that wasn't a random drive-by and eventually it will occur to them to come here. Money or no money, you ought to leave. We can just go downstairs and go out the front door."

"Joel would kill me," said Eddie, shaking his head.

"OK, let's just go back downstairs," said Vivian. "If we're lucky

Joel will have shot Chucky and we can all move on with our lives."

Eddie half-chuckled. "Chucky? Do people call him that?"

"It's what I call him," said Vivian. "He's a douchebag."

"Yeah, that's for sure."

"I'll look at the rest of these piles," said Vivian. "But it's not here. Then we go back downstairs."

"Yeah, OK," said Eddie, plucking nervously at the cuff of his sweatshirt.

Vivian flipped through the other piles. They looked like the usual conglomeration of random notes, instructions, receipts, and other detritus of modern living, but none of them were legal documents. It had been nearly ten minutes, so Vivian finally stood up and walked toward the door. Eddie shrugged and went with her.

She wondered what he'd do if she turned right instead of left at the bottom of the stairs and just went out the front door. But she wasn't ballsy enough to try it so they walked back to the kitchen.

Joel had run a dish towel over the trail of blood on the floor and thrown it on top of Dave's body. Chucky sat at the kitchen table, checking his phone and talking as if his mouth was on autopilot. As she watched, Joel pulled a jug of orange juice from the fridge and tipped it straight into his mouth.

"And that's another thing," continued Chucky.

"Not there," said Vivian, not bothering to wait for Chucky to stop talking.

"Then where did he put it?" demanded Chucky.

"I don't know, Chucky," said Eddie. "Maybe he shoved it up your ass."

Joel laughed around the jug of OJ and then had to wipe a dribble off his chin.

"My name is Charles!"

"I like Chucky," said Joel. "I think your name is Chucky."

"It's Charles," hissed Chucky.

Above the window sill, behind Chucky, a small device

appeared—like a camera on a stick. Someone was outside. She looked around the kitchen. Was Rowan on his own? Would he be able to take all three of them? Would it be better if she separated them? Could she separate them?

Eddie started to turn toward the window.

"I think I know where the will is," Vivian blurted out and they all focused on her again.

"You just said you didn't," said Chucky. "You've been saying you didn't this whole time."

"Yeah, but I think I just figured it out," said Vivian.

"Fine. Where is it?" Chucky sounded like he didn't believe her. She supposed that no one could be as stupid as he looked.

"Well, you said you searched upstairs. And I know it wasn't at work. That means it's in the office here."

"I didn't see any papers on that trick desk," said Chucky. "Is there a secret drawer somewhere or what?"

"No," said Vivian, trying to work it out as she spoke. "Nadine said that he came home from golf with your father and went directly into the office."

She remembered that the computer screen had been the work log-in and realized what Howard had done. He'd come home and gone directly to the office to get the document securely into the work records. That meant he'd scanned it. She was going to bet money that if she searched the database the will would already be there. But she didn't want to tell Chucky that because if she was right, he was already shit out of luck.

"I think he went to photocopy it and got distracted. I bet it's still in the copier."

Chucky rolled his eyes. "Old men can't even figure out how to work their phones. Who was ever going to look *in* the damn copier?"

"Not you apparently," said Joel. "Go get it."

Chucky reached out and grabbed Vivian by the arm.

"You don't have to push," barked Vivian, sharply shoving

Chucky's hand away.

"I will push whatever I want to," snarled Chucky.

"Stop touching the girl and fucking go get the will," snapped Joel. "I want to get out of here."

Chucky looked angry but didn't say anything. Vivian stomped down the hall.

"Look," she said loudly, swinging open the office door so it made a loud bang.

Vivian hoped she was loud enough to keep the two in the kitchen distracted, but she didn't know if that was the right thing to do or not.

"You can just take the will and get out of here," she said keeping her voice loud.

"Yeah," said Chucky. "That's what I'm going to do."

"Why are you even bothering?" demanded Vivian crossing the room to the desk. "You are getting money one way or another. What do you care if it's got an extra zero or not?"

"What do I care? That is *my* money."

"It's your father's money," said Vivian.

"It's mine. I have had to put up with all of his wives and all his stupid ass shit for too many years to get cheated now. I'm not forking over one single dime to that harlot of a wife of his or her brat."

"You mean your sister."

"Maybe she's my sister. Maybe not. He never got a paternity test like I told him too. That money is mine."

"And for that, it's worth killing Howard?" Vivian asked, lifting the lid of the scanner on top of the printer.

Sure enough, there was a document inside.

"Don't kid yourself, Vivian. As soon as I get that will, I'll have Joel put you in the pantry next to Dave."

"Too chicken to do it yourself?" asked Vivian looking down at the will.

"Why should I get my hands dirty? Although, if you made it

worth my while maybe we could come to some sort of agreement."

She had reached out to pick up the will when she felt his hand on her ass. The anger that had been welling up inside her suddenly crystallized into something hard and sharp.

"Get your damn hands off me," she said straightening up.

"I'll be fucking you one way or another, you know," sneered Chucky. "It doesn't really matter. You don't have any *friends* with Ferraris around to protect you. You should be nice and maybe I'll be nice to you."

There was a shrill yell from the kitchen and a bang as if something very hard had been hit by something else.

"What—"

Chucky turned toward the noise, his gun swinging away from her. Vivian whirled, clamped one hand down over the gun, forcing it even further away from her. With the other hand, she hauled back and punched Chucky as hard as she could in the eye. He staggered, and she wrenched the gun away as she hit him again and then a third time. He seemed disoriented, but that wasn't good enough. She reached out and grabbed the decorative stone plinth off the table next to the armchair and swung for his head.

He finally let go of the gun and toppled over, hitting the carpet chin first. She spun the gun around in her hand so it was pointing at Chuck and stopped, panting, when he didn't move. The door slammed open, bouncing off the wall, and Vivian raised her plinth and the gun.

Rowan stood in the doorway, a rifle pointing at Chucky. His frame was tensed, pushing forward in carefully restrained energy and a grim expression on his face, but he was the most beautiful thing that Vivian had ever seen.

"Rowan, I don't want to see you Monday," Vivian wailed, dropping the gun and *objet d'arte*.

"What?" His gun came down and instead of feeling better, Vivian burst into tears.

"I love you," she sobbed.

"Baby," he said, coming forward and putting an arm around her.

She tried to say all the things, but between the tears and her face being stuck in his chest, it probably sounded like a Muppet in a windstorm.

"You love me and we got in a fight and all you got to say was that you would see me on Monday?" he asked, holding her tight and kissing the top of her head.

"Yes!"

"It's OK," he said, soothingly. "I knew that was what you meant."

"Rowan?" someone yelled down the hall.

"Yeah!" Rowan yelled back. "We're good."

"Is Vivian OK?" asked Tyrique appearing in the doorway. "Jake's sitting on the other two."

"She's upset because she said she would see me Monday."

"Um…" said Tyrique.

Vivian straightened up and tried to wipe tears off her face. "Nadine is going to be so mad," she said looking down at Chucky. "He is bleeding all over her carpeting."

"Yeah," said Tyrique, nodding. "Rowan dented the fridge with that other guy's head too."

"Fuck that guy," said Vivian.

"Baby, I really do love you so much," said Rowan.

"Aww," said Vivian, and melted against him. She knew she probably looked a mess, but it didn't matter when he kissed her.

37
Vivian

LEADERSHIP QUALITIES

Vivian knew she only had one shoe on, but she stared at her phone while holding the other high heel in her hand.

They had been at the police station most of the day answering questions and filling out statements. Vivian had gone with one of her more lawyer-y looks with heels and a dress that hugged her curves, but ended below the knee. Rowan thought the police just didn't like them for going rogue. But the detective had treated her like an idiot when she'd shown up in leggings, so Vivian had thought it was better to dress like a boss. The police still hadn't liked them today, but the District Attorney appeared to think they were excellent witnesses, so the dress had been the correct decision. The detective had also let slip that they'd pulled Howard's phone records and discovered that Chucky had been the one to call Howard and lure him out to the curb. Teddy finding the vehicle had been the nail in the coffin when it came to the case and because of that Vivian thought Rowan and the rest of the team would skate by without any reprimands. Ms. Branch had shown up to the bail hearings to personally ensure that Joel, Eddie, and Chucky wouldn't be getting out any time soon. Making enemies of lawyers had consequences and Hoskins, Branch, and Kato wanted everyone to know it.

And that had been their day. It had been tiring, but at least it had felt like Chucky and the others would get what they deserved. Vivian had answered a phone call from Father Fred right after they'd gotten home and stopped in the living room while Rowan went to change. Rowan was utterly oblivious that TikTok had nominated gray sweatpants as the male outfit of fall sexiness, but he inhabited the trend like the daddy he was.

"Baby? You doing OK over there?" he asked as he went toward the kitchen.

"Ashley…" She paused, uncertain about how to explain the phone call. "She did what I didn't want her to do."

"What did she do?" he asked coming back into the living room.

"She told Father Fred about this crazy idea of hers."

"Which one?"

"The one where I apply to be the next Executive Director of Victory Mission."

"Mm," said Rowan, nodding.

"You're not laughing."

"Why would I laugh?"

"Because… I'm not a director of anything?"

"And I wasn't a CEO until I was," said Rowan with a shrug.

"Well, she told Chappie and of course he thought it was a great idea and then he…" She rubbed at her neck nervously. "He floated it by the Board."

"Oh. So, we're moving on this."

"You're still not laughing."

"It's still not funny. What do we do? Do we need to make you a resume?"

"Um… Yes. I'm supposed to officially submit a resume and a letter of interest so they can vote on it."

"But he wouldn't tell you to do that unless they were going to vote yes."

"Apparently, me bossing everyone around at the gala was considered very impressive and displayed leadership." Vivian looked down at the shoe in her hand, trying to remember how it got there.

This time, Rowan did laugh. "I told you I thought the tactical response went well. You even paused to make a statement to the press that made Victory Mission and Valkyrie sound like fucking rockstars and worked in a mission statement and where to donate. Who does that?"

"I'm pretty sure I can do a *where to donate* in my sleep. Chappie did say our donations have been up since the incident." She slipped out of the other shoe and put the pair next to each other on the floor.

"Yeah. They'd be idiots not to give you a shot. You are leadership material AF." He went back into the kitchen and opened the wine fridge.

"What are you looking for?" asked Vivian, trailing him into the kitchen.

"Champagne. I'm going to be sleeping with the boss."

Vivian laughed. Rowan found a bottle and pulled it out.

"You don't think it's a little premature?"

"Uh… no. The bad guys are in jail and you just got invited to submit a resume. *Invited.* That is code for you got the job. If this isn't a champagne night, I don't know what is."

Vivian watched as he unwound the wrapper from the bottle.

"Wait until I tell the guys," he said. "They really are going to start calling you General." His smile stretched from ear to ear. He was proud of her. Vivian's heart did a little flip-flop and for some reason she wanted to cry.

"I want to see how far I can launch the cork," said Vivian. "Can I do that?"

"Yes," he said laughing. "Come on. We'll go out on the deck."

The backyard was still a mud pit from all the construction equipment. The landscaping was set to go in next week and then there would be a firepit with seating and a full outdoor kitchen. Vivian tried to ignore that she was dating above her income level, but she couldn't help being excited about some of the amenities Rowan brought to the table. Girl's night with s'mores was going to be a thing. She also couldn't help but notice that Rowan seemed to have designed his remodel with others in mind. There were four bedrooms and extra bathrooms and a big dining room so that there could be a whole group in the house. Rowan had designed a family home—not a bachelor pad.

"Here you go," said Rowan handing her the bottle of champagne. "Knock it out of the park."

The air was cold, but for once the sky was clear and the setting sun painted everything in mottled shades of orange and pink. The water sparkled in the distance and a light ray shone on the oil plant across the water at Gas Works Park.

But after a few seconds of trying, Vivian gave up with a laugh. "I'm not knocking it anywhere. I can't get the stupid cork out."

"I got you," he said wrapping his arms around her and adding his hands to hers on the neck of the bottle.

"Teamwork," said Vivian, wiggling herself tighter against his him.

"Mm," he said, half laughing, and nibbling at her earlobe. "I like your idea of teamwork."

"I just want to pop the cork!" protested Vivian, knowing that it was a straight-faced lie.

"You're going to if you keep rubbing up against me like that!"

Vivian giggled as he took a firmer grasp of the bottle.

"OK," he said. "On three. One, two, three!"

She had felt the cork wiggling, but it still surprised her as it shot off into the air, arcing high off the deck and into the mud somewhere. She laughed in surprise as the champagne splashed over their hands. He lifted the champagne bottle and offered it to her.

"Congratulations, Ms. Kaye."

She took a heady swallow of champagne, the bubbles sparking and fizzing down her throat. She handed him the bottle and watched as he took a drink—his eyes still on her. She didn't understand how she had gotten this lucky.

She reached behind her and tugged at her zipper, but didn't let it come down more than a few inches.

"I think I need your help opening something else."

"Do you?" he said, taking another drink out of the bottle.

"Yes," she said. "I'm stuck."

"In your dress?"

"Mm-hmm," she said taking the champagne bottle back. "Very stuck." She tugged at the neckline of her dress, dragging it down a few inches. He grinned as she took another drink.

"Vivian, I think you are…"

She backed away slowly, heading back inside. He came after her, shaking his head, but when he reached for her, she darted toward into the living room.

This time he laughed and gave chase. He zagged around the armchair while she zigged and he pinned her against the couch. With a quick he spun her around and quickly cleared her hair off her neck.

"Funny, but you don't seem very stuck," he said kissing her neck as he dragged her zipper down. She giggled and took another drink of champagne. The dress parted for him and she shivered in delicious anticipation as his hands caressed her skin. Pushing the sleeves from her arms, he worked the dress off of her, leaving her in what she thought of as her serious underwear because it was black and a bit strappy with dominatrix vibes. It also made the girls look amazing.

"Mmm," he groaned as he ran his hands over her breasts. She opened her eyes and realized he could see her in the mirror on the other side of the room. She rubbed her ass up against him, and watched the way he snapped his teeth together, biting air.

"Naughty girl," he purred.

Vivian closed her eyes again, and took another drink. The champagne bubbles popped in her mouth, bright and sharp as his mouth made lazy warm kisses on her neck and his hands made little trails of heat down her body.

"Mmph," she pouted as he stepped away from her, taking his

heat with him. But a moment later, he was back and he was all skin and muscles, pressed up against her. The sweats were now in a pile on the floor somewhere. She could see the bandage on his arm, but he didn't seem bothered by it.

"How about this thing?" he said, tugging at her bra strap. "Having trouble getting out of that too?"

"So much trouble," she murmured, twisting to kiss him.

Her bra went ping and then the girls were no longer being held up and as he gently pulled it off her. She needn't have worried about a lack of support because his hands took over. She breathed out in a soft moan. Being with Rowan meant that she didn't have to think about anything. He was the ultimate sinful decadence for a woman—he was the ability to stop worrying.

She pushed away from the couch, trying to kiss him more fully, and his hand slid between her thighs, gliding gently along the outside of her panties.

"Nope," he said abruptly pulling back.

"Mm?" Vivian looked up at him in confusion.

"I was thinking about the couch. And nope. I'm all for furniture fetishes, but right now I want you naked on my damn bed and I do not fucking care if I get champagne all over the sheets."

Vivian giggled and lifted the bottle to her lips and filled her mouth enough that trickled down her throat and onto her cleavage.

"Works for me," she said. "Race you there."

She meant to run off directly after that, but he was too quick. He wrapped an arm around her waist and hefted her off the ground. She shrieked in laughter as he put her over his shoulder and marched toward the bedroom.

She was slung down on the bed and relieved of the champagne bottle and one smooth move. Vivian put her hands behind her head and stretched out on the bed, letting him get an eyeful while he downed the wine. Then he stretched out his arm and dribbled champagne right onto her stomach.

She gave a little squeal, but he was on her in a second, licking the cold liquid off with his hot tongue. Bubbles frothed over her breasts, followed by his mouth, sucking, licking, and making her moan. By the time he poured champagne into her open mouth, she was wet from more than just the wine.

"Rowan," she gasped.

He pushed inside her and Vivian let out a groan of pure satisfaction. Each thrust was glorious perfection. As the heat began to rise between them, Vivian clung to him. She wanted the moment to last forever, but could feel her orgasm building. She alternated between gasping for air and holding her breath, unable to control even her own lungs.

"Oh God," she moaned. "Please Rowan. I need..."

His fingers clenched in her hair at the nape of her neck, forcing her to arch and it was just what she needed.

"Oh God, yes, yes, yes!"

He finished a moment after her and Vivian wrapped her arms and legs around him, trying to squeeze him so tight to her that he would feel all of her love.

"I love you so much," she whispered.

He pushed away from her, looking down at her with his golden hazel eyes. She thought he would speak, but instead he shook his head and leaned down to kiss her. His mouth was a tantalizing butterfly that teased her before pressing into her with a deep hunger.

"I love you literally more than I can say," he whispered back.

EPILOGUE
ONE WEEK LATER

Rowan leaned back on the couch and watched Vivian in the kitchen dancing to whatever she'd put on the stereo. Some band he'd never heard of called Teddy Swims. The groove was hot. But then, anything Vivian danced to was all right with him. The Halloween Festival had been an unmitigated success. His brothers had been charming, and Olly had been a delight. Vivian's Halloween costume of Miss Frizzle from the Magic School Bus had the toddler seeing stars.

Rowan pulled out his phone and put in a message to his brothers.

I'M REALLY GLAD YOU GUYS HIT IT OFF WITH VIVIAN. I PROBABLY SHOULD HAVE MENTIONED THAT SHE MOVED IN WITH ME, BUT IT FELT WEIRD TO TELL YOU THAT WE WERE DATING AND LIVING TOGETHER ALL IN THE SAME CONVERSATION. I GUESS I DON'T HAVE MUCH PRACTICE WITH INTRODUCING YOU TO MY GIRLFRIENDS. LIVING IN THE SAME TOWN WITH YOU IS KIND OF NEW TERRITORY.

Ash's response came through almost immediately.

OK, THANKS FOR CLARIFYING BECAUSE I WAS TRYING TO FIGURE OUT HOW TO ASK ABOUT THE LIVING SITUATION WITHOUT ASKING. FOR THE RECORD, I THINK VIV IS AWESOME. NO CLUE HOW YOU GOT THAT LUCKY, BUT TWO THUMBS UP.

Rowan nervously tapped at his phone, waiting for Forest to reply.

OLLY MAY BE CALLING HER MISS FRIZZLE PERMANENTLY. TELL HER SORRY IN ADVANCE.

Ash tagged Forest's message with a laughing face and sent a Miss Frizzle gif.

I THINK OLLY CAN CALL HER WHATEVER HE WANTS. SHE JUST SPENT FIVE MINUTES TELLING ME HOW HE WAS THE MOST ADORABLE

THING ON THE PLANET. AND THEN FOLLOWED THAT UP WITH HOW LUCKY I WAS TO HAVE SUCH NICE BROTHERS. I KNOW I'M LUCKY, BUT YOU GUYS HELP ME LOOK GOOD. THANKS.

His phone was now full of Olly and Vivian pictures. Tentatively, he picked out one with Chloe, Forest's new nanny, Vivian, and Olly and sent one to the family text thread.

Ash immediately responded with a picture of Rowan, Vivian, and Olly. And then a moment later, one of Chloe, Forest, and Olly.

Rowan hearted both of them.

A second text bubble popped up from Ash.

OK, YES, I LOVE VIV. SHE'S SMART, PRETTY, YADA YADA YADA. CAN WE TALK ABOUT CHLOE AND FOREST?

Rowan laughed.

"Something funny?" called Vivian.

"Ash wants to talk about Chloe and Forest."

"Oh, my God, yes!" Vivian came out of the kitchen waving a wooden spoon. "What was that? Tell me I'm not the only one who thought there was a thing there?"

"No, I thought there were definite vibes," said Rowan and Vivian nodded, pleased with his agreement, and returned to the kitchen.

VIVIAN THINKS THERE'S SOMETHING THERE.

DO YOU THINK THERE'S SOMETHING?

Rowan couldn't tell what tone Ash meant the text to have.

YES, BUT I THOUGHT THERE WAS SOMETHING WHEN HE SENT THE PUDDLE VIDEO. DON'T GIVE HIM ANY CRAP. YOU KNOW HE'S BEEN GUN-SHY SINCE VERA.

Over on the family thread, Forest sent a pic of Ash and Olly. Then, an actual message.

WE NEED TO GET ONE OF EVERYBODY TOGETHER AT THANKSGIVING.

Rowan breathed out a sigh of relief. If Vivian was included in what Forest thought of as everybody then everything really was fine. He thumbsed up the message, just as one came through on Ash's private thread.

I DON'T WANT TO GIVE HIM ANY CRAP, BUT SHE'S THE NANNY. THAT CAN'T BE A GOOD IDEA.

Rowan shook his head. Ever since dating Emma, Ash had acquired a snooty streak. Not that dating the nanny couldn't get complicated, but Chloe had seemed so genuine that Rowan couldn't help thinking that she was precisely what Forest needed.

CLIMB DOWN OFF YOUR HIGH HORSE. BESIDES, IT MIGHT NOT BE ANYTHING. IT MIGHT JUST BE FOREST REMEMBERING GIRLS EXIST.

That got a laughing emoji.

"Ash is laughing at Forest," said Rowan, raising his voice to carry to the kitchen. "I hope he doesn't do it in person. Forest has been through the wringer. He deserves someone as sweet as Chloe."

"No one laughs harder than someone who is *not* in love. Wait until it happens to Ash. Then *we* can laugh," said Vivian.

LAUGH ALL YOU WANT. JUST DO IT BEHIND HIS BACK. FOREST DESERVES SOMEONE WHO MAKES HIM HAPPY.

Rowan didn't want Forest to get hung up because Ash made fun of him.

HE DESERVES THE WORLD AFTER WHAT HE'S BEEN THROUGH. HE'S STILL A DORK.

Rowan gave that comment a laughing face, but it occurred to him that sometimes it felt like he didn't really know what was going on with Ash.

Vivian came to the edge of the kitchen area and looked down into the den. She's left the spoon somewhere.

"Rowan?"

"Yeah?" He reached for his wine glass but looked up at her, caught by something nervous in her tone.

"I want babies."

He froze, with his wine glass halfway to his mouth.

"Uh. Now?"

"Not next year, but the year after. So I have a full year at Victory Mission."

"And that's the plan, General?"

Which worked conveniently well with his plans. He'd get the house tidied up, finish the warehouse, and move the company over there, and then they could have the wedding in early September and babies the following year. He liked plans.

"Well... it will be the plan if you agree to it," said Vivian. "I thought I should tell you where I was heading in case you weren't on the same page. But I think we could make cute babies." The last part was said in a hushed whisper.

He grinned. Olly's existence was a persuasive argument in favor of Valkyrie babies.

"I'm in," he said. "And our babies will be the cutest. Now get over here so we can practice the pre-parenting portion."

"Pre-parenting?" she asked, looking puzzled.

"Baby making," he supplied.

Vivian giggled as she scurried across the room and flung herself into his arms. She was still laughing when he planted his mouth on hers.

"You know, Ms. Kaye," he said, pulling back. "When I got in that elevator, I really did not think this was where I was going."

"It's been a bit of a ride."

"Yeah, but I think we should take this one all the way to the top."

"Yes, Mr. Valkyrie," Vivian whispered and kissed him.

THE END

Find out if Chloe and Forest can
catch their own elevator ride to happiness
or if they'll get stuck...

LOVED IT?

WANT A FREE BOOK?

For a free e-book visit:
www.**bethanymaines**.com

Blue Jones just stole Jake Garner's dog. And his heart. But technically the French Bulldog, Jacques, belongs to Jake's ex-girlfriend. And soon Jake is being pressured to return the dog and Blue is being targeted by mysterious attackers. Can Jake find Blue and Jacques before her stalkers do? For Blue, Christmas has never been quite so dangerous. For Jake, Christmas has never been quite so Blue.

WANT MORE ROMANCE FROM BETHANY MAINES?

TRY THE DEVERAUX LEGACY SERIES

The Deveraux Family: wealthy, glamorous, powerful… and in a lot of trouble. Senator Eleanor Deveraux lost her children in a plane crash, but she has a second chance to get her family right with her four grandchildren – Evan, Jackson, Aiden and Dominique. But second chances are hard to seize when politics, mercenaries, and the dark legacy of the Deveraux family keep getting in the way.

TAKE A SNEAK PEEK AT BOOK 1

THE SECOND SHOT

SATURDAY

Maxwell Ames

I have better uses for my mouth.

The words were etched in his brain.

Maxwell Ames looked across the room at Dominique Dever-aux and felt himself physically flinch at a memory-driven whip of embarrassment.

An eighteen-year-old Dominique had arrived at college with an ice queen reputation and a pair of legs that had fueled half the hot dreams on campus. But it hadn't been the legs that had gotten to Max—it had been her lips. Max had taken one look at Dominique and decided he wanted, no, *needed* to know what those lips felt like on his body. And he'd declared, drunkenly, to an entire frat party that he would melt the ice queen. He hadn't doubted for a minute that he could do it. He was a senior. He was a nationally ranked college wrestler—his body showed his effort—and he rarely had to do more than lift a finger to get panties to hit his floor. Perhaps it had been the liquor that had made him stupid, but whatever the reason, he'd simply walked over and told her what he wanted her to do to him. He recognized his mistake the second he heard the words come out of his mouth. Her horrified expression only confirmed how bad-ly he'd misjudged. Then she'd gone from shocked to furious, but instead of slapping him, she'd pulled herself up to her full height, looked him in the eye, and declared loud enough for the rest of the room to hear: *I have better uses for my mouth.* And then he'd stood there and let her pour the entire contents of her red solo cup down his front.

And now, six years later, his father had dragged Max into the

Galbraith Tennis and Social Club and directly into revisiting one of his top ten stupidest moments.

"Dad," said Max, turning to look at his father.

"She donates two-k a year," said his father, staring across the party hall at a woman in beige everything. "She's worth like eighty million. Would it kill her to scrounge a little more change out of the couch cushions for needy kids?"

"Dad," said Max again.

"Yeah, what?" asked Grant Ames, finally making eye contact.

"You didn't say this was a Deveraux party."

"Uh, yeah?" said Grant, looking away again—probably scanning the crowd for more targets. "Oh, that's right. You went to school with them, didn't you? Dominique and Aiden? They're probably around somewhere if you want to dig them up. Eleanor usually commands appearances from the family at these little shindigs."

Eleanor Deveraux was running for congress. Again. Or still. Whichever. These *little shindigs* were fundraising events masquerading as cocktail parties. Max didn't know why she bothered. Her nearest competitor was a bitter Republican that sounded crazy even to his constituents. But his father, always on the hustle, spared no thought about why the party existed—he simply enjoyed that it did. And of course, it hadn't occurred to Grant to mention to Max who was hosting.

After the frat party incident, Max hadn't even had the courage to apologize to Dominique. His only consolation was that during all their other encounters she had treated everyone in the room with an equal amount of cool disdain—he hadn't been singled out. Generally, she hadn't even acknowledged him, let alone what had happened.

"You said we wouldn't be here long," said Max, looking back at Dominique. Her golden blonde hair was longer than the last time he'd seen her, laying in soft waves against her pale skin. Those lips that had made him lose his judgement were painted a wine red that emphasized their size. Her conservative pencil skirt and long-sleeve, high-necked blouse should have taken her allure down a notch, but as far as he could see, she was even more gorgeous than she had been in college.

Max had been with plenty of beautiful women—hell, his last girlfriend had been a model-slash-actress. Dominique shouldn't have been able to make the impact she did. But here it was, six years later, and Dominique still hit him like a Mack truck to the libido even when the only skin he could see was her knees.

"We won't be long, I promise," said Grant, scoping the room, oblivious to the direction of Max's gaze. "I need to make the rounds. Say hi to a few people and then we'll be off for burgers."

It was a lie. Max didn't know why he'd thought his first visit to his father's in over a year might warrant special treatment—particularly, since his entire childhood held evidence to the contrary. He wondered if there was a point in adulthood when a parent's failings stopped mattering so much.

Dominique nodded along as the guy next to her talked. He was a lean, good looking twenty-something with black hair and a designer suit. Max watched in surprise as Dominique burst out laughing at whatever he'd said—Dominique had never been very demonstrative in public. Her laugh made the guy grin, but, still talking, he leaned over and snagged something off her plate. Dominique smacked at his hand, but the man leaned further away, dragging the morsel with him, and popped it into his mouth. She flicked at his ear, miming patently faked annoyance. In equally mock penance, her companion lowered his head and held out his plate and Dominique made a show of selecting something in recompense. The only person he could remember bringing out that sparkle of playfulness in her had been her brother, Aiden. It seemed that the ice queen had been melted after all.

Still chewing his stolen goods, Dominique's companion looked up and scanned the room, homing in on the location of the other Deveraux family members. Max followed the man's gaze to the matriarch, Dominque's stately and poised grandmother, Eleanor, holding court by the bar at the far end of the long, narrow room. Then he shifted to Dominique's red-headed investment manager cousin, Evan, amongst a bevy of Wall Street bros in the middle of the room. And last, Dominique's brother, the equally blonde Aiden, hovering by the buffet table in front of a wide expanse of floor-to-ceiling windows.

All of the Deveraux children had lived with their grandmother after a plane crash had left them orphans sometime during their early teens. Max remembered thinking how nice that had sounded when his father had missed every single one of his college meets and was late for graduation. He supposed it hadn't really been pleasant for the Deveraux cousins, but at least they'd had each other and Eleanor.

Max realized, too late, that the scan was continuing on to the new arrivals in the room, which, in this case, were Max and his father. Max found himself awkwardly making eye contact with the guy and knew that he'd been busted staring at Dominique. He broke eye contact and turned to follow his father.

Max pretended to be absorbed in his father's conversation with a white-collared, black-shirted Jesuit priest. After a few minutes of discussing the endowments and scholarship funds, Max's eyes glazed over and he looked around the room, desperate for anything to take his mind off his desire to blurt out a question about pedophiles. How did anyone take priests seriously anymore? He found himself fidgeting with one of the tiny decorative pumpkins placed on the bar-height tables and biting his tongue.

With Halloween and the election around the corner, the party was decorated in a patriotic harvest theme. The red leaves and orange gourds seemed attractive, but Max thought the hay bales by the buffet table seemed a bit too folksy for the Deveraux, not to mention the tennis club locale. He suspected that the entire reason for their existence was to support the stars-and-stripes-bandana-wearing scarecrow. After all, a politician couldn't fundraise without at least a nod to the flag.

He snuck another glance at Dominique and realized that her boyfriend was scanning again. Same pattern—Deverauxes first, then new arrivals, then the rest of the room. There was something professional in the appraising stare, and Max felt the weight of it resting thoughtfully on him. Max checked his watch and angled so he could watch Dominique and her guy. She chatted in an easy, unaffected way, but at a minute fifteen, her boyfriend made another scan. Then again a minute later. It was definitely a more than a casual glance. Max tried to get a better look at the guy. What was he? Boyfriend, bodyguard, security? The suit was expensive, but he was drinking water as he watched the crowd.

Dominique reached out and put her hand on his arm, tugging impatiently, demanding attention. The guy laughed and complied, turning toward her with an affectionate smile. He was definitely not the hired help. For some reason, that burned. In the intervening six years, Max had put Dominique out of his head. Mostly. Sort of. Max would never have admitted it out loud, ever, under any circumstances, including a court of law, but Dominique had always been one of his go-to fantasies. He was perfectly sure that she hadn't thought about him once in that time. So why did he feel jealous of this guy?

Max turned back to his father and tried to focus on the conversation. Dominique was none of his business. What did he care if she dated someone with an over-active sense of security? None. Of. His. Business.

Grant moved on and Max followed him dutifully, the same way he had when he was twelve. He was a prop to his father's socializing. He met a dozen people and forgot their names instantly. Finally, he turned away from a blocky woman in a Chanel jacket and found his father about to introduce him to Dominique and her date.

"Max, I don't know if you've met Jackson, but you went to school with Dominique. Max is staying with me for a few weeks while—Hey, Frank! Frank! Be right back. I've been trying to get five minutes with that guy all month." Grant buzzed off and left Max staring uncomfortably at Dominique and her date.

"So, Max," said Jackson, his expression derisive, "do you need Dominique to get you another drink? We could send the catering staff out for some beer and solo cups."

Max glanced at Dominique, who was visibly restraining a laugh.

"No," said Max, trying not to feel like an ass—any hope that she'd forgotten him or the incident slipping away. "I think once was enough." Did she really have to tell everyone?

Dominique actually did giggle this time and her boyfriend looked amused by her laughter, but his attention was pulled away.

"Nika, what is Aiden doing?" asked Jackson, looking past Max.

"Um," she squinted toward the door, "exactly what you told him not to do?"

Jackson sighed. "OK, I'll be right back." He ducked around Dominique, his jacket swinging open. For a second, Max clearly saw the strap on a shoulder holster and outline of a gun. Max looked back at Dominque, but she seemed not to notice. She was watching her brother attempting to sneak out of the room and biting into her bottom lip with a frown. She transferred her gaze back to Max and smiled, but it was the same old cold smile.

"I'm glad you can laugh about that uh... incident," he said, deciding to man up and do what he should have done six years ago. He glanced down at the floor and realized that she was only conservative from the ankle up. Her heels were stacked, strapped, and had a black satin bow at each ankle that begged to be untied. "I really apologize for that," he said, tearing his eyes off her feet.

She looked startled and suspicious.

"I was a total asshole," he added.

"Um." She frowned, then smiled—a real smile this time. "Well, apology accepted."

It was his turn to feel surprised. He hadn't expected her to simply believe that he was sorry. "And I wouldn't say total. I'd go ninety-eight percent."

"Ninety-eight percent?"

"Well, I'll give you a one percent discount for being young, dumb and in college."

"Yes," he agreed fervently.

"And another one percent for standing there for the entire cup of beer."

"I knew I'd earned it," he said. She glanced over his shoulder, still following the action across the room.

"Your boyfriend's a little intense," he said.

"My boyfriend? You mean Jacks?"

He wanted to comment on the intimate shortening of their names. Jacks seemed weird, but he liked Nika. On the other hand, it really was none of his damn business.

"Does he always carry a gun?" he asked instead.

"Oh, you know…" she said, trailing off and not answering the question. Max decided that meant the answer was yes. "Grandma has gotten some… Well, they're death threats, really, in the last few weeks. She's chairing that Senate Committee Hearing on Absolex. And nothing brings out the crazies like Big Pharma."

"I don't understand," he said. "I thought that was about government fraud?"

"Absolex falsified research and then sold their drug Zanilex to the VA as a solution to treat complex PTSD. Suicide rates sky-rocketed. Turns out that, in fact, it makes the symptoms of PTSD worse, particularly the paranoia and depression. Or at least that's what Grandma intends to prove. She's going to haul the CEO out on the carpet next week. But ever since the hearings started, she's been getting hate mail."

Max looked around the party. "Where is the Secret Service?"

"None of the threats have been active. It's all kind of vague. And she's not a party leader or anything. So, no Secret Service."

Max frowned. If he had been Eleanor, he would have been

putting his foot down and demanding an investigation. He also wouldn't be hosting a party and looking as relaxed as she did.

"Besides," continued Dominique, "we have Jackson. Although, even he couldn't get her to cancel this stupid party. She claimed that we all just didn't want to go."

He raised an eyebrow and she looked guilty.

"That may be partially true. Anyway, Jacks said if she was going to insist on having the party, we should at least be smart about it. He gave us all rules and hired additional security. Of course, Aiden is not following the rules. I would accuse him of being willful, but it's more likely that he's just not taking the threats seriously."

Max nodded. His memory of Dominique's older brother was a sunny personality to whom nothing serious was allowed to adhere and who never seemed to get mad about anything.

"I expect Jacks will tell him about a secret stash of bourbon under the bar and rope him back in."

"Sounds like Jackson knows what he's doing then," said Max, turning to look at the two men who were now making their way back toward them. Aiden stopped to adjust the bandana on the scarecrow with a disapproving shake of his head.

"He does," agreed Dominique, looking up at him with a flash of a smile, "but Jackson isn't—"

Whatever she had been about to say was drowned out by the sound of a car engine and then a thunderous crash as a car exploded through the windows, slammed through the buffet table, plowed across the room, and buried its nose in the far wall.

FIND OUT WHAT HAPPENS NEXT IN...

THE SECOND SHOT

FOR MORE HILARIOUS MYSTERY...

Book 1 of the San Juan Island Murder Mysteries

An UNSEEN CURRENT

You never know what's beneath the surface.

When Seattle native Tish Yearly finds herself fired and evicted all in one afternoon, she knows she's in deep water. Unemployed and desperate, the 26 year old ex-actress heads for the one place she knows she'll be welcome – the house of her cantankerous ex-CIA agent grandfather, Tobias Yearly, in the San Juan Islands. And when she discovers the strangled corpse of Tobias's best friend, she knows she's in over her head. Tish is thrown head-long into a mystery that pits her against a handsome but straight-laced Sheriff's Deputy, a group of eccentric and clannish local residents, and a killer who knows the island far better than she does. Now Tish must swim against the current, depending on her nearly forgotten acting skills and her grandfather's spy craft, to con a killer and keep them alive.

CHAPTER 1

FIRED VS. QUIT

Personally, I blame the New Kids on the Block.

Tish arrived at Winthrop Design, a premier Seattle architectural firm, in a sunny mood on Monday after a three-day weekend – her first full weekend off in over six months – and went to her desk.

"Did everything go OK on Friday?" asked Tish, sliding into her chair and booting up her computer.

"As far as I know," said Sarah. "I didn't hear anything to the contrary anyway."

"Oh good," said Tish, heaving a sigh of relief. "I just hate leaving Carl in charge of anything, much less a million-dollar proposal."

"All he had to do was look it over, approve it, and hand it to an admin to deliver, right? How badly could he screw that up?" asked Sarah rhetorically.

"Is he in yet? I should ask him about it."

"Haven't seen him," said Sarah. "But you know it's just now eight, so…"

"So he won't be here for at least another hour. Right," said Tish, rolling her eyes.

Or maybe I should have taken a Motrin.

"Hey, has anyone seen Carl?" asked Tim, walking around the corner into the marketing cube nest.

Carl Lyns, the Marketing Director, was a mid-size man who seemed hell-bent on jumbo-sizing himself. In college, he'd born a strong resemblance to Dennis Quaid, with sandy hair, dimples, and an effuse charm that people naturally gravitated to. However, as he moved to the other side of thirty-five, his trendy fitted sweaters had given way to looser and looser shirts that couldn't hide the expanding paunch, and his ebullient personality could no longer disguise an essentially childish nature that resisted any rules or guidelines, even the polite ones – like alerting co-workers to when he wouldn't be present.

"No," said Tish, smiling apologetically at the tall, lanky architect. "We don't expect him for another hour or so."

"But he's scheduled for a meeting with my team on the Henderson project," protested Tim.

"We can try his cell phone," suggested Sarah half-heartedly. She'd given up apologizing for their boss's inability to show up anywhere on time.

"The meeting's in fifteen minutes," said Tim with a sigh that expressed both frustration and a lack of surprise. "Can I just have someone from marketing?"

"Can't have me," said Sarah. "I'm in the Regency meeting in a half hour. Maybe Marta?" Sarah clicked open the group calendar.

"I think I'm free," said Tish looking over her shoulder at the screen. "And apparently Carl's got a doctor's appointment right now, so that's why he's not here."

Among Carl's many faults, besides leaving leftovers at his desk for a week at a time and a refusal to wear headphones because they "hurt his ears," was his failure to adjust the privacy settings on his calendar. Which is how they'd all known about his colonoscopy last month.

"Is he really scheduled to be in Mexico for two weeks next month?" Tish blurted out, pointing at the calendar on-screen. She felt a surge of rage. Carl routinely came in late and left early, all while exhorting them to work extra hard; the unfairness of two weeks off in Mexico made Tish grind her teeth.

"Apparently," said Sarah, shooting her a don't-air-our-dirty-laundry-in-front-of another-department look.

Tim shook his head but didn't go so far as to comment on Mexico. "Well, if you're free, Tish, that'd be great."

"Yeah, she's free till after lunch," said Sarah. "I now pronounce you meeting buddies. Go forth and meet."

Tim laughed. "Thanks. I'll see you in fifteen."

Or maybe it was the six months of reduced pay, increased hours, and the "just shut up and be happy you have a job" attitude.

The meeting rolled into lunch, followed by another meeting. By three, Tish had barely sat down at her desk when Louis rushed up to her desk.

"Didn't the submittal get turned in?" gasped Louis, his eyes wide in panic.

"Yeah, admin drove it over on Friday," said Tish, smiling reassuringly at the Land Use specialist, a quick-witted Texan transplant with curly red hair and a quirky personality. They'd both spent the previous week sinking long hours into a proposal that, if they landed the job, would prevent more layoffs for the Land Use Department.

"I just called my friend at the city building, and he said he hadn't seen it!"

"What?" Tish felt her pulse leap with an involuntary surge of adrenalin. "No… I'm sure he just missed it."

"What if admin took it to the wrong building or something?"

"I went over the address with Everly myself," said Tish. Everly, a middle-aged mother of four, ran the admin staff with an iron fist and mom hugs. Messages delivered to Everly did not go astray.

"Can we check?" asked Louis, tugging nervously at the color of his button-up. "Yeah, we'd better," agreed Tish, already standing.

They found Everly staffing the front desk and the multiple phone lines with a smile.

"What can I help you two with?" Everly asked, smiling even wider.

"The submittal delivery on Friday," said Tish. "Did everything go… OK?" She didn't know how to ask if it had been done at all without sounding rude.

"Jill went over to Marketing at two, like we arranged. Do you want me to page her here and ask?"

"Could you please?" said Tish relieved by Everly's natural handling of the situation. Jill appeared moments later in answer to the overhead page.

"Oh, hey, Tish," said Jill as she approached. "What's up?"

"The submittal delivery on Friday," said Tish for the second time. "How did it go?"

"Oh, I was going to ask you about that," said Jill, a crease forming between her eyebrows. "I went to marketing like you told me to, but Carl said that there wasn't anything to be delivered."

"He said what?" asked Tish, gaping.

"I tried to look on his desk, but he kind of covered up and shooed me away."

"So you didn't deliver anything?" asked Louis, looking white and slightly ill.

"No," said Jill, starting to look scared. "Is everything OK?"

"Carl," hissed Tish. "I knew it! I knew better than to leave him in charge of something important. I bet it's still on his desk."

Storming back to the marketing area trailing Louis and Jill, Tish marched straight to Carl's desk.

Carl's computer was piping out the 1990s R&B and pop that he somehow considered work appropriate. The unholy mix was a perpetual assault on all within earshot, which, thanks to the open concept office, was pretty much everyone in a fifteen-desk radius. Currently, The New Kids on the Block were doing it *Step by Step*. She remembered, with loathing, the way her older cousins had played the song non-stop the summer it came out.

Gritting her teeth, Tish dove into the mountain of papers on the desk, unearthing three work-request slips for projects that were due today, five unsigned expense reports, a birthday card for Marta that they'd ended up replacing, a bag of donuts, and a pair of shoes. Tish

tossed the shoes angrily onto the floor and picked up the next item –
a brochure for Vertical Banded Gastroplasty at the Cosmetic Center
of Mexicali, Mexico – and underneath, saw her proposal with a glob
of marinara sauce on the custom cover she had designed.

"What are you doing?" boomed Carl, striding into the office.

The tinny, synth-pop sound of NKOTB filled her ears as she
pivoted around to face her boss.

Or maybe it really was just the New Kids on the Block.

"Me!" gasped Tish, whirling around to face Carl. She could feel
her face flush with a riptide of anger. "What the hell do you think
you're doing?!" She shook the submittal in his face. "I left you with
one thing to do. One thing! Hand the submittal to Jill. That was all
you had to do!"

A crowd was beginning to gather now, but Tish couldn't seem
to stop herself from yelling. Dimly she was aware that this was the
point of no return. This was her chance to close her mouth and
storm off; she'd be in the doghouse for a week, but she'd probably
keep her job. She tried to think about that, but all she could hear was
the bass beat of the New Kids song.

"I don't appreciate your tone!" yelled Carl.

"And I don't appreciate that you blew off a million dollars worth
of work that would save your co-workers' jobs because you were
too busy eating a meatball sandwich and thinking about getting your
stomach stapled, you lazy, slacker bastard!" bellowed Tish, using all
of her training to make every word reach the farthest corners of the
office.

Carl went white. "Fired!" he burst out. "You're fired. You are
FIRED!!"

"You can't fire me," said Tish, suddenly calm. There was a
speech in her head somewhere about Carl's dire lack of self-aware-
ness, management skills, and fashion sense. But, as per usual for
Tish, when she was acting without a script, it didn't come out right.
"I quit. I won't work for someone who hasn't bought a new album

since 1992."

Carl went from white to lobster red. His mouth opened and closed a few times then he spun on his heel and marched from the room. Tish dropped into his seat as though her knees had given out. Around her people were drifting off, distancing themselves from the animal who was being culled from the herd.

"We'll help you clean out your desk," said Sarah, clearing her throat softly. "I'll get you a box from the stock room," said Louis.

"Thanks," whispered Tish.

The HR manager had magically appeared moments later. There was paperwork to fill out. Apparently, one could not just stomp out like in the movies. Fortunately, Louis and Sarah had finished the packing while she was away, so all that was left for Tish to do was hand over her building key and collect her box of stuff. Exit stage left with her boxes of samples, postcards, and trinkets.

She arrived at the apartment she shared with her useless cousin Sean, parked in her spot, heaved her box onto her hip, and trudged up to her front door, a tear dribbling down her cheek as she went. She had been intending to find someplace else to live since she moved in due to her cousin's loser, pothead friends, bartender's hours, and the permanent layer of debris that spread across the apartment despite her constant cleaning efforts. But somehow, she never seemed to have the time to apartment hunt.

I guess I'll have time now.

Tish pulled up short as she saw their landlord standing with a locksmith in front of her door. "Is there a problem, Mr. Garrity?" asked Tish, sniffing fiercely.

"You're evicted," said Mr. Garrity, turning sharply toward her and thrusting a piece of paper her way with angry energy.

"What?" Tish gaped, unsure if she'd actually heard him correctly. Mr. Garrity put the legalese-riddled letter on top of her pathetic white box full of used-up work things. The word "eviction" popped out at her from the top paragraph.

"You two haven't paid the rent in three months," he said with a shrug. "I sent you notices. I talked to Sean. What am I supposed to do?"

"But... But..." Tish stammered, swimming in uncertainty. "But I gave Sean money. He said he wanted to pay on his credit card to get airline miles."

Mr. Garrity looked at her pityingly and even the locksmith turned around to give a look of disbelief.

"Tish, you seem like a nice girl. I don't blame this on you. I know that pretty much all you do is work."

I'm going to start crying and I already have a lot of snot going on. I'm going to blow a giant snot bubble all over Mr. Garrity.

"And if you want to go in and collect some of your things I'll let you, but why on earth would you give a cokehead like him money?"

"Cokehead?" repeated Tish. "No, Sean is... he's a little troubled, but he's..."

"Sniffles all the time, manic moods?"

"He's got allergies," said Tish.

And I'm an idiot. Sean never had allergies when we were kids.

"He's a cokehead," said Mr. Garrity cruelly. "Who hasn't paid rent in three months. And unless you pay the back rent today, you're out, and I'm confiscating your shit to sell."

"You can't do that," said Tish, her eyes tearing. The snot bubble was imminent.

"Sure I can," said Mr. Garrity. Tish opened her mouth and shut it a few times. She didn't know what to say. "Look," he said, sighing, "Like I said, you seem nice. I've got some stuff to take care of in the office. Whatever you can haul out in the next hour, I'll let you take with you, but after that, you're out." Mr. Garrity stomped away, and the locksmith, apparently done with changing out the locks, picked up his gear and followed the landlord, shaking his head.

With nothing else to do, Tish pushed open her door and went inside. The living room was startlingly bare. Her cousin's usual collection of takeaway boxes and empty booze bottles were still in place, but the couch had been removed, and so had the flat-screen TV Tish had bought herself at Christmas. Tish continued into the kitchen. The fridge was gone. They didn't even own the refrigerator – it came with the apartment. Her bedroom had been equally destroyed. Her jewelry box had been emptied and the antique dresser removed – her clothes left in heaps on the floor. There was nothing of monetary value left in the apartment.

She had a distinct memory of Sean belting out the lyrics to *Step by Step* in the backyard the day the policeman came to tell them her father was dead.

Tish collapsed onto her mattress, her life in ruins around her.

What am I going to do now?

FIND OUT WHAT HAPPENS NEXT IN...
AN UNSEEN CURRENT

ABOUT THE AUTHOR

 Bethany Maines is the award-winning author of action adventure and fantasy tales that focus on women who know when to apply lipstick and when to apply a foot to someone's hind end. When she's not traveling to exotic lands, or kicking some serious butt with her black belt in karate, she can be found chasing after her daughter, or glued to the computer working on her next novel.

ALSO BY BETHANY MAINES

CARRIE MAE MYSTERIES
Bulletproof Mascara
Compact With The Devil
High-Caliber Concealer
Glossed Cause

SAN JUAN ISLANDS MYSTERIES
An Unseen Current
Against the Undertow
An Unfamiliar Sea
An Unfinished Storm

SHARK SANTOYO CRIME SERIES
Shark's Instinct
Shark's Bite
Shark's Hunt
Shark's Fin
Peregrine's Flight
Shark's Blood

THE DEVERAUX LEGACY
The Second Shot
A PNWA Literary Contest Award Winner
The Cinderella Secret
The Hardest Hit
The Fallen Man

THE SUPERNATURALS
Wild Waters
A Little Red **(3 Colors #1)**
A Deeper Blue **(3 Colors #2)**
A Brighter Yellow **(3 Colors #3)**
Maverick
Hudson **(Rejects #1)**
Killian **(Rejects #2)**
Alekos **(Rejects #3)**

GALACTIC DREAMS
When Stars Take Flight **Vol. 1**
The Seventh Swan **Vol. 2**
A Book Excellence Award Winner
The Beast of Arsu **Vol. 3**